WHIP

Novels by Martin Caidin

Whip
The Last Dogfight
Three Corners To Nowhere
Marooned
The God Machine
Four Came Back
Almost Midnight
Cyborg
Operation Nuke
High Crystal
Cyborg IV
Devil Take All
No Man's World
The Mendelov Conspiracy
The Last Fathom
Anytime, Anywhere
The Cape
Maryjane Tonight At Angels Twelve
The Long Night

MARTIN CAIDIN

HOUGHTON MIFFLIN COMPANY BOSTON

1976

Library of Congress Cataloging in Publication Data

Caidin, Martin, 1927–
  Whip.

  I. Title.
PZ4.C133Wh [PS3553.A38]   813′.5′4   75-40221
ISBN 0-395-20707-X

Printed in the United States of America

c   10   9   8   7   6   5   4   3   2   1

for

AL CASAROTTO

This one is on me . . .

AUTHOR'S NOTE

ALTHOUGH the characters in this novel are fictional, the combat is real — even the final great battle. There *was* a B–25 bomber group very much like the one in this book and it fought with deadly effectiveness at treetop and wavetop level. Even Whip Russel has his real-life counterpart in Bill Bagwell, a pilot for all seasons and a flying friend of many years.

MARTIN CAIDIN

WHIP

1

THE HEAT ROSE about them in shimmering waves so that the horizon was buried within a shimmering heat carpet. It was savagely bright. Glare does that. The air glowed with the naked sun, intensely painful to the unwary, and past headaches brought experienced men to seek the rare vision-comforting shadows of the northeastern Australia scrub-land. More than sun this day, really. Dust fine-grained and pervasive thickened the air. It was stinking weather in a stinking land, where men sought any distraction to veer their minds from oppressive tedium and inescapable discomfort. Yet at this moment, wherever they were, whatever they were doing, they slowed in their efforts or stirred from their glazed-eye trances, for there had appeared an intrusion unexpected in their miserable lives. In this nothingness of the parched land splashed forever around Townsville in northeastern Australia, scattered about lackluster airfields with their tents and shelter halves and weathered shacks, and the aircraft, some whole but more broken in many different ways, events dragged haltingly to a stop. It took no small thing to do that, to lift a man's head from his dejection with diarrhea and cramps, with skin rot and malaise.

The intrusion was a sound. The sound of engines, and that in itself was a surprise, because they'd by God heard enough engines throbbing from the sky and from the ground to last their lives, and they heard them all the time, day and night, as if the country just beyond sight were occupied by huge swarms of mosquitoes that never shut up. After all, aircraft and engines were the only reasons for this forsaken hellhole and the only justification for the men suffering as they did. It was here that old and battered machines staggered in to be repaired or modified or cannibalized and engines ran whenever men brought them to readiness, and the engines ran low and slow, popping and snorting, and when they were run to full power and propellers slid into flat pitch, they howled and screamed. So they were accustomed to it, it was part of their lives.

But there was a subtle difference to this engine sound. It took an experienced ear to detect it, but Garbutt Field ran thick with men capable of such distinction, and so they shook themselves free of the moment, and looked up and squinted into that goddamned glaring sun and sky.

Synchronized thunder. A beat of sound that came from so many engines that it should have been garbled, an accepted cry of rumbling discord, but it wasn't, and then they saw what they knew must enter that glaring sky, the black, winged shapes far off in the distance, and with only that first glance, that momentary pinging on the eye of the shapes, they knew this outfit differed from any other they'd known before. Garbutt Field was home to sick and broken machines, and when the bombers staggered onto the dusty runways they were flown by men often as weary and bone-bent as the aircraft in which they sailed the skies. No, these strangers were different, already recognizable as twin-engined, and from the high-shoulder-wing configuration and slab sides no question they were B–25s.

What snatched at the attention of the men across the parched ground in this early fall of 1942, in a world where the Japanese were triumphant and near-masters, was the way those people up there were flying those machines.

There is a *touch* to certain pilots and it is created, it is never simply born, of discipline and pride and confident skill, in themselves and their fellow pilots, and whatever it was, those men up there had it. No one aircraft chased another. They flew formation, tight, riding easily the thermals and the spinning slipstream of great propellers and the vortices pummeling back from wingtips. But other men also did that well, so this was not the siren call that beckoned attention from the ground. There was some invisible mark that etched this formation growing in size as it approached Garbutt Field, and for the watching men, for whom defeat and misery were no strangers, a surge of pride stirred somewhere deep within them.

It was precision to such an extent it was beautiful, and as the machines continued their approach they could see more clearly just how beautiful was that formation. They flew as if one man touched the controls of all eleven aircraft, and the men watching from the ground, knowing that distance has a habit of glossing over imperfections, held their breath and wondered if this also would mar what had grasped at them. But as the thunder swelled and the machines enlarged with decreasing distance they saw there were no imperfections, and Jesus, but they're holding it in *tight,* all bunched together as if they were in a goddamned aerial parade with the air soft and untroubled, and the widened eyes were joined with grins and startled exclamations. Everyone who could hear and see was looking into the sky, screw the sun and the glare, and they watched the eleven bombers as they came on down low, very goddamned low, right onto the bloody deck, thank you, until their thunder was a massive pounding and the watching men knew that the eleven pilots at the controls also knew just how good they were, were trying to impart that pride and confidence, and there wasn't any better way of doing it than what they

were doing, rushing now with furious speed and hammering
sound waves over the dusty earth, and *oh, Jesus, but they're
beautiful.*

They were even more surprised when the Mitchells came
close enough for details to be seen, for most witnesses from
the ground had assumed these aircraft to be new replacements from the States, pilots with fresh uniforms and
factory-new machines, smelling that mysterious new-air-
plane smell, untouched by Japanese steel, in their last
moment before the acid test of the agile Zero fighters. But,
no; they were wrong. These airplanes were worn, battered,
beaten, holed and scattered across their metal surfaces with
their smallpox scars of tin covering bullet holes and patched
over gaping tears made by exploding cannon shells. Just
what in the hell were these men *doing?*

By now the commanding officer of Garbutt Field had
emerged from his makeshift office, trailed by his staff, *and*
the cooks and administrative and hospital personnel, and
everyone on the field who could walk, because the thunder
of twenty-two engines close up was overwhelming,
pounding the earth, sending dust flurrying upward in a fine
mist, and the strange B–25s flattened it out on the deck,
smack down the runway, all eleven of them holding what
everyone knew by now had to be their combat strike
formation, and as they swept by, they came hauling up in a
sudden, steep wild climb, the first nine bombers in a vee of
three vee's, then the last two, and they were really hauling
coal now, flashing before the blazing sun, as they rolled
smoothly, beautifully, out of their climbing turns, their
thunder more ragged with the thunder of those great props.
They seemed to ease into an impossible floating movement
as the pilots let up on the power and from every bomber,
virtually at the same moment, flaps were sliding back and
down from wings, the three legs of the landing gear of each

bomber jutted stiffly into the wind, as the watchers below
strained to make out more details, because the first three
B–25s had curved gracefully, like fighters, through the
pattern of the airfield, and rolled around, sliding into final
approach, *still* in tight formation, and staying tight, and
"Holy cow! Look at 'em!" and they looked and another man
shouted, "Them crazy bastards are gonna' *land* like that!
Jesus, in formation, yet!"

You just didn't do that at Garbutt Field. The runway was
all screwed up with undulations and dust and rocks, and it
wasn't that wide, it just wasn't the place to pull off this kind
of superprecision crap, but no one had told those pilots up
there, and they *were* doing it, and every man on the ground
who knew what the inside of a cockpit looked like knew also
that the manifold pressure gauges and the revolutions per
minute and fuel pressure and oil temperature and the rate of
descent and the air-speed needles and the gyro compasses in
each plane were dead-on, every set of instruments in each
plane like those of its companion aircraft. If the instruments
worked, that is.

They came sliding down their invisible rail in the sky,
glued together and all of them shimmering in the heat rolling
off the runway, and as the earth came to meet them, the
pilots had their trim set just right and they flared, control
yokes easing back with practiced skill, without deliberate
thought, for this was rote and instinctive motion, and the
nose of each bomber came higher as they bled off air speed
and ghosted their descent to earth, looking for all the world
like three great stiff-feathered creatures about to alight in
their desert nest, and then the main gear wheels spurted
back dust and they were rolling, no longer flying, rolling on
the main gear and as speed fell away the noses came down
and the single wheels before each bomber touched and then
from three airplanes there were nine trailing dust plumes, all

three aircraft holding position, still tied with their invisible knots. Thunder rumbled easily along the ground as the pilots fed in a touch of power and taxied in formation to the end of the runway, to a cleared area for parking where a startled lineman had run and began motioning with his hand signals. They wheeled about in line formation, the black airplane in front turning smartly with deft bursts of power and the B–25 came to a stop, rocking gently on its nose shock.

The other two bombers aligned with the first ship, the black killer, and the men in the cockpits were busy with their checklists, shutting down systems, attending to power and flow and pressure, but not yet cutting the final umbilical of power. Behind them, down the far end of the runway, the next vee of bombers was lightly treading dust, and the men on the field watched and marveled, feeling the pride that had been so long missing.

2

CAPTAIN WHIP RUSSEL released his seat belt and freed his shoulder harness, sweat springing from where the webbing had pressed against his body. He pulled open side windows and watched his copilot do the same, so some breeze would be caught from the flailing propellers and thrown through the sweltering cockpit. Russel half stood behind the control yoke of the pilot's side of the cockpit in the black B–25. He paid no attention to First Lieutenant Alex Bartimo to his right or to the other three men in the aircraft. They would go through their shutdown checklist without comment from Russel.

The little man in the pilot's seat, all 138 pounds of him raw nerve and rubbed tendon and fierce intensity, had no eyes for what transpired within his own aircraft. Whip Russel had brought his eleven bombers into Garbutt Field for major modification work, and first impressions were important on a field where priorities came from scheming and where regulations were archaic memories. They could mean the lot between getting what he wanted or running into the stone wall of a fast administrative shuffle. This was the first time Garbutt Field had seen the 335th Bombardment Squadron, Medium, and Whip Russel was determined they were damned well going to see some professionals at work. He glanced through the plexiglas of his cockpit, studying the other bombers rolling down the runway, the third trio about to set down, as the two Ass End Charlies cut it in close.

"Keep it in tight, you bastards," Whip growled into his microphone. No one bothered to answer. No need. These cats had it all together and Whip's radio call was more conversational than required. They feathered down from the glaring sky, raced ahead of their dust plumes to the roll-off point and one by one lined up and stopped, *exactly* so, engines on all the iron birds still running, but now with a sound that made a mockery of the sweet precision thunder of flight. A Wright Cyclone on the ground is music to no one save a pilot or a mechanic.

The watching men were still motionless, caught up in the powerful display of flight and touchdown, and now they waited to see what these strange pilots would do with their battered aircraft. Whip Russel was satisfied now. He knew that in each cockpit the shutdown procedures had been started and the pilots and copilots were waiting on his word, and he grinned as he thumbed his mike. "All right, troops. Everybody cut 'em." In eleven cockpits hands moved mixture controls and throttles and adjusted switches and twenty-two engines expired, by no means in unison, because there aren't any men born who can bring that many Wright Cyclones to perform their last exhalation on command, but still there was a mass rumbling to a halt, metal bodies and wings shaking as the engines gave up their power, the great propellers twitching in their final revs.

The silence was incredible.

It was the signal to resume human activity, and the men drifted forward, looking up at the planes, gesturing or shouting greetings to the men who slid down through the belly hatches, gawking and wondering at this quiet curtain to the unexpected performance. There was more to stare at than just airplanes. These bombers were marked and not only with the telltale signatures of Japanese bullets and flak. On the nose of the lead B–25, the black machine, beneath

the cockpit windows on each side, was a macabre death's
head, a skull with a bullwhip handle jabbed mockingly
through one eye socket, twisting in upon itself so that it
assumed the appearance of crossed bones beneath the skull.
There were Japanese flags and the half-silhouettes to mark
sunken ships and rows of bombs to indicate missions flown.
This was a hardened, combat-tested outfit.

Now, more than the planes, the men stationed at Garbutt
Field waited to see who commanded this maverick bunch
who flew with angel touch on their controls. Because now
the word was spreading through the clustered onlookers.
They knew this outfit. The carved notches in the form of
painted markings identified the killers.

The Death's Head Brigade. Sometimes they were called
the 335th Special. They were famed throughout the Southwest Pacific, and their leader was more than that. Infamous
would do. Whip Russel. They knew his name, and they'd
heard stories of how he'd made a mockery of both the high
command in Australia *and* the Japanese in their own
territory. There were stories that General MacArthur would
have personally liked to have killed Whip Russel because
of his incredible insubordination, but he didn't, and he
wouldn't, because the 335th was more of a pain to the
Japanese than it was to headquarters, and God knew we had
few enough outfits who could hold their own against the
enemy, let alone run up the devastating success enjoyed by
the 335th Special. The Japanese, of course, also would have
relished Russel's demise, but unlike MacArthur, they were
doing their very best at it, and failing.

Understandably, the men crowded forward to see this
phenomenon who had defied MacArthur and the Japanese
and seemed to have survived both in excellent health.

His crew was already on the ground, standing in the
shade beneath one wing as the engines crackled and popped

as they gave off their heat, when Whip came down through the forward hatch, the last man to descend from all the bombers. No one could miss that lithe and fluid motion.

A voice rang out from the watching crowd. "Shit, he *is* a little dude, ain't he." Some laughter followed the remark, but it was friendly, even admiring, because a long time ago these people had learned the physical size of a man didn't count for much in hauling an airplane through the sky, especially not when you enjoyed the reputation of *this* man. They pressed closer, wanting to see him better, to watch him move, to listen to him say something, anything, when the sounds of an approaching jeep with horn blaring began the dispersal of the still-gathering assembly.

The jeep came to a halt in a cloud of its own swirling dust. Seated by the driver was an enormous man. Not simply big, but fat, almost corpulent, and no one needed to ask to understand this was a civilian rushed into uniform for whatever skills the army wanted so badly it would overlook his physical grossness. He sat quietly, one thick leg on the edge of the jeep, his khakis stained with sweat and coated with various layers of dust and oil and grease from airplanes. His hands were dirty. Beneath his nails was a grime that could not be removed for months, compounded as it was from the lubrication of warplanes and his own hard work. Finally he rose, so that he could rest his massive forearms on the windshield runner of the vehicle, surveying the line-up of bombers, until he halted his gaze on the man who commanded the Death's Head Brigade. For a long moment no one spoke. Then the fat man, whose colonel's eagles were barely visible against the stains of his uniform, spoke slowly. His deep voice carried surprisingly strong through the air.

"Captain," he addressed his words to Whip Russel, "you are a goddamned disgrace."

No one moved.

"Captain, you are out of uniform."

Which Whip Russel certainly was, since he wore only boots and faded shorts and a .45 automatic strapped to his right side. His body was a strangely lined mixture of dark tan and white stripes from bandages worn in the sun while he recovered from wounds he refused to allow to keep him out of his cockpit. Above the heavy combat boots his legs were bandy-muscular, almost ludicrous. The faded shorts could have come from any decade preceding the present. His stomach was braided muscle, he carried a three-day growth of beard and his hair was unkempt.

No question of the reaction to the colonel's words. The men watching the scene showed disbelief and open contempt for the observation. Jesus, here they were in this freaked-out desert of northern Australia, with the Japs just over the horizon kicking the shit out of everybody save *this* one outfit, and all this fat bastard of a colonel can do is complain about how this little guy dresses. Jesus, no one in the whole outfit had a complete uniform!

Whip Russel strolled lazily from beneath the wing of his bomber to the jeep. He stopped, dust scuffling about his boots, and he looked up at Colonel Louis R. Goodman, Commanding Officer of the 112th Maintenance Depot, that took in Townsville and Garbutt Field and a dozen other airstrips scattered across the parched Australian countryside.

"And you, Colonel," drawled Whip, "are one fat son of a bitch."

Men gawked. And shook their heads, and waited for the fireworks.

Colonel Louis R. Goodman grinned hugely. "That I am, Whip," he boomed jovially, and the two old friends who'd not seen one another in nearly two years clasped hands. "Get in, you little bastard. I'll buy you a beer."

3

"YOU LIVE in a lousy neighborhood, you know that?" Whip gestured lazily from the back seat of the jeep, leaning forward as they drove from the flight line.

"Well, I can't hardly argue with you," Goodman replied, his gaze following Whip's gesture. "It's all pretty obvious."

It was. About them, near and far, were dispersed aircraft and teams of mechanics and air crews in what was virtually raw desert country. Scrub trees showed haphazardly, augmented by low, stunted plants unfamiliar to Whip. "What I don't understand," he said to the colonel, "is why people this far back from the shooting have to live like this." His reference was to the "permanent" frayed tents and other makeshift dwellings.

"Because we ain't got nothing better," Goodman grunted. "Hell, Whip, look around you. See those canvas sheets over there? We don't have anything with which to build what might even pass for a hangar. When we tear down an engine we build a tent around it, otherwise the dust would get into everything and the engine would tear itself apart the first time it flew." Goodman sighed. "Man, we're not just short of the right equipment, we don't have *any* right equipment. This whole complex is the biggest scavenging yard you ever saw. My people are even making their own tools, for Christ's sake. We can't get sheet metal for repairs. The only way we've stayed in business is by stripping old cars and trucks and cannibalizing planes we don't believe should be sent back into the air. I've been screaming to headquarters just for the tools to do the job. Never mind that half my men are sick to death from lousy food and our medical supplies are a joke and they sleep with scorpions and God knows what else. They'd accept all that and just bear up under it, *if* they could only do the job we need doing. And that's patching up the worn machines and modifying the others that come in here." He cast a baleful look at his passenger. "I imagine we'll get around to what you want before too long."

"Uh huh. Before too long."

About them, in the individual stands back from the road, were bombers standing without purpose, awaiting long-overdue repairs. Their wings and bodies showed scars and gaping holes, and Whip studied with his practiced eye the black punctures where Japanese bullets and cannon shells had ripped through metal skin and structural members, leaving the aircraft dangerously weakened until the metal could be made whole again.

"You still carrying operational groups from here?" Whip asked.

Goodman nodded. "We do. Its a case of their patching airplanes together until they have enough to go on a mission. We've got the 19th Bomb Group right here at Garbutt — you can see a few of their B–17s over there — but they don't fly too often. The only way they can stay in the air with the Japs, flying the small formations they do, is to get upstairs where the Zeros can't hack the thin air. The problem, Whip" — and again there was that sigh that reflected incessant, nagging problems — "is that the super-chargers on those things are a mess, and we're short of oxygen equipment, and every time they try to fly to thirty thousand feet they're lucky to stay up."

Goodman motioned for his driver to turn left. "Over there

we've got two squadrons from the 22nd Group. Marauders. They've got the 33rd Squadron out at Antill Plains, about twenty miles south of here. Their 2nd and 408th Squadrons are at Reid River, another twenty miles to the south. Whip, they got an out-of-commission rate of about fifty percent. We just can't keep those things flying without parts. Hell, when they're grounded, the crews live with their airplanes. They got live rounds in their weapons to keep the other crews from stripping their machines."

Lou Goodman shook his head. "Before I got into this side of the war I thought I knew men pretty well. I didn't. I didn't know a goddamned thing about how people could put up with absolute hell, and do everything they could to stay in the fighting. You'd think these crazy bastards would welcome the chance to stay the hell away from the Japs. But it doesn't work that way. I was talking before about the 19th, the people in the B–17s. Their morale is so low it wouldn't reach the bottom of a cat's ass. Their planes are wrecks. I wouldn't want to fly one around the pattern. No supplies. Nothing. They were scheduled to fly a mission up to Rabaul with ten bombers. It was the goddamndest joke you ever saw. They scraped parts and pieces from all the planes so they could get just *two* airplanes off the ground. And one of those had to turn back when the oxygen system went out." Goodman paused and dug in a shirt pocket for a sweat-stained cigarette. "The other plane went all the way to Rabaul."

Whip raised an eyebrow. "Alone?"

"Alone. They didn't come back either. The crew that had to turn back were almost mad with frustration. Felt that if only they'd gone along they might all have made it."

Whip shook his head. "Don't count on it. Two B–17s is like waving a flag up at Rabaul."

"I know, *I know*. I'm just telling you about the crews. You've flown out of Seven-Mile, right?"

Whip pictured one of the main airfields in Papua, the southern half of New Guinea. Seven-Mile Drome lay seven miles outside the harbor town of Port Moresby on the south coast of New Guinea. "Yeah, I've been there, Lou."

"Then I don't have to say anything about it, do I." It was more a statement than a question.

"No, Lou." They both knew the score about Seven-Mile and the other fields around Moresby, where everyone was a lot closer to the enemy. Seven-Mile was also the advance combat base through which Australia-based bombers staged for refueling on their way to strike at Japanese targets. Crude and rough were kind words for the field which the Japanese used for target practice several times a week, day and night. What Whip thought about, and he knew his thoughts were shared by Lou Goodman, was that as bad as it was for the men who flew, it was sheer murder for those who patched and fixed and worked to keep the Marauders and Mitchells going.

The world in all directions from Seven-Mile was a bitch. In the summer the grass burned into brittle straw, and the only thing worse than the hordes of insects were one special breed — the Papuan mosquitoes, which were numberless and maddening by day and by night. A man couldn't accustom himself to the weather, because he had to endure the weird combination of choking dust from the airstrip and dank humidity from the surrounding jungle and the sea. Yet this was only the backdrop to the real problems. Men can endure almost any type of weather or terrain, but they've got to have a fair chance at their game.

Not at Seven-Mile. When the Mitchell bombers, and others, went to Seven-Mile, it was usually to stage out of the airstrip for a series of swift and hazardous strikes against the Japanese. They had to be swift because of enemy attacks against Seven-Mile, which were always extremely hazardous because of the quantity and the quality of the enemy's fighters. The pilots and air crews knew their chances for survival left much to be desired, but few of them would have willingly exchanged places with the men who kept their battered machines in the air.

The ground crews knew an existence limited strictly to bone-weary sleeplessness from work day and night. The groggy state into which they fell while they worked was broken only by the shriek of Japanese bombs or the stutter of cannon fire from Zeros sweeping up and down, strafing at treetop height. It didn't do their morale much good to see Japanese fighters in tight formation performing loops and other aerobatics directly over the field in a nose-thumbing challenge for the American or Australian fighters to come up and do battle. Which, wisely, the pilots who flew the P-39s or P-40s refused to do. There are few ways to commit suicide faster than to try to fight a Zero from below.

Whip Russel recalled one time in particular when they came back from a mission. Taxiing down one side of the runway he saw two Buddhalike figures in the parched grass on the far side. There, two of his mechanics — Sergeants Charles Fuqua and William Spiker — were sitting perfectly upright. Their legs were crossed beneath their bodies, and they were sound asleep. These two men, and the others who worked with them, if luck proved to be on their side, might average three hours' sleep a night when the raids increased in tempo. They considered five hours at any time a delectable luxury.

Whip shook his head. For this moment he had shifted from the rough jeep ride to the north, beyond Australia and across the Coral Sea to Papua and that triple-damned operations area of Port Moresby. Those mechanics . . .

"Lou, you know what's worse than all this?" Whip waved his hand to take in all the wretchedness and scrubland and rotten facilities. "Here, and at Seven-Mile, and wherever else we've been in this godawful country?"

"I think I do," the colonel said warily, "and when I think about it I get sick."

Whip couldn't hold back the words. There was just no goddamned escape from this crap. "It's the men, Lou. What the hell keeps them going? Working for us, the pilots and crews, the way they do?" He spread his hands and looked at the palms as if seeing them for the first time. "I've had these guys working with open cuts and sores in their hands, for Christ's sake."

Goodman nodded. "Despite the fact that almost every man jack out here feels he's been written off."

Goodman motioned for the driver to turn back to the right, to take them through the B–17 dispersal area. The Fortresses were great ships but Russel was glad he didn't have to drag one of those big bastards and their four engines through the air. It was like trying to run a railroad when you flew a bomber that big. And when you sat in that left seat on the flight deck you didn't really have the chance to fly *and* fight, you could only fly, while a whole team did battle. It made you feel like a sitting duck. Not that these Fortresses were doing very much of fighting a war, either like a sitting duck or a busted swan. There wasn't a single bomber in commission, and —

"What?" Whip turned suddenly at the sound of Lou Goodman's voice. "Sorry, Lou, I was looking at — "

"I know. A mess."

"What were you saying?"

"That we almost had a riot on our hands here last month."

"Here?" Whip looked around at the great expanse of nothingness. "What the hell about?"

Goodman shook his head. "Not here. Some of the men wanted to go south to Brisbane and a few other cities and bomb the waterfront."

The incredulous look on Whip Russel's face spoke his questions without need for words.

"Oh, they've managed to keep it pretty quiet, and, well," Goodman hesitated, "when you've been fighting side by side with the Aussies, it seems almost impossible to believe, and — "

"What the hell are you talking about?"

"Would you believe," Goodman sighed, "that the Australian dock workers refused to unload some ammo ships?"

"Refused?" Whip knew his echoing sounded stupid, but he couldn't figure what Goodman was trying to —

"There were some ships in Melbourne. Bombs, ammo, spares; the lot. We had trucks, even a few planes, waiting to rush the stuff up here. Then it started to rain. The stevedores walked off the job."

Whip stared at the other man. "I don't believe it."

"You'd better. I was there, trying to hustle the stuff back up here. I *saw* it, Whip." He motioned at his face. "With my own two beady eyes. They had a union contract that they didn't have to work in the rain and so they walked off the job."

"Just like that?"

"You called it."

"I hope what happened is what I think happened."

Goodman laughed. "I didn't even recognize myself. I was speechless when it happened. I've heard of union rules but this was just so ridiculous it went beyond — "

"I wouldn't call it ridiculous. Or insane. There's another word for it. Treason."

"Just how I felt. Next thing I knew I had that damned forty-five in my hand and I was climbing onto the ship, and I went into the cab of that crane, you know, the one that unloads from the cargo holds?"

Whip nodded.

Goodman chuckled with the memory. "I never thought, not once, about what I was doing. But I went into the cab of that crane, or boom, or whatever the hell it is, and I stuck the barrel of the forty-five in the guy's ear, the operator in there, and I told him quietly, very quietly, I think, that if that crane wasn't working in two seconds flat I would smear his head all over the windows of his cab."

Whip paused. He had a thin smile on his face. "Would you have pulled the trigger, Lou?"

Goodman didn't return the smile. "You've seen how my men live. You bet your sweet ass I'd have pulled."

Whip's smile broadened. "I really think you would at that." He slapped Lou Goodman's shoulder, then changed the subject, pointing to a weird antenna jutting upward from several camouflaged vehicles. "What the hell is that?"

"Our pride and joy, Captain. That is a radar set. The finest in the world, I'm led to believe."

"Radar? You mean you can get warning of somebody in the air with that thing? Long before they're in sight?"

"So they tell me."

"So they *tell* you?"

"We have a problem. It doesn't work. There are no parts and there's no manual to run the thing and nobody has ever seen one before. But it's pretty, isn't it?"

Whip shook his head. "You got flak positions scattered pretty good around here. I knew the Japs had torn hell out of Darwin. You getting any company in here?"

"Not that much, really. We have people stationed up the coast and we've equipped some boats with radio gear. We use the old Chinese system of lookouts calling in by radio or land line. The Japs have sent in a couple of long-range flying boats to try to catch us napping. They can be pretty mean, especially if they ever get through without warning. I've never seen anything like them. They're faster than you'd believe."

"You get any of them?"

Goodman shook his head. "No such luck. But we just happened to have a bunch of B–26s coming down from Moresby when two of those things made a pass at us and lit out for home. The 26s went after them with everything wide open. They chewed one to pieces and the other made it away in some clouds."

"You lead an interesting life, Lou."

The jeep pulled up before a primitive mishmash of weathered boards, tarpaper and canvas. Goodman climbed heavily from the front seat and nodded his head in the direction of the structure.

"Be it ever so humble, Captain, this is it."

4

PLYWOOD SHEETS divided the interior of the makeshift headquarters into office cubicles. Lou Goodman nodded to his staff as he led Whip to the rear of the building and went through the one interior door into what passed for his office. He closed the door behind them and waited several moments for Whip to look around. What he saw was an utter shambles. Or what passed for one, with plywood filing cabinets and a bulletin board that filled an entire wall with notes and work orders. Yet Whip knew that where Lou Goodman was concerned appearances were deceiving. He remembered other offices just as much of a mess as this one, but the man who sat behind the weathered desk knew where everything belonged. And that from the paper jungle there emerged a pattern of orders with meaning and purpose.

"It stinks, but it's home," the colonel said without apology.

Whip draped his body across a couch assembled from packing-crate boards. "All you're missing, old man, is that cold beer you promised."

Goodman grinned at him. He crossed the room to a curtain strung from a cable. "Whip, my lad, you know I never jest about serious matters. Behold my pride and joy." He pulled aside the curtain to reveal coiled tubing, copper tubs coated with dripping condensation and a small motor that thumped noisily, rattling the floor beneath. "The best of Rube Goldberg," Goodman admitted. "One of our mechanics was a refrigerator repairman. He rigged up a cold box for us. Once in a while, by persons unknown, whose names I am sworn forever never to reveal, I am brought certain luxuries of a life we may remember dimly from our past, and — "

"Lou, do you really have a cold beer inside that thing?"

"I have."

"Well, Jesus, man, I mean — "

Goodman opened a heavy door. Even from across the room Whip felt the unspeakably delicious draft of cold air. Goodman turned with a flourish, holding forth a beer can in each hand.

"You look like you're seeing a ghost."

"I *am*."

Goodman punched open the cans. Whip held the cold metal to his lips for a long moment. He took his first sip slowly, incredulous that the taste could be so alien, so marvelous to him. The cold liquid struck his throat with a feeling of pain. He swallowed several times, slowly, then released his breath in a long sigh. "I still don't believe this," he said at last.

It was the moment for a long pause, to open mental doors and bring the past into the room with them. No more colonel and captain, two old friends looked across the room at one another.

"It's been a long time, Whip."

The younger man finished a long swallow and gestured with the beer can. "Yeah. It's been that, all right. A long time and a lot of miles and maybe a couple of lifetimes."

Whip tilted his head slightly to one side in a gesture the colonel remembered from way back when. "When was it I last saw you?" Whip asked, and in bridging the past, he was suddenly softer, a bit warmer, Goodman reckoned, than any of his crews had ever seen him. Whatever he said, Lou

Goodman knew how to judge men, and this was an old friend, and he was coming to realize just how stiff and Prussian this captain was — had to be — to keep his men alive.

Goodman chewed the question. "It was that last big rally, wasn't it?" he ventured. "Three hundred mean and lean cats on motorcycles. The whole Hellfire Club, if I recall."

Laughter spilled easily from Whip. "They were all lean and mean except you, Lou. You were mean enough, but — "

"I know, I know," Lou chuckled. "You used to say half of me hung over the sides of the bike when I rode."

"You were something, that's for sure." Whip studied Goodman. "You know something, Lou? You're . . . different. I'm trying to figure it. What's different, I mean. I think, maybe, you *care* now about what's going on."

Goodman didn't answer for several moments. "Could be. You're not the same cat with a chain on the end of a billy club either."

"No, I guess not." Whip took another long pull from his beer can. "The flying is when it all began. The changing, I mean. For me, for you. Most of the guys."

"Uh huh."

They didn't need to verbalize that period of change. Whip Russel and a mob of toughs were the first real motorcycle gang in southern California. They were more hell-raisers than people on the make for trouble. But when you've got that many free-wheelers out in a bunch, clogging the roads and scaring motorists half to death, the fireworks were inevitable, and they had their private rumbles with other fast-growing clubs, and a lot of heads got bashed and bones broken, and *then* there was the law.

In southern California, in 1939 and 1940, the cops could be and often were mean. Very mean. The busted heads were shared on both sides. It could have been the last wrong road to follow except that Lou Goodman ran both a sprawling motorcycle shop in south Los Angeles and a private airport thirty miles beyond. Whip and his cohorts knew Goodman from the bike shop, and they trusted the big, fat man who was as quick to cover for them with the law as he was to chew them out personally. When they'd had a particularly bad time with another club, and Whip and three other riders had ended up killing one of their friendly enemies, they lit out for a place to hide. At four in the morning they rode into Goodman's airport, lights off, busted off the lock from a hangar and stashed their bikes inside.

Lou Goodman got to the field at eight. He'd heard about the confrontation. The killing gave the cops every advantage they needed to crack down, and no one was out to protect a gang of marauding bikers. Lou Goodman told Whip and his three friends that a whole convoy of police was scouring the local countryside and working their way right to where they were at that moment.

"No use cutting south or east," Goodman told Whip. "They've got roadblocks on every road that way, and there's no country you can break out from." He smiled without humor. "And you sure can't cut west. Those bikes don't float very well."

It was then, for the first and the last time in the years that he knew him, that Whip Russel laid it on the line. "We need your help, Lou."

Goodman studied the small, wiry kid with so wild an aura about him. He was different this moment. He still had that awesome energy within him, that indefinable charge of leadership, but he was idling his power, running his personality in a gentle cruise rather than throwing everything he had at Goodman in an effort to secure the big man's assistance. Goodman looked from Russel to the three toughs with him. They *were* mean bastards, but their blank

faces told him only what he already knew. Whatever came
by the boards with Whip was the way they'd go.

Goodman sighed. "I'll hate myself for this." He started
for the hangar where the motorcycles had been hidden, then
turned. The four bikers hadn't moved an inch. Sudden fury
assailed them from the fat man. "You asked for my help,"
Goodman snarled. "Now *trust* me, goddamnit."

Whip led off, the others following. In the hangar, working
against time, Goodman and the four bikers heaped dust and
sawdust from the floor onto the motorcycles. Rags and a
canvas cover were tossed loosely onto the bikes and the
floor surrounding. Without saying another word Goodman
led the way to the rear of the hangar, motioning the
foursome to climb through the entrance door of a silvery
twin-engined Lockheed 10. Still angry at what he was
doing, bewildered by his motivation, Goodman yanked the
chocks and entered the airplane, stomping up the narrow
aisleway to the cockpit. He hardly noticed Whip cautiously
easing into the copilot's seat, he was so busy in his mixture
of self-anger and starting up the Lockheed. The engines
banged into life and with only a passing glance at the gauges
Goodman taxied toward the active runway. He was turning
into the wind for his run-up when he saw a dust cloud
rapidly approaching the field.

"Shit." He said only that one word, fed power to the right
engine and rolled onto the runway, violating the cardinal
rule of checking out the engines and aircraft systems. No
time. He knew, and so did the others the moment they saw
the nearing cloud, that the police were rushing toward the
field. It didn't matter any longer. No one had seen Whip
and his toughs come onto the airport. If the motorcycles
were found, they had already cooled and their metal would
be cold to the touch. Even if the cops saw through the dust
and rags tossed about.

Goodman's right hand went forward on the throttles.

With full power the tail came up quickly and he sped along the runway, easing into a turn away from the field as he came off the ground and punched up the gear. All the cops had was a glimpse of a silvery machine disappearing in the distance.

Goodman's plan was simple. Just fly the four of them to a field about a hundred miles away. Make a telephone call from the isolated airport to a friend who had a motorcycle shop in the small town. Two hours from then, Whip and his friends would ride *into* Los Angeles, not away from the scene of the killing. It was a good plan and it worked, but not exactly the way Goodman had planned.

He was at four thousand feet when he finally glanced to his right. He was so startled he was unable to voice the anger that had continued to build within him.

Whip Russel sat in a half-trance, fingers caressing the control yoke, his eyes wide and staring. Lou Goodman knew the signs. The anger melted away. "All right, kid," he said as softly as he could over the hammering roar of the engines. "You take it."

Whip looked at him, startled and delighted. Suddenly the tough kid from the motorcycle gang was another youngster to whom the sky had miraculously beckoned. Lou Goodman told him what to do, how to handle the yoke gently, to pick a point on the distant horizon and fly toward that point, how to mix experience with feeling. He let Whip stay on the controls with him during the flight and the descent into the small field, and after he made his telephone call to the friend with the bike shop, only three of the gang rode motorcycles back to Los Angeles. Whip returned with him, never off the controls for a moment, never thinking of anything but the flying that had so abruptly, exhilaratingly, overwhelmed him.

"They never did tumble to what we did that day," Goodman said.

Whip sprawled across the packing-crate couch. "You'll never believe it." He grinned crookedly. "I got a job. Down in San Diego. I got a job and I spent every goddamned dime on flying lessons. Later, I guess it was about two months before Pearl Harbor, I got my civilian license and signed up. They were really pressing for people. I didn't meet their two years of college, but since I had my ticket, they looked the other way, and the next thing I knew I was in flight school as a cadet."

"You seem to have done pretty well, son."

Whip kept his gaze on the can in his hands. "It's been a long road, Lou." He looked up slowly. "I lost touch. What happened to you?" He laughed suddenly and the crinkles appeared in crow's-feet back of his eyes, above his cheekbones. "I just never figured you for a uniform."

Goodman grunted as he heaved his bulk to a more comfortable position. A cigarette appeared in his mouth and he scraped a kitchen match on the floor beside him to light up. "I never figured on it myself," he agreed. "Right after you disappeared, the government sent people around looking for maintenance facilities. Well, I had the bike shop, and that auto repair station, and I owned the airport and part of another one, and before I knew what the hell was happening I had contracts up the gazoo for rebuilding engines and airplanes and starting contract flying schools. Everyone knew the war was coming, Whip, and they were dishing out the money like it was coupons. Christ, I was making a bundle." A long sigh came from the man fondly remembering better days. "Then suddenly it was December seventh, and I wake up in the morning, and I'm an expert in aircraft maintenance. I didn't tell the army that; *they* told *me*. The next thing I know I'm sworn in as a major and they tell me I'll be fixing their goddamn airplanes, and they sent me to Pearl to pick up some of the pieces there. I told them to junk what was left, and they put me on a boat loaded everywhere with parts and pieces and a bunch of kids who were supposed to be mechanics, and — " He shrugged to bring the story to its conclusion. "I've been here ever since. Oh, I make the rounds from here to Moresby and down south, and that sort of thing, but Garbutt Field" — he thumped his desk — "this is home plate."

Whip locked eyes with him. "They tell stories about you, Lou. They call you the miracle man."

"Sure, sure, Whip. I build iron airplanes out of straw and scorpion crap. Don't believe everything you hear."

"Never figured you for being modest."

"They said it was part of being a colonel."

Silence came gently between them for long minutes. Finally Lou Goodman shifted uncomfortably in his chair. "Whip." He saw the other man look up, knowing they were about to cross sensitive ground. "I don't want to walk around it, Whip. I heard rumors. You know, about Melody."

He saw Whip's eyes narrow, and the cold steel that came into his face made Lou Goodman begin to believe the stories he'd heard about Russel from other pilots. What he'd seen when those bombers came into Garbutt Field was signature enough to any pilot with experience: there had been a touch of brilliance in that flying and the man who'd led the formation. But this went beyond that. A legend had been growing in the theater about the man who flew the bomber with the death's head painted on each side of the nose, who did things with the Death's Head Brigade that should have been impossible.

There was pain in that expression, as well, and Goodman knew they were both seeing Melody Russel. Remembering what she looked like. The young girl who adored her brother, who went everywhere she could with him until she signed up as an army nurse, and was rushed through training, and was sent overseas in the late fall of 1941. To a place called Bataan, in the Philippines.

"I don't know too much, Lou." The words came forth strained, tinged with a bitterness that had to be there. "The last report I got was that she was captured. That last stand at Corregidor. She was supposed to fly out, all the women were, during the last evacuation. They took out the women by submarine." Whip blinked rapidly. "But she wouldn't go. She refused to leave the wounded."

He didn't say any more, and Lou Goodman didn't press it, because what the hell was there to say? They both knew what must have happened.

Lou Goodman was surprised, then, when Whip found his voice again. And what he told the colonel also told Goodman, more than anything else, just how extraordinary a change had taken place in this man.

"I try not to think about it too much. It could kill me, and some other people too. This hate thing. If I hate that much I don't think, I just see red and all I want to do is to kill. But that's a mistake because then I'm going up against the Japanese with hate as my overriding compulsion. I had a hell of a time fighting that down. I mean, you can't go into this war without thinking ahead every step of the way. Every step you can, anyway. Otherwise you make mistakes, the kind the Japs love you to make. They've got us outnumbered and the Zero is a killer, it's a hell of a lot more fighter than our people have to fly, and there's nothing more those guys would love to find than a bunch of B–25s without some real discipline to the way they handle those bombers. So I try, I try as hard as I can, not to hate, because it will eat me alive." He gestured to push away what might have been an obvious but wrong conclusion on the part of his audience. "Oh, I think about her, Lou, but I try to remember what she was like, that she'll be the same way, older and

more experienced, when I see her again, but she'll still be my
kid sister and . . . and, oh, shit, Lou, you know all the
words."

Lou Goodman gave him a few moments. "Sure, kid, I
know." He forced life back into his own voice. "I hear you
cut your teeth at Midway."

He could almost feel the relief in Whip at the change in
subject. Whip nodded slowly. "It was Midway, all right.
We were flying the Marauders then. The same 22nd Group
you got here at Garbutt." He laughed harshly, but without
bitterness, because Whip, Lou Goodman was learning
quickly, was never bitter about the business of killing with
airplanes.

"Midway. What a hell of an introduction to a war . . ."

5

AT THAT SAME MOMENT of reminiscence between Whip Russel and Lou Goodman, shared over the precious cold beer dragged to its last regretful swallow, Midway was also the topic of discussion elsewhere on Garbutt Field. The men of the Death's Head Brigade had assembled within what was laughingly called the Officers' Club, a tarpaper-covered wooden shack embroidered with grass and reed walls. However, despite the warm beer and the stale cigarettes and the scratchy phonograph and the brutal heat and the insects that crawled, buzzed, burrowed and stung, it was infinitely to be preferred to the drab nothingness of the tents assigned to the newly arrived men as temporary quarters. The tents shared with the club the same heat, dust and insects, but lacked the beer and heat-warped records scratching away their memory-jogging tunes of distant dance halls and Saturday night dates.

Captain Benjamin Czaikowicz, fondly christened "Psycho" by his fellow pilots, looked sadly about the dusty abortion of a club. Psycho was a Polish boulder of brawn and muscle and a gifted pilot, almost blind in his devotion in following Whip Russel in combat. Psycho flew the number two slot in the 335th Bomb Squadron, to the left and just behind the black airplane that led the pack.

Psycho shook his head. "There's a breeze in here," he murmured. "I think." He gestured to the other men. "There must be a breeze. See those flies over there?

They're doing slow rolls where the breeze comes around that corner. But maybe it's not a breeze at all, hey? Maybe it's the flies. Maybe they make the breeze."

First Lieutenant Alex Bartimo leaned against the bar with elbows at perfect angles of ninety degrees, fingering the dust on his beer can. Of all the men suffering the dusty heat and the insects, only Alex jarred the eyes. He didn't *fit*. The other men were slobs. Theirs was the uniform of the day, and the night, and it didn't matter because they had nothing to wear but ragged and stolen clothes. Alex Bartimo, who flew copilot in Whip Russel's airplane, was not and never had been a slob. Never. No matter what he wore, which at this moment consisted of old trousers cut into shorts with neatly hemmed edges, a shirt fashioned into what might pass for a rakish vest, and, sneakers. *White* sneakers. In a supply situation generously described as chaotic, Alex had discovered by the peculiarities of the quartermaster a case of white shoe polish. His sneakers were always white. No socks. Yet the man — not his attire — was impeccable. He was a polished reflection of hygiene and a once-upon-a-time social world. He was also an enigmatic sore thumb in a crowd of ragamuffins.

Alex sighed at the question of flies and a breeze murmured by his hulking companion. "Wrong, old man," he said in clipped, precise wording. "They do not maybe make the breeze, to quote your colorful and oafish term. They are adept and adroit, but I daresay you are too thick in the skull to appreciate aerobatic skill. It lies beyond your comprehension, which is why the Japanese do so much damage to that crudely flown machine of yours."

The other pilots of the Brigade smiled tolerantly. Psycho always walked into the verbal sandtraps and Alex always neatly buried him. Yet a man would have to be blind not to discern the deep bond between the two pilots.

There were other pilots in the club, too, men from the B–17 bombers, others from the Marauders, still others from transports and still more without any aircraft at all. A few fighter pilots sat at a far table, uncomfortable in the midst of bomber teams who went to war at a range beyond the reach of the fighters.

A B–17 pilot edged to the bar with Psycho and Alex. He motioned to the latter, receiving the cool response of a nudged eyebrow. Alex Bartimo was clannish to a fault with his own men. But this man eased his curiosity into the open. "You're the copilot for this Russel, aren't you? The guy who leads your outfit?"

Alex Bartimo blinked his eyes. Once.

"I hear they call him Whip. Like that bullwhip he's got painted on your airplane, with the death's head. Is what they say about that guy true? Really true, I mean?"

It was a mistake. It could have been a mistake. Conversation among the Death's Head Brigade crews went stockstill. The pilot who'd voiced the question stared from one unmoving face to another. The B–17 driver stiffened, staring from one man to another. "Hey . . . come off it, you people. What the hell did I say to rattle your cages?"

Psycho leaned sideways on the bar, massive forearms bearing his weight. The dumb Polack was suddenly gone, and in his place was a very large, very sensitive man. "We're touchy about the captain," Psycho rumbled, and you could tell from the tone of his voice that it *was* Captain, and not captain. "Very touchy. Most of us would be dead without that — that guy, as you call him."

The B–17 pilot, Tod Chippola, shook his head. "You people are reading me all wrong." He hesitated, and they waited. "You fly in here like a parade review at Kelly Field, and we recognize the things you're flying, and it dawns on us what outfit you really are. We've heard a lot about you."

He laughed harshly. "You're touchy about the captain?" He laughed again. "I'll tell you people something," he said as he looked around the club. "Any son of a bitch in this room wants to give up a seat in one of those B-25s, I'm your replacement." Again he looked around. "No takers? Shit." He stared directly at Psycho, and he wasn't backing down an inch. "You think we'd rather sit here on the ground with that wreck we got out there in the desert? I'll *buy* a pilot's seat in your outfit, for Christ's sake."

Tension flowed away into the heat. Psycho took the measure of the other man, rested a beefy hand gently on his shoulder. "The next one is on me, friend."

"Sure."

Czaikowicz pushed a beer slowly at the B-17 pilot. The barriers came down even more. "You want to know about this fellow who leads us?" He jerked a thumb at the man in shorts and white sneakers. "You ask him," he said of Alex Bartimo. "He's been with the captain longer than any of us." Psycho grinned hugely. "They flew and fought together before the rest of us ever met Whip Russel."

Chippola looked up at the suddenly open door, and Psycho carried it just a bit further. If Bartimo didn't want to pick it up, that was up to Alex. "They were together at Midway," Psycho added.

Tod Chippola showed his surprise. "So was I. Flew a B-17 there." He studied Alex Bartimo. "I thought I knew most of the people who flew Forts at Midway. I don't remember you."

Alex sighed. Ordinarily he would never have responded to this man. But Psycho, and the others from the 335th, had picked up the deep strain running through these poor bastards at Garbutt, and the empathy had worked its way into the open. If Psycho had given him this much lead, well, what the hell.

Alex Bartimo turned his eyes to Chippola. "You were too high to see us," he said at last.

The B–17 driver nodded slowly and they saw he'd put it all together very quickly. "B–26s. I remember now. There were four Marauders there. Two from the 22nd and two from the 38th Bomb Groups. You were all under navy control from Midway." He snapped his fingers. "Sure. That's right. You carried torpedoes." He stared at Alex Bartimo in a new light and with open respect. "Jesus, you poor bastards went in *on the deck*." He shook his head. "We could hardly see the goddamned Japanese fleet, we were so high."

A deep moan swept overhead and then there was the rush of thunder and wings passing by. "P–39s," someone called out. "They keep away most of the flies."

"They sure as shit don't bother the Zeros," came another catcall, and the laughter followed the fading moan of Allison engines.

It was a pause for searching back through the months. They all remembered the Battle of Midway in June. The first week of the month. Hell, *yes;* we won that session with the Japanese. The biggest air-sea battle since the war started, for Christ's sake. Everyone knew what the Japanese had in that engagement: an armada of six aircraft carriers, seven battleships, sixteen cruisers, forty-five destroyers, twelve transports and hundreds of fighters and dive and torpedo bombers. They outnumbered us by three or four to one and before the whole thing was over we had broken the back of the whole Japanese fleet and —

They drew up short in their introspection. Let's keep it straight, they might have said to themselves. The *navy* won that battle. Because sure as hell the Army Air Forces did *not*. Not because they didn't try. Everybody tried, and for most of the way through that savage melee the Japanese beat the absolute living shit out of the army, the marines and the navy. Not until the very end of things, when we were on our way to one of the most disastrous defeats in our history, with consequences far more critical than resulted from the battering at Pearl Harbor, did the navy dive bombers cut loose and run.

The Japanese were busy tearing the hell out of torpedo bombers trying to get through to the Japanese warships. And while they were enjoying their massacre of the hapless souls flying just over the waves, the SBD dive bombers rolled into the screaming plunges that ended with the enemy carriers gutted and exploding.

Tod Chippola openly studied Alex Bartimo. You could almost hear the thoughts rustling through his mind. Bartimo didn't look like the kind of man you expected to find in a flying wreck in the midst of a brutal air war. Especially in a hell-bent-for-leather outfit that was scoring hard against the Japanese. No matter those carefully patched rags and sneakers. You couldn't miss the signs. Alex was a fancy, a smooth dude, and he hadn't spoken more than a few words for Chippola and the other crewmen in the club to recognize he was no American pilot.

"Underneath all that fancy spit and polish, gentlemen," Psycho announced suddenly, "we got a pure naked Aussie. A renegade from this godawful continent on which we now stand ass-deep in dust."

Goddamn if that big hulk wasn't right. Somehow Alex seemed, *was,* different. He stared unblinking at the scrutiny to which he was being subjected.

"I was supposed to fly that mission," added Czaikowicz. "Fly right seat for the captain. We were in the 22nd then. Two of our B–26s and two more from the 38th, and they stuck torpedoes under our bellies, Jesus, I'd never even seen what the hell a torpedo looked like before that day, and they were gonna send us out with six of them new Avengers the navy got in a hurry to Midway." He shook his head with self-chagrin. "There I go again, making it sound like I was on that run. I was supposed to, but I can't go." The look on his face even now showed his incredulity at what had happened then. "Food poisoning. Of all the rotten luck. Can you believe it? Food poisoning, for shit's sake. Anyway, I'm all doubled over with cramps, and I can't even stand, let alone fly, and Alex was there, and . . ." Psycho let it hang. He knew someone would ask the question.

"What the hell was an Aussie doing at Midway?"

Alex smiled, and the deeply tanned face with the thin white mustache took on a rueful look. "Navy, you know. *Our* navy, I mean. Australian. Liaison officer with your people. Why" — he shrugged to encompass the enigmatic workings of government — "I never did know, really. Ours not to question why, but only to stumble forth and, well, and all that sort of rot." He sipped at his beer and smiled.

"After all, I was a pilot. A ruddy good one, I might add. I thought I would be flying in this war. Certainly I had every intention of it. Shooting down Zeros left and right in my trusty Wirraway, you know."

Laughter met that last remark. The pilots recognized the Wirraway. An American trainer to which the Australians had added a more powerful engine than the original model, and then with no more than ghostly faith and monumental courage, was sent out to battle with the tigerish Zero fighters, which with appalling ease tore them to shreds.

"But everything became scrambled," Alex went on. "My rotten luck not to have one of those splendid machines. Someone goofed. I was shipped off by flying boat to Midway to coordinate with your navy on our fighting the war together. Of course, I appreciated the faith my government had in me, since I was *all* the Australian forces on

Midway. I found myself, bluntly, with my thumb stuck up
my ass. Not a thing to do, everyone too busy to talk to me.
So I watched what was going on. The big battle was
shaping up. And the aircraft they brought in."

"I saw those brand-new TBFs, those Avengers, that were
going out to destroy the Japanese fleet." He shook his head
and they saw he was serious. "Poor, misguided souls."
Alex Bartimo seemed to come alive as his words shifted to
the machines in which they were so interested.

"And the Marauders. Those Martins you people call the
B-26. A lovely airplane, really. They were trying to sling
torpedoes under them. I was in the operations center, the
war room, I suppose they called it, and people seemed quite
mad the way they dashed about. Then, in the middle of all
this profound insanity this little fellow came in. Whip
Russel."

Alex chuckled with the memory, and suddenly he became
aware of just how intent was his audience. Including his
own men. Alex realized — funny he'd never thought of this
before — that not even Whip's men had ever really known
what happened that day at Midway.

"Well." Alex took a longer swallow. "He was in a real
snit. I didn't know him then as Whip, of course. Captain
Russel. He came storming into the war room and no one
paid him the slightest. Just ignored him. Froze him out.
They were rather busy, to give them their due. Whip took it
for a few moments, I imagine he was sizing up the situation.
Suddenly he shouted, 'I need a goodamned pilot!' Just like
that. No preamble, no how-do-you-do, my-name-is-so-and-
so. Just opened his mouth and out came this bellow as from
a drill sergeant. If his intent was shock, he succeeded.
Certainly he attracted my attention. I attracted his, it
seems. Or rather, the wings on my tunic. Everyone stared
at him, but he was staring at me."

Alex Bartimo sighed, mixing the sound with a smile. "He came slowly up to me until we were only inches apart. I'd never felt the aura from another human being as I felt that moment. His eyes were wild. I imagine the look on my face by now was one of mild shock, or whatever, but the wildness went out of his face, and he knew quite precisely what he was doing. I was suddenly aware that I was a white sheep in a room filled with very dark and woolly animals. There I stood in all my glory, resplendent in my white uniform and R.A.A.F. wings and all that sort.

"The little captain tapped the wings on my chest. 'Do you fly?' he demanded. I mean demanded. He didn't ask.

" 'Not without an airplane, old chap, I told him.' He quite ignored my quick wit, I should add. I'll never forget his reply.

" 'I got a goddamned airplane and a copilot who's in the barracks throwing up blood and he can't walk and the Japanese fleet is out there just waiting for you and me to show up. You want something to do to get the crease out of those goddamned clothes?'

"Some high-ranking officer, I really forget what he was, had listened to us, and he finally came over and told Whip Russel he couldn't take me in his machine, that it was against regulations. He had quite a bit of horsepoop to say, but somewhere in the middle of his speech my new-found friend offered to kill him right on the spot. Grabbed his attention, it did. Then he turned to me. 'You know where we are on the flight line. We take off in twenty minutes.' He turned around without saying another word and walked out the door and I thought to myself, My God, that's the kind of man who may yet win this bloody war."

Bartimo shook his head and smiled. "Would you believe it really happened, just as I've said it? I did fly with him that day, you know. Flew the right seat as copilot in a machine the inside of which I'd never seen until I climbed through the ruddy hatch. Ridiculous, really, you must understand. But I will lay claim to one distinction for the Battle of Midway."

They waited through his pause. "I'll tell you this, gentlemen. *I* was the best-dressed pilot in that entire battle."

He lapsed into silence, another quiet long swallow of his beer and lighting a cigarette. Pilots and crewmen in the club looked at one another, not speaking, waiting for one man to say the words for all of them.

"Lieutenant."

Alex turned to the major who'd said only that one word. He simply waited for the other man to go on. The question came quietly and it came with total sincerity.

"What was it like . . . on the deck, out there?"

Alex fingered the beer can. "I was afraid someone might get around to that," he said.

He was surprised when Psycho nudged him, gently, with a thick forefinger. "It's all right, Alex. Just tell them."

6

"Well. You all know, of course, what those machines look like. The short-winged killers. It's difficult to describe, but they gained a special sense of a killing machine with those torps slung beneath. Of course we were all feeling the tremendous tension from the day before. The Fortresses had gone after the enemy from high altitude, and the Nips simply shrugged them off. During the night following some very brave idiots went out in PBYs, flying as close to the water as they could, and I imagine they were doing all of ninety miles an hour when they drove right at the Japanese. They were using radar, as I recall, and they managed to put a tin fish into the side of a tanker. Of course, none of this really bothered the Japanese, when you consider the size of the fleet they had going for them. Anyway, earlier that same morning, it was the fourth of June, the day of the real confrontation, the marines went out to intercept a force of Zero fighters. Buffaloes and Wildcats, and the Zeros came down on them. If you didn't know what happened I'm sure you can figure it for yourselves. Carnage. A bloody slaughter. The Zeros tore the marines into little pieces. We had just gotten the news of that mess when we started turning over our engines. We had four Marauders, as you know, and we were intended to perform in concert with those six Avengers. Anyway, the two Marauders of the 38th Group held lead and right-wing position. Whip was holding down left wing, and we had another ship from the 22nd behind us to fill the slot. We were only fifteen minutes out from Midway when we sighted them. The whole bloody horizon was filled with Japanese warships. Difficult, I daresay, to forget that moment. The time was precisely five minutes past seven. Not the most auspicious start for a day . . .

"Pity the poor bombardiers. Month after month they'd trained with their Norden sights and their fancy gadgets, and now that the enemy was growing ever larger on the horizon, all they could do was check their sights and activate their arming devices and turn everything over to the pilots. We weren't going to make any bomb runs, of course, we were going as low as we could and aiming was nothing more than the pilot pointing his machine where he hoped the enemy vessel would be, and sending his torpedo on its way. Sounds terribly simple, but it isn't, really.

"Anyway, things were happening quickly now. I mean, we saw the warships, and the Japanese saw us just about the same time. Whip was talking with the other pilots so they could each select a different target, and the gunners were on the line now, rather excited, and difficult to blame them, even for shouting the way they did, because directly before us, about twenty miles away, were more fighter aircraft than I'd ever seen in my life. Two large formations of Zeros cruising in wide circles.

"I'd always prided myself on being cool in a nasty situation, but I found I wasn't cool anymore. I was cold right down to my toes. I realized quite suddenly that all those fighters out there were going to do everything they could to keep us from getting to the carriers. You can guess that's what Whip selected — the largest carrier in sight.

"The tempo began to pick up. Whip firewalled the throttles and eased ahead on the yoke. What he calls balls to the wall. The Marauder is fast, and we were squeezing from them everything they had to give, and the dive helped.

But the torpedoes slowed us down and just gave the Zeros more time to make their move. I should add that the Zeros were high, oh, perhaps fifteen to twenty thousand above us, so they could pick exactly how they were going to make their runs on us, with all the advantages of speed picked up in their dives. They could trade off height for diving speed and perfect positioning, but I imagine you're all quite familiar with this sort of thing."

A voice came quietly from the group. "Amen."

Alex smiled. "Our gunners called off at least eighteen Zeros peeling off on us. I found myself admiring those pilots. I mean, they didn't break formation or throw their advantage away. They wheeled about smartly and came at us in precision, where they could do the most damage.

"Well. By now I could make out the shape and disposition of the fleet getting closer with every moment. What I saw did nothing to inspire confidence. The warships were deployed miles deep, arranged in a loose box formation, with the carriers moving swiftly. This way they kept plenty of maneuvering room for evading our attacks, and still they retained the protection of all the other warships. I imagine that totaled several thousand antiaircraft weapons of various calibers, and the fighters, to say nothing of the carriers themselves."

Alex went quiet for several moments. The muscles in his left cheek twitched visibly. But there was no quaver or change in his voice.

"Anyway. It was obvious the Japanese were going to give us what you Yanks so quaintly call the old one-two punch, first with the defending fire of those warships, and then with the Zero fighters. One sight I will never forget. For a moment I thought I'd gone mad. The whole fleet seemed to have exploded into flames. Then I realized that every gun of those warships had opened fire, and the brilliant flames I was seeing came from the flashing of the guns. One rippling blast of flame after the other.

"We'd hoped, of course, to hold a tight formation so we might better defend ourselves against the fighters. Not much of a chance there, however. The Japanese were firing everything up to and including their sixteen-inch rifles, and their first salvos fell short of us. Impossible to miss, because the ocean erupted in towering geysers where their big shells struck the water. It's a frightening thing, really, to see those spouts of water. Must have been hundreds of feet high. You run into one of those and it's like hitting a tree. It's all over right then and there.

"That wiped out our neat formation, to say the least. We began to dodge. Whip at once skidded off to the left of the lead aircraft. The way we were bunched in there, one salvo and its waterspouts could have creamed all of us. So we spread out and began to jink about. We were really dodging the great spouts of water, flying between and around them and trying to stay one jump ahead of the Japanese. Yet, the man who was leading the show, I think his name was Carter, was quick. He estimated the Japanese had shot their load with those heavy salvos, and that now they would leave it up to the fighters to attend to us. So he called out for everyone to close it in tight again, and we did just that, back into the diamond formation."

"We got down to the thin skin of it all when the Zeros made their move. They came at us in line-abreast position, and the fun began with the first sweep of six of the bastards. You all know the sight when they're firing with their cannon and guns, but you rarely have a delayed view of all those Zeros with their noses and wings sparkling like that. They opened fire with their nose guns. *Then* we saw the wings come aflame. The color was darker and had black smoke, and that meant, of course, they had opened up with their cannon.

"It was quite eventful, really. There were still some odd waterspouts about and before us, so in effect here we were rushing in like some bloody fools to take on the whole Japanese fleet, and we were actually trapped. Remarkable, when you think of it. We didn't dare climb because that would slow us down and open us up to lighter flak, and everybody would have a piece of us. We still had some altitude because our dive was rather shallow. Carter, who was leading us, had a rather terrible decision to make. Did we give the nod to the guns or the Zeros as the greater evil? The man deserves enormous credit for split-second thinking. The instant he saw the black smoke from the wings of the Zero fighters, he made his decision. I was still sitting there with visions of cannon shells coming at us when all four Marauders went down steeply. Very steeply, because I had a marvelous view of the ocean rushing up at us. The air was more than rather bumpy, of course. All those exploding shells were throwing out their shock waves. Most interesting effect, really.

"Well, what Carter had done was to think that one vital moment ahead of the Japanese. Our sudden dive, and still in formation, took us right down to the water. It threw off the aim of the Zero pilots in their head-on pass at us, and also gave our turret gunners a chance to have a shot at the fighters as they passed overhead. It was a marvelous payoff for us, for we rushed ahead of that wave of fighters, and the short dive gave us some extra speed.

"I haven't had much to say about those navy machines. The poor bastards in the Grummans. They were quite a bit slower than us and trailing well behind. What worked for us didn't do a thing for those blighters. I had a chance to look back and to my right.

"Nasty back there. The Zeros were dead-on in their aim. Almost at the same instant I saw two of the Grummans explode. One moment they were holding their tight formation, incredible discipline, really, and then two of them were just fireballs and going into the water. A third one lost its wing and cartwheeled into the sea. No one had a chance, of course.

"It was at this point that we were cutting to the right, and I still had those Grummans in sight. Three of them had gone down in less time than I've told you. Another one flew into one of those waterspouts from the exploding shells. With all that had been happening I was still startled. The effect of hitting that column of water was, well, it was like a giant hand came out of nowhere and just slapped the machine into the water.

"Then there was no time to look. The Zeros were back onto us. By now we were closing rapidly on the warships and the fighters were going crazy after us. A few of them singled us out and — " Alex blinked several times; the onrush of memory was hitting him faster than he could bring it to words. He took a deep breath and looked about the club. Most of the men watching him were aware that Alex didn't see them. He was embroiled in that misty tunnel of months before . . .

"You know, the sequence of . . . I mean, things were now happening so bloody fast. We had no more formation. Impossible to hold. We were ten feet off the water, absolutely no more. It looked like we were flying straight into the ocean, all the time skidding and weaving madly to throw off those fighters. They were more of a nuisance than ever before. You've heard the old expression about flying through a storm of bullets and shells. Once I laughed at clichés. No more, because that *was* a storm of bullets and shells.

"Do understand" — and they could see Alex straining to paint them into the pictures flashing through his mind — "that it had all become quite the madhouse. The sounds

. . . our engines, of course, the banging on the wings and fuselage from enemy bullets. Every now and then a cannon shell would hit. You've all heard that sound, you know what it's like, but it's so difficult to tell anyone who hasn't. It's like putting your head inside a bucket and then having someone fire off a shotgun, also *inside* that infernal bucket. The gunners were shouting back and forth to one another, calling the fighters as they made their runs, and our turret guns were firing, and the tail gun, and the two waist guns as well. I'll never forget Whip during that long run toward the aircraft carrier.

"He wasn't flying anymore. Too soft and easy a word. He'd become a part of that machine. Every muscle in his neck and his face was as tight and visible as braided wire, and you could see muscles snapping, his nerves taut as he slammed his feet — yes; *slammed* — back and forth on the rudder pedals, and the yoke was working constantly. We weren't flying, actually, we were being thrown constantly forward through the air. I paid close attention to it all, because I knew that if Whip took a bad one, it would be up to me to take over. So I had my hands and feet ready to go to work, and it was positively maddening.

"I don't like the Japanese. Nasty beggars and all that, but you had to give them credit, the way they came after us. Their air discipline was beautiful. They closed to absolutely pointblank range, ignoring our gunners as if they didn't exist, firing in short, steady bursts. I said pointblank range? They were closer than that. It looked as if they might even ram us.

"Then they finally found our number. Our turret gunner, his name was Gogoj, tried to get them off us, and Ashley, in the tail, was doing the same thing, but the Japanese just ignored them. Three fighters picked us out and the next thing we knew the machine was filled with buzzing, screaming hornets. The bullets were literally that thick, and every now and then we heard that terrific whacking bang of the cannon shells going off.

"Gogoj took the worst of it. The fighters went for his turret to get him out of the way, and they shot the plexiglas covering of the turret into a shambles. Pieces whipping away in the wind, that sort of thing. We, gentlemen, fly inside the cockpit. Can you imagine what it was like when those shards, those jagged pieces of plexiglas, whirled about? We were doing something like three hundred miles an hour, and the torn plexiglas ground Gogoj's face, instantly, into raw hamburger. You must understand I didn't know all of this at the moment it happened; I'm recounting, to some extent, so forgive me if I seem to have been everywhere at the same time. Gogoj was torn to ribbons about his face and neck, and the exploding shells and the wind quite literally blasted him out of the turret. Blood was everywhere. His face was spurting blood from a dozen wounds, there were slivers of skin hanging from his cheeks, his nose and chin, his forehead. He was in agony, and there he was on the floor of an airplane that Whip was throwing about as violently and as constantly as he could, to throw off the aim of the Zeros. And it kept getting worse for Gogoj; you see, as Whip kept jinking so wildly it threw the sergeant against the sharp mechanism of his turret and opened up even more wounds.

"We went through a wild turn, a long skid, to be more precise, when one of our machines bought it. I was watching this Marauder, flying along, and the next instant there was this long streamer of brilliant flame coming back from a wing tank. I never believed fire could spread that quickly. It raced along the wing into the cockpit, kept right on going and ignited the engine on the opposite side. Thank God it didn't last long, for you all know what it was like inside that airplane. The tanks exploded. I know I was thinking that that airplane could be *us*. For an instant all we saw was a fireball and then pieces of wreckage struck the water. They must have bought it instantly.

"We didn't know, not then, that at that very same moment, the fifth Grumman had also gone in. That left one of those Avengers still in the air. Only that one. Not a very auspicious start for the machine, what?

"Anyway, as my friend Psycho is wont to say, things were going to hell in a handbasket for us. Back in the fuselage, that remarkable man, Gogoj, bleeding everywhere, was heard screaming curses into the intercom, and actually forcing his way, and with a great deal of pain, I should add, back into his turret."

Alex took a deep breath. "The worst was the wind? Not so, I imagine, for frustration must have exceeded even that. This man had forced himself back into his turret and was swinging his weapons around, but he never had a chance to fire. Zeros came in from both sides and they chopped us to pieces, and poor Gogoj again caught the brunt of it. This time the poor bastard took a cannon shell almost in his face. He was still staggering from the blast — and there is no way this man could have lived, but I assure you he did — when he was surrounded by buzzing hornets. Would you believe a bullet tore away the charging handle of his left machine gun, right out from under his closed hand, without injury to the hand? At the same time the turret control handle was shattered, the triggers were mashed to pulp and the turret wiring was cut in a hundred places.

"Now, imagine this if you can. The turret was dead, the man was critically wounded, and he waved away all help, because he figured if he stayed at his guns, he might bluff the Japanese pilots into thinking his turret was still danger-ous and they might be more cautious in their attacks.

Alex gestured easily. "Don't let me take away from anyone else. I mentioned Ashley in the tail turret. That poor bastard took five bullets in his hip and knee, and all at about the same moment. He was thrown back into the fuselage, and he crawled out of the way, bleeding and in agony, so that Melo — he fired the tunnel guns — might get past him to the tail, where the gun position was much more vital.

"Melo, it turned out, hesitated just long enough to make Ashley comfortable, and he paid for that little bit with a slug across his entire forehead. Would you believe that this man also ignored the pain and the blood and forced his way into the tail turret? I should say, he tried. Because he took another bullet, this time in his right arm near the shoulder. Two more slugs went into his side, raking his ribs. Still he went for the turret. A cannon shell exploded and put something like fifty or more pieces of hot metal into his leg.

"*Then* he made it to the turret. He wasn't there long before he discovered his back was on fire. Incendiaries; they'd set aflame the seat cushions in the tail. Melo carried the blazing cushion to the open space by the tail and hurled it away. The wind threw it back into his face and set *him* afire. He beat out the flames with his bare hands, snuffed out the fire in the cushions and turned around to see flames everywhere.

"He tried to call us in the cockpit, of course, but the intercom was dead. All the radios and wiring had been shot away. Melo went back to the tail gun, but it was shot up and jammed. Somehow, in that wildly flying machine, Melo came forward through the fuselage, along the catwalk of the bomb bay, through the small circular hatch, down into the radio compartment and then up to us. He grasped Whip's arm, shouting that everyone in the airplane was badly wounded and we were on fire.

"For the first time in this insane mission *I* finally had something to do. Poor Melo collapsed, but I had no time to help him, of course. Whip ordered me back to the tail. When I got there I had a bit of tidying up to do. Most of the seat cushions were burning away merrily, and I managed to fling them away through one of the side gun positions.

"I didn't know the tail gun was wrecked, so I thought I'd have a go at it. I had a perfect view of what was going on behind us, and I was just in time to see a Marauder take a full dose from a couple of Zeros. It exploded and went straight in. I tried to fire and found the gun useless. So I went forward again. It was quite a journey. Whip was jinking about so violently I was thrown from side to side and more than once knocked off my feet. How Melo, wounded as he was, had done this very same thing was a mystery to me. I came upon him by the cockpit and started to give him some first aid, but he brushed me off, murmuring that Captain Russel might need help at the controls.

"Back into the right seat I went, and I was startled to see blood trickling down the side of Whip's face. He'd taken a grazing bullet along his scalp, and he ignored the wound and the blood. What I didn't know was that Whip had a few pieces of cannon shell in his left leg, and that flying the aircraft through its maneuvers had been sheer hell for him. But he never let on.

"No sooner was I strapped in than we seemed to be in the middle of the whole bloody Japanese fleet. I've never seen so many warships before or since. They were everywhere. Just before us an aircraft carrier swelled in size as we raced at it. The entire side of the vessel, as well as the nearby warships, blazed with fire — all those guns having a crack at us. We were so close — I hope I never again have the pleasure — that even the smaller cannon and the machine guns were firing, and the air about us had come alive.

Tracers, all kinds. Glowing, burning, shining; whatever. It was all there, and we were flying right through the middle of it. Have you ever flown at night in a snowstorm and put on your nose light? The whole world is incandescence rushing at and around and all about you. It was something like that.

"Funny. Until now, with the war some six months old, I'd never seen a Japanese flag. I thought about it right then and there because I was being provided my first view. Overdramatic, of course, but there it was. The Rising Sun, fluttering from the carrier's mast. I stared at the flag, and Whip bored straight in toward the carrier, absolutely ignoring the hundreds of guns firing pointblank at us.

"Those Japanese were fast. The carrier was already heeling over, turning into us, as Whip held the Marauder straight and true. Then he shouted his command, and waved with one hand to the bombardier, his name was Johnson, down in the nose, to yank the release. Johnson gave it a go and the torp dropped away, and everything quite became a blur in here because we were almost onto the carrier by now. I mean, it was still well *above* us. Whip shouted, *'Pull!'* and I grasped the yoke with him and we both hauled back as hard as we could. I still remember all those Japanese staring at us with their mouths open as we raced scant feet over the deck. How we missed the planes there, and the masts, is a mystery I'll never fathom.

"The moment we crossed the deck we dropped back to the water, dodging a destroyer that had opened up on us. We had more speed now because we'd lost the drag and weight of the torp and we'd burned quite a bit of fuel. Whip was actually banging on the quadrant, beating his fist against the throttles and prop controls, trying to get more speed out of the aircraft. It seemed to work, and we were truing out at better than three hundred, and the Zeros coming after us weren't doing very well. We were too low and too fast for them to fly a pursuit curve. They had to hang in straight behind us. Johnson was out of the nose now, and he went aft to see what he could do to help those poor fellows back there.

"I hadn't realized how badly the Marauder was shaking. Whip's face was white from his wounds and the strain, and he told me to take it, to stay low and just keep flying as fast as we could go. He sat there, utterly exhausted.

"Johnson worked his way back to the radio compartment to get a homing signal from Midway. Useless. Everything had been shot to pieces and the antennae were all blown away. But at least we had a real chance now. The Zeros had given up their chase, and I pulled up a bit and came back on the power. The engines were badly overheated, and easing the power also saved us from the wild buffeting and vibrations that had been getting worse all the time.

"Our navigator, despite some rather nasty wounds of his own, had Johnson hold him up so he could use the small plexiglas dome to shoot the sun and get our bearings to return to Midway. It wasn't quite that easy. Something came loose, somewhere, and the aircraft began to shake worse than before, and one man couldn't hold her. Whip and I flew together and it took all our strength to hold her in the air.

"We were afraid we might explode at any moment. Fuel was coming out in a heavy spray from the tanks that had been holed. One spark and that would have been it. I'd been telling you about Gogoj. He came up front, looking all the world like a giant blood-soaked rag, and he went right to work, transferring the fuel into the two tanks that were still whole. Otherwise we'd never have made it back.

"You can imagine what the machine was like. She was a wreck, from nose to tail, and I still don't know how we kept her in the air. I'd never handled a B-26 before, and now was not the time to start taking lessons. So Whip flew, and I helped, and it was the most incredible piece of flying I've ever seen. He came in to Midway holding hard right aileron and left rudder, like a drunk sliding out of the sky. When we'd put down the gear and given it a visual, we saw that the left tire was all chewed to ribbons. An absolute mess. A wrong move and the gear would have snapped, and we would have ended all that with a cartwheel down the runway. But Whip played her like a master, holding her off the left gear, until finally she settled. We went hard for the brakes. Nothing. They'd been shot away. The impact of hitting that gear and riding on metal was unbelievable. We were banged about so badly the entire instrument panel tore completely off its fastenings and ended up in our laps. But we made it, stopping in the center of the runway.

"I had to walk around that machine, to see what she looked like from the outside. And I didn't believe it. The left gear, the doors, the whole bottom of the nacelle was a shambles. Fuel dripped from the tanks, hydraulic fluid and oil spattered on the ground. She leaked in a dozen places. Every one of the eight propeller blades was chewed into a jagged mess. The entire top edge of the left wing had been blown away. All our antennae had been shot off. The engines were filled with holes. The rear turret was a bloody mess. There was blood all over the interior, and some of it had sprayed outside. The tail turret was a sieve. There were more than five hundred major holes, rips, gashes, tears and, well, we quit counting on only one side of the machine. It didn't seem much use to go on, because obviously that airplane was unflyable long before we got past that carrier."

There was a long silence. Someone pushed a fresh beer at Alex. Men began to move their bodies. They'd been oblivious to heat and dust and their own stinking perspiration.

A captain rose to his feet. "Lieutenant, would you mind just one more question?"

Alex shrugged. "Be my guest."

"What," asked the man, "the hell are you doing with the Death's Head outfit?"

Alex chuckled and even the ponderous Psycho grinned hugely. "It's very simple, really," said Alex. "I like them."

"Man, that's for sure. You're with them even though you don't have to be here. But that's what I mean. I was trying to figure out how the hell you get away with it. You're Australian, and yet — "

Alex gestured to stave off the rest. "Who, my dear fellow, is going to tell?"

The pilots laughed and the captain waved his capitulation. "Lieutenant, it sure as hell ain't going to be me. Welcome to the crowd."

7

COLONEL LOU GOODMAN had spent the last hour in his quarters, rummaging through the memories the appearance of Whip had brought surging to the forefront of his mind. Funny how these past six months had so effectively obliterated his past immediately before that period. Pearl Harbor had come with a clamorous explosion to his enjoyable, albeit hectic, life-style, and it had wrecked the affluence he had grasped. Yet, and he was not slow to make the self-admission, he had found a strange and stirring new purpose in what he'd been selected to do. A military figure Lou never had been and never would be, and his corpulence was tolerated only because of his brilliance in patching together combat aircraft from the lowest part of the scavenger barrel. In this respect he was a genius and his men recognized him as such, and without exhortation on his part — for the fat colonel was likely to be found in the depths of engines or under broken wings as often as his men — they would do anything for their commanding officer. Goodman would never have understood that he was an inspiration to his men. His sense of their belief and confidence in him was enough. Lou Goodman had not yet come to the realization, although it hovered along the periphery of his consciousness, that he was a man who felt and enjoyed immensely the fact that he was making a vital contribution to staving off the Japanese in this desert-ocean-mountain hellhole that formed the bottom of the bucket called the Southwest Pacific.

The appearance of Whip Russel had jogged him back to certain unpleasant memories he had forgotten with ease. Whip and his friends saw Lou Goodman as the ultimate wheeler-dealer, the man who had his ins with the law, who knew how to move through the thickets of a thousand shady deals, who knew who and what and where made the right wheels turn to his satisfaction. They had never known of a wife even fatter than he, to whom he was chained by his own honest love, and the knowledge that without his support, financially and emotionally, Rachel would disintegrate into a mass of frightened human blubber. Lou Goodman had made the wise move of sliding into his home his wife's favorite sister, a woman of lesser girth but possibly even greater ugliness, so that the two women might present an impenetrable wall to the stares and remarks of neighbors and what passed for friends. It worked well for Lou Goodman; his patience and largess was not unappreciated, and his wife kept for him an expansive study and bedroom, where by unspoken but mutual agreement he was not to be bothered by anyone. It was a welcome and an accepted haven within his own home, so that Rachel and her sister, Rebecca, would see Lou only at his own pleasure, or when some minor emergency required his decision-making powers.

Away from this quiet, regulated home life, Lou Goodman took to his daily affairs with what was almost a vengeance. He found himself unable to run his motorcycle shops, his airfields and his growing aircraft maintenance facilities without increasing involvement with the young men who gravitated to these interests. At a later stage in his life, when he should have been fading into obscurity, his being was filled with purpose, in the intricate interweaving of his own experience and essential wisdom with the problems and headaches of those who came to him.

Yet, and he was deeply satisfied with the realization, it was on Whip Russel that it all focused. That day in the Lockheed, the sudden flight to escape the police, he had gained a level of emotional consummation he was astonished to find in himself. Lou Goodman had never admitted it then, and he had never pondered the matter since, but now, at this moment, in his ramshackle, stifling office on Garbutt Field in northern Australia, he became aware that more than anything else, he identified with Whip Russel, his own — Goodman's — thwarted dreams of his own youth. There it was, he realized, and he was amazed with the growing sense of reality about it all: that moment in the Lockheed, the caressing touch, the gaze of wonder, the song the skies were singing so subtly but powerfully to that young man . . . there it all was. Oh, Lou Goodman flew, and he was a good pilot, but he'd never known the furious joy of throwing himself with wild abandon into the heavens. He wanted, urgently, that this might be the chosen lot of the fierce-eyed youngster, and yet, Goodman knew as well, he must walk a careful line indeed through Whip's emotional instability. Whip could not be jerked suddenly from his world; it would be a gross violation of his own ethics; if nothing else, young men like Whip stood to the very end by their word.

He could not be thrust from his circle, but he could be weaned. And of all the difficult decisions Lou Goodman had made, it was *not* to press too greatly against the youngster. Lou Goodman could do no more than simply be there, to let Whip reach out of his own accord.

He flew him in different machines, he explained, he answered questions, he taught him to fly, and finally he reached the pinnacle of stepping from the airplane so that Whip might take to the air for his first solo.

It went as he expected. Whip flew the small aircraft better than well. The touch of the born pilot, the hesitancy that could not disguise the brilliance still waiting to be fulfilled — it was all there.

When Whip landed, Goodman walked back to the flight line, as Whip taxied the bright yellow Cub with gentle bursts of power, walking the rudder carefully, holding the stick well back. Lou Goodman stood to the side and waited until Whip shut down the Cub, until he tied the machine to the earth, closed the aircraft to the world.

He told Whip Russel only one thing. "I want you to remember this," he said. "No matter what happens in the future, no matter what you decide you want from the sky, no matter how tough you may find life, keep this in mind. No pilot ever has more than one first solo. You've had yours. You're now a part of that fraternity most pilots seem to talk about but can never really identify when someone calls them down for an explanation of what they mean." Goodman smiled. "That's because it's tough to talk with your heart."

He had said no more, and they had drifted apart. And then there had been that grim and bloody disaster on the morning of December 7, and the world turned savagely upside-down, and Lou Goodman had lost him.

It was "down there," in the dust-choked outback of northern Australia, that he heard again of Whip Russel.

There were stories of a lunatic who flew his B–25 as if it were a bullwhip. Just the one word, that sound of bull*whip,* when first he heard the stories, brought Lou Goodman to the realization that this might, it could, it *must* be that same kid who had first tasted the sky by Goodman's side. The crew of an A–20 Havoc had flown into Garbutt Field in an airplane holed and sieved and badly in need of work, an airplane that was as close to unflyable as it was for a machine to be and still stay in the air. Lou was in the shack they called a clubhouse when the A–20 crew made sounds of relief as they drained nearly forgotten beer.

Goodman caught snatches of conversation and found himself leaning to these men who were strangers but so closely of the same breed he feared no breach of crossing lines. He rose slowly and went to their table, excusing his intrusion, which was all the more remarkable because he was a colonel and they were all far down the ladder of rank. They also knew, in that certain instinct of the veteran, that this colonel gave not a damn for his own rank, or, theirs.

"This, ah, fellow you've been talking about," Lou Goodman said quietly. "Have you flown with him?"

"Not exactly, Colonel. I mean, we joined up with his outfit for a strike against some shipping at Finschhafen, off the Huon Gulf. You know, just — "

"I know where it is, Captain."

"Right. Anyway, we had three A–20s, and this outfit, which was led by some lunatic in an all-black B–25 with some sort of death's head insignia, he led the strike with five ships from his squadron. The eight of us amounted to everything we could put into the air." The captain shook his head and grinned. "I'd thought I'd seen it all, Colonel. Until I saw this guy fly that day, and then I knew maybe I was all wrong and I really didn't know that much about this business of driving iron birds through the air."

"What was so . . . unusual?"

"Well, the target was a bitch. The Nips had moved in some barges just loaded with flak. A real shitty mission, because we had to get in close and it was like getting right in the middle of a whole nest of wasps. They had fighters in the area, also, and the odds were — well, frankly, Intelligence estimated we'd take about one-third losses. That don't make the odds so good."

Lou Goodman nodded. "No, Captain, that don't."

They saw he was as serious as they, and the captain went on. "We *should* have taken those losses, and we would have, except for this guy who led the show. The moment we got within range of the Japanese he called for everybody to firewall their throttles, give out all the power they could make and stay close to him. You ever see this man fly, Colonel, and you'll know what a joke that is."

Goodman thought of a youth caressing the first control yoke he'd ever seen, and — he forced the past away and concentrated on the man before him.

"I've never seen or even known of a bombing run like that one. Jesus, we were in a long shallow dive all the way into the target, getting all the speed we could, and this black B–25 seems to go crazy. Follow him? Oh, man, it was like watching a snake with wings up there. The damn airplane was undulating. That's the only way to describe it. He's making subtle changes all the time in his approach, and the flak is all around him but he's just not taking any real hits. He's weaving and jinking *all* the time, he's throwing off the flak, and the fighters that are coming after us now haven't got a chance to set us up, and all this time this guy knows exactly what he's doing. I mean, when the Japs least expect it, when they figure the man in that lead ship has got to be scared shitless of all the flak and the rest of it, he goes forward on the yoke and he's in a steep dive now, closing to the target, and, well, we were full up on power, the props flat out and the engines ready to come apart, the airplane shaking and vibrating, and we see that black bomber firing with all guns, and he's *still* all over the place and, well, all of a sudden he comes out of a diving skid, a falling turn, but with lots of power and speed, and suddenly he's all through with this nonsense. I mean, we're almost there, and we should be trying to dodge everything when he, this cat in that lead B–25, all of a sudden he's not twisting or turning anymore, he comes out of that snake dance of his, and his airplane is flying now like it's on a set of rails.

"It's like, well, it's like all this time he's been throwing his arm forward, holding a whip, and now he's cracked the whip. See, all this time he's set up the target, he's got us past the fighters and through the worst of the flak, and now what's left is dumping our bombs right where they belong. It's straight in and to hell with everything, and would you believe, that son of a bitch creamed a bunch of barges, and we were hanging on to his tail feathers for dear life, we were scared shitless of losing him, and when we came out of it, every goddamned one of us was still in the air."

The other crewmen nodded slowly in full confirmation of their pilot.

Goodman drummed his fingers on the table, looking from one man to another.

"Uh, Colonel? You said, I mean, it sounded like this man is a friend of yours. Excuse me, sir, but can you tell us his name?"

The disappointment showed on Goodman's face. "I was hoping you might be able to tell me that."

"I'm sorry, Colonel," the captain said. "I wish I knew it. Because me and my whole crew are lined up ready to kiss that man's ass, anywhere he says."

"Including Macy's window during the lunch hour," another man offered.

Goodman laughed. "Did you know what outfit he was in?"

"Yes sir. The 335th. Medium. But we never got a chance to track it down."

Goodman rose heavily to his feet. "Thank you, gentlemen." He turned and walked away slowly.

They kept their eyes on him as he left through the far door.

"You know something?" They turned to their pilot. "I'd almost swear he was talking about his own kid."

8

THEY TROOPED in slowly, hesitant, following the easy stroll of Captain Whip Russel, but, and it was obvious to the private amusement of Lou Goodman, without their leader's confidence in what the meeting would produce. As soon as they settled on old chairs and ramshackle furniture Whip introduced them to the commander of Garbutt Field.

Goodman took careful measure of each man as Whip went the rounds. "This is Captain Ben Czaikowicz. We call him Psycho, for reasons that become clear the longer you know this loony bin. But he flies a mean airplane." Goodman didn't miss the affection, or the total acceptance, as Whip spoke of the man who flew number two position in the Death's Head Brigade.

"Lieutenant Alex Bartimo, sir." Goodman shook hands with the ludicrous figure, the combination of stiff upper lip with rags and white sneakers. There was something else that tugged at Goodman's attention. Ah, there it was. A certain way of rising to his feet with the introduction, the unique formality of address to a superior officer. It tagged Bartimo, and when Goodman got it all sorted out in his mind he grinned hugely. "You're Whip's right-seat driver?" Goodman queried. The response was clipped and precise. "Well, Lieutenant," Goodman said, "whoever you are that's an interesting skeleton you carry around with you." He caught the briefly revealed surprise that even Bartimo's self-control failed to hide. "It's all right, son," Goodman rumbled. "Whatever's your secret I'll leave it between you and your captain."

Goodman smiled to himself. Alex Bartimo would spend the rest of their meeting trying to figure out just what the devil this fat old colonel knew — and everyone else, save Whip, would be curious to discover *how* he'd overturned Alex's private rock.

There were other pilots brought into the meeting, but they were passed over lightly by Lou Goodman. It was the men who took care of the planes who really mattered. One look at the grizzled face of Master Sergeant Archie Cernan told Goodman he was in the presence of one of the well-experienced old-time line chiefs. Hands scarred and grimy, skin leathered from exposure to the sun from working outdoors for years on planes. This one was better than good and he was more than a mechanic; he was midwife to creatures with iron wings.

Lieutenant Dick Catledge wore pilot wings but wasn't on the list of active flight personnel. Young-old, reckoned Goodman. A man familiar with death and the dealing of same, and Goodman offered himself a private pat on the back when Catledge was identified as the squadron ordnance officer. That's why, mused Goodman, the smell of death with this man. It was his profession in more ways than one.

Goodman made a special effort in studying Captain Elmer Rankin. Bookish, yet, *that* didn't fit, and it took several moments of trying to draw his own picture of Rankin before Goodman realized he was dealing with an unusual brain. "How come you're not with headquarters?" Goodman snapped. It was a demanding question and its verbalization was much too sharp for the tone of this particular gathering. It almost put the captain on the spot. Rankin glanced at Whip but received only a thin smile in response. It told him to play it alone.

"To be frank about it, Colonel, I've been avoiding them like the plague," Rankin said carefully. He was testing Lou Goodman as thoroughly as the colonel was running him through the mill.

Goodman took note of the thin blond hair, the misleading build of the athletic body. He would have described Rankin as a man with haunting eyes. Goodman was almost sure he had it. He wanted to reach his own judgment before it was offered too easily. Rankin did it for him.

"Sir, uh, would you mind my asking why you brought up headquarters?" Rankin was out of water. No one had lifted up his mental shirttails for a long time.

"Headquarters," Lou Goodman said slowly, "is beating the bushes in every direction for people who know the Japanese better than other people." The look of surprise on Rankin's face was matched by every other man in the room, and they shared the same unspoken question. How the hell did Goodman know about —

"Does it bother you, Captain," Goodman went on, "to kill the Japanese?"

Even the manner of wording the question was enough for the two men to understand one another. The look on Rankin's face sewed it up. He nodded his head slowly, then stared directly into Goodman's eyes and gained all the more respect from the colonel. "Yes, sir, it does."

"You speak the language well?"

"Yes, sir."

"Where did you live in Japan?"

By now every man in the room save Lou Goodman and Elmer Rankin were staring open-mouthed at the two. Not even Whip Russel had known what he was hearing for the first time.

"Nagoya. Off the main drag of the town. Near Higashi-yama Park. A small school there." A thin, humorless smile appeared. "I think of *those* people, Colonel Goodman, and yes," he reaffirmed, "there are times when it hurts."

"I'm glad to hear that," Goodman said quietly. "There's hope for the rest of us then."

He swung his bulk about to face Whip squarely. "All right, Whip," he said brusquely, "you've been priming my goddamned pump for two days now. Every single thing that's happened since you and your band of roughnecks showed up has been aimed at softening up the fat old bastard. You can open your fists now and let me see what you've been hiding. Are you going to deny setting me up like a clay pigeon?"

Whip held his right hand over his heart. "Who? Me?" He leaned forward, his elbows on his knees, and the physical tightening of his body was almost a visible thing. His face took on an aspect Goodman hadn't seen.

"I want some airplanes that will let me fight." The words came out flat, no-nonsense. It wasn't a request or a demand. It was a statement.

Lou Goodman didn't answer immediately. Let it come out. "The B–25 you're flying," he said. "Not good enough?"

"Shit, no, Lou. Those airplanes of ours. They're good ships." He made a wry face. "Or they will be as soon as your people and mine have the chance to cure them of their leprosy. That isn't the point. Even when they were brand-spanking-new, when they came off the line, they were good airplanes."

Whip shifted in his seat. He was into it now and he was comfortable. Screw the fight he knew he would have with Lou Goodman. He had his teeth into it. "That's just the whole point, like I said. They're good *airplanes*. But for what we need they're not good enough."

Goodman toyed with the cigar butt. "I want to stay with you. Take it step by step. You're not talking about getting another type of bomber?"

Whip shook his head. "Hell, no. You're a miracle worker, Lou. I never called you a magician. There *aren't* any other bombers."

"You are so right," Goodman sighed. "So what you're talking about is changing what you've got."

"Not changing, sir." Goodman turned his head to Lieutenant Dick Catledge. "That's not enough. Improving what these machines can do."

"You're the expert with the guns." Another statement from Goodman.

Catledge started to reply and was cut short by a gesture from his commander. "You've seen those reports from Eglin Field?" Whip threw in.

"I've seen them."

"Is that all the hell you've got to say?" he demanded.

"That depends," Goodman told him. "It depends upon many things, Whip. It depends upon where you are. It depends upon what you've got to work with. It depends upon what regulations say you can and can't — "

"Screw the regulations."

Goodman shrugged. "Okay. We'll play it your way. Screw the regulations then. That doesn't change what you've got to work with." Goodman shook his head in mild self-rebuke. "I'm getting ahead of myself again. You tell me what you want."

"Okay, Lou. You know that we can change these airplanes we have. Turn them into something that can survive in the air with Japanese fighters. Right now our outfit has used up all its luck and borrowed a hell of a lot. Most other outfits, I don't care what they're flying, if they get caught by Zeros and there's no fighter escort, it's slaughter time. Our people get creamed."

Goodman's face was like stone. "I know *that* too."

"We're losing almost as many people to ground fire — ground and ships — as we are to the fighters. Why?

Because we're not flying these things the way the people who built them intended them to be flown. If we were going by the book we'd be upstairs anywhere from eight to fifteen thousand feet, dressed up in perfect formation and dropping our bombs in patterns. The trouble with all that — and, goddamnit, Lou, I know you know this also, but you told me to spell it out — is we aren't flying that way. If we played tin soldier games at those altitudes and the Zeros latched on to us there wouldn't be room on their fighters for all the pretty American flags they'd be painting.

"So" — and Whip's shrug was as eloquent as his intensity — "we go down low. That way we know we can hit 'em where they live. We can put the bombs where they do the most damage, and on the deck we've got a better chance against the Zeros. They can't come up beneath us in belly attacks. They've got to play it topside all the way and that gives our gunners a better chance. Not much of a better chance, but you take everything you can grab. But it's *still* not enough."

Whip took a deep breath and suddenly he bolted from his chair. It was another sign of that band-saw impetuosity, the staccato movements of a man's body trying to keep up with his mind.

"I don't want a goddamned medium bomber, or a light bomber, or even whatever it is they call an attack bomber. That's all fancy-name crap for airplanes that are getting shot to pieces. You know what I want, Lou?"

Goodman waited, impassive.

"I want a *gunship*." Whip stopped his pacing as if he'd smacked into an invisible wall and he turned sharply, a fist thudding into a palm. "A *gunship,* damnit. I want to be able to take my people on a run right into the teeth of the Japs and all their flak, and I want me and them to have the chance to come out of that run, and all in one piece. I want to be able to go into a bomb run and I want to chew the hell out of the flak positions that are waiting for us. I want more firepower going *at them* than they can throw up at us. You ever see those Jap destroyers, Lou? They're fast and they're good but their sides are made of tin, *tin,* goddamnit, and if I've got enough punch I can blow holes in those things with just my guns. The guns I want. The guns, damnit, that we *need.*"

Whip turned and his eyes bored into Lou Goodman. "We're the best," he said, suddenly quiet, but with no loss of the intensity that had gripped him so fiercely. "But time is running out for us too. If we don't get better equipment in the air, well . . ."

He threw himself back into his chair. "We've got to change the odds. We've got to turn our airplanes into weapons, for Christ's sake, not some toys from a Sears catalogue."

Lou Goodman let the silence hang in after Whip's mixture of tirade and unspoken plea. He knew what was meant. There had been those reports from Eglin Field in Florida. New experiments with bombing. They'd thrown away the book because everyone knew the book was a joke.

The new concept was skip bombing. You came in on the deck, you came in low and you stayed low, and the theory had it that if you dropped your bombs from a certain angle and a certain speed the bombs would skip — bounce — across the water just like a kid skipping a flat rock across the surface of a pond. And it worked. That was the real wonder of it. The damned thing *worked,* and it promised an accuracy of delivery that was almost too much to believe.

But it wasn't enough, because a bomber had to hold that run on the deck, and during that long, intolerable period of boring into the target you were a setup for flak. You had to have a way of knocking out, suppressing, the hellish fire-power the Japanese threw up at you.

Lou Goodman created a vision of a B–25 bristling with

fifty-caliber machine guns. It would be a bitch. There would be bracing problems, vibration, center of balance to consider, ammunition supply and feed and —

"It's not going to be that easy," Lou said, the quiet in his voice matching that of his friendly adversary. No one else in the room spoke. It was between these two.

Whip had a look of sudden disbelief. "Who the hell said it would be easy? Jesus Christ, Lou, its an engineering problem we're talking about. I don't want a goddamned miracle! I want solid engineering, ordnance work. Cutting, sawing, hacking, bolting together." Again he was intensely alive, springing back into the thickets they faced. He threw out his arm, stabbing the air.

"You know what we brought with us in those planes of ours? The best mechanics in our outfit. The *best*. And we scraped together every goddamned piece of metal we could find. Parts and pieces and bits. Aluminum and steel and galvanized iron and tin and God knows what else. We borrowed and stole every tool we could find. Those ships of ours are flying junkyards. Every one of my men is here to work on those planes. They're going to work day and night with your people, Lou. Day and night and I don't give a shit who sleeps or doesn't. But we're going to rebuild those airplanes into gunships and when we go back north we're going to make it a whole new ball game."

Lou Goodman had made a steeple of his fingers and he peered over them, owl-eyed. "I repeat, it's not that easy. I — "

"*Jesus!* Don't tell me how hard it is! Tell me *how* you're going to do it!"

Goodman stirred. He stalled for time so he could speak with the kind of clarity that would have meaning to these people who strained so hard to get back into a war with the right kind of weapons.

"Okay, Whip. Now you listen for a while, all right?"

"I — "

"Just can it, Whip."

Whip Russel narrowed his eyes and the two men stared at one another, but there was more bridge than gulf between them, and Whip nodded slowly.

"All right, Whip. Let me take it from your point of view for a moment. We're agreed that between my men and yours we have the bodies to do what you're planning. Gunships out of B–25s. We agree it's never been done before — "

"Catledge has worked it all out."

"Just shut up," Goodman went on smoothly. *"It's never been done before."* Goodman's repetition was quiet, forceful, and it hung in the air, visible for them to see and to ponder. "Until it's a fait accompli we don't know what problems will crop up. All right; we'll accept there are, there will be problems, and like all other horseshit like this, we'll cross those bridges when we come to them. We'll do what has to be done.

"We know generally what we need; armor plating and the galvanized metal and the bracing and the ammo feed chutes and the gas exhaust blowbacks, and all the thousand little things for this job. We'll accept that. I'm short on manpower here on Garbutt, but you know that and you've filled in the holes with your own people. They may know a hell of a lot less than either they or you think they do, but we can teach 'em in a hurry. We've got a whole field of wrecked and broken airplanes and I think we can convince the people from those iron birds to give up a few points. As for the rest of it" — Lou Goodman coughed gently and shifted again in his chair — "well, the food stinks and the beer is warm and the women they all got warts and chancres — at least from what somebody told me because I haven't seen a dame in months — so we don't have to worry about social life interrupting what has to be done."

For the first time a small ripple of laughter went out among the men in the room. Jesus, the old man's bought the idea! The thought swept among them and they eased their tension and —

Lou Goodman dropped his bomb in the midst of their uplifted spirit. "There's one problem."

You had only to look at his face to understand that the colonel meant what he said. No levity, nothing hidden. The room sobered — at once.

Goodman gave it straight out. "We don't have the guns. We do not have the machine guns you need to do what you want with your airplanes." The finality of Goodman's tone matched his words. "There's no use crapping in the sand about this to any of you. We can handle everything, even the ammunition. We've got boxes of fifty-caliber ammo up the gazoo. Only God, and not even Douglas MacArthur, knows how the supply system works. So we have more ammo than we know what to do with, but we do not repeat do not have the machine guns for this job."

Goodman waited out the silence and the inevitable questions. Dick Catledge was first to break the ice. "There are other planes on the field. Maybe — "

"Would you give up *your* weapons from your aircraft for another outfit?"

"No."

"Forget it then."

"Isn't there anything in the pipeline, Colonel?" Rankin asked.

"If there is, I don't know about it. Besides, nothing comes to us directly. It goes through the system, friend. From the Pentagon to Pearl Harbor to MacArthur's headquarters and then to Far East Air Forces and then it gets spread out wherever the head people say. It's a big and a clumsy system and in many ways it's stupid but it's there, like God, and you got to go to their church."

Whip gestured idly for Goodman's attention. Of all the men in the room he alone had caught the drift of what Goodman was trying to tell them, but without spelling it out like an instruction manual.

"If you don't have, ah, access to this stuff, Lou, who does?"

Goodman didn't answer at once. He swung around to face his desk and for several moments he shuffled papers idly. "According to certain records which mysteriously, and by persons unknown, somehow ended up on my desk, two days ago, at a dusty little hellhole known as Bowen, a cargo ship unloaded several dozen crates. From what I understand, those crates contain certain critical war items. They were unloaded at Bowen because the ship suffered damage in a storm and the captain was afraid it would never make it to South Australia. The plan was to drop it off at Bowen and then take it south on the coastal rail line."

Lou waited for the questions that came like arrows from the group.

"*What* certain critical items?"

"They include air-cooled fifty-caliber machine guns. The M2 model, I believe."

"Where the hell is Bowen?"

"Due south of here there's a fair-sized harbor facility known as Rockhampton. Between here and Rockhampton, isolated from the rest of the world except for a narrow road and the rail line, lies the port of Bowen. There are no Americans there. Just local people. Perhaps a handful of Aussie troops with antiaircraft, bored to death."

Whip rubbed the stubble on his cheek. "If they got these fifties there why the hell don't you just go get the damn things?"

"A good question, Captain," Goodman retorted. "They

have not been assigned to Garbutt Field. I have no authorization to simply take them. I *did* try, as a matter of fact. I made a signal — Christ, I'm getting to sound like these people here — I sent a priority message to FEAF. I pleaded and cajoled to the best of my ability, which is considerable. No dice. The guns are assigned to some purpose the meaning of which is clear only to MacArthur and his minions."

Whip looked at Psycho and Alex Bartimo, and leaned forward on his chair.

"Lou," he said. "Tell me more about the setup at Bowen . . ."

9

BAKED TO A GRIZZLE by the remorseless sun, a pimple on the long rail track running along the eastern coast of the huge island continent, injected with a semblance of purpose because of its crude port unloading facilities, grim and weathered as they were, Bowen felt the war only from a distance. It was a war in which they had never seen the enemy, although he was not safely far from where the citizens of Bowen plodded through their days and nights. The Japanese presence was threatening, yet had no more direct substance than heat waves shimmering in the pitiless sun.

The vision-slurring heat was another matter; its effect upon the skin was immediate and real. The *unseen* presence of the Japanese was worse, for the war had moved inexorably closer, and when it became a bitter struggle in the mountains and jungle and grassy hills of New Guinea it had its own frightening overtones, for parts of New Guinea were administered by Australians. It was an extension of the island continent, it was a touch, an arm, a moment of the people and its land. The Japanese came in and they smashed aside the courageous but woefully inadequate defenses of the Australians, and the people of Bowen, who had never seen a Japanese soldier or heard a Japanese airplane, knew that this invisible enemy was killing and maiming Australian soldiers. But no one *really* believed this pissy little place would be selected for the attention of the

Imperial Emperor, or whatever it was they called that funny little man in Tokyo. After all, when you really gave it some thought —

So early the next morning, with the sun huge and eye-knifing just over the horizon, the people of Bowen were totally unprepared for the swift strike from the eastern sky. In a classic move the enemy struck directly from out of the sun so the hapless defenders on the ground could barely see a thing as the bombers thundered overhead. The townspeople for a long and terrible moment were convinced their end had come, but the garishly painted Japanese bombers howled overhead and went into steep turns that took them directly for the port's dock facilities. From the center of town there was only that one clear look at the enemy planes and the orange ball marking the wings and fuselage; then the bombers were some distance away, hammering at their chosen target.

Brave Australians fired ancient rifles and the one machine gun assigned to the community defense, but everyone knew the effort was little more than a display of local honor. And they were more than willing to let the Japanese tear up the makeshift docks at the close of the rail spur, which immediately after the bombing attack began was enveloped with a thick pall of acrid smoke, drifting before the wind upon the town and nearly smothering its inhabitants.

Samuel Arthur Beddingford, the mayor and home defense leader of Bowen, ensconced in his crude basement shelter with a crowd of curious onlookers, fiddled with the dials of a military radio set that had been provided to the community for emergency communications. He looked up at the others with triumph as a Japanese voice came through clearly, barking out commands to the pilots even then hammering the dock area.

Mayor Beddingford, to his surprise, discovered the tele-

phone lines were still working, and he rang through at once
to Melbourne, punctuating his report with curses that "even
as I'm talking with you, mate, I can 'ear the bloody Nips
giving out orders to blow us all to hell and kingdom come!"

An emergency signal was flashed to the nearest military
airfields, including Garbutt. There the frantic call from
Melbourne was received with incredulous looks. Nonethe-
less, Major Tim Benson, airdrome defense officer, scrambled
every available fighter ready for takeoff. Two P–39s and
one P–40 got into the air approximately fourteen minutes
later and headed south, quite convinced nothing would be
found.

In the interim the people of Bowen remained under cover.
They looked at one another with shared satisfaction that the
town itself was being spared. Let the slanty-eyed bastards
have their way up at the docks and the rail spur. Just keep
your fingers crossed, mate, that they stay the hell away from
us . . .

Whip Russel looked down from his B–25 as he brought
the formation about in a tight turn for another attack run.
In the number three position Captain Elmer Rankin gabbled
away in fluent Japanese, although no one save the captain
knew what he might be saying. By agreement the other
pilots maintained strict radio silence.

Alex Bartimo looked across his cockpit at Whip Russel
and shook his head. "If anyone, if *anyone*, had ever told me
I'd be bombing an Australian town . . ." His words trailed
off in disbelief as the bombers swept earthward again,
laying a string of 100-pounders neatly in open ground, but
dangerously close to the loading docks where they could see
the crates piled along the shore. They banked sharply along
the beaches and machine guns poured their fire into the surf,
sending up geysers of spray and foam.

"You're not bombing a damned thing except desert," Whip grunted at him. "We haven't even mussed anyone's hair." He studied the hills to the north. "Any sign of the trucks?"

Alex nodded. "There. That dust cloud. That's them."

Whip fingered the intercom button and called Staff Sergeant Joe Leski, his radioman-gunner. "Joe, we're going to swing around in front of the trucks. Give them a couple of green flares."

"Yes, sir. Two greens coming up."

They swept low over the road, just before three trucks speeding south toward the dock area. Two green flares arced away from the bombers and they saw men waving. Whip took them back for another "bombing run" and again the air was filled with the chatter of machine guns and the slapping concussion of exploding bombs.

The timing was everything. The three trucks cleared the last rise overlooking the town and the dock area, and with the "attack" at its peak, the trucks pulled up in heavy smoke alongside the crates. Men heaved and cursed and sweated as they grabbed boxes of machine guns and parts. Several men pointed to a stack of large crates and they were manhandled into the trucks. Not a moment was wasted. The racketing thunder was keeping the locals under cover and the trucks pulled away from the dock area, speeding north, and within seconds over the hill and beyond sight of anyone who might venture forth from ground shelter.

By the time the attack dissipated and the first people clambered into the streets within the rapidly thinning smoke, there was nothing to be seen but a final glimpse of the yellow-ugly Japanese raiders heading out to sea.

The townspeople moved cautiously, still coughing and wiping away tears from the biting smoke. But the skies remained quiet, and people turned their attention to the expected damage.

Not even the docks had been hit. The shock of the bombing attack turned to elation when the townspeople discovered how badly the enemy had done. "Damned buggers can't even shoot straight," crowed the mayor.

No one had counted the crates when they'd been brought ashore from the crippled freighter. In the delight of survival without damage after the raid, no one bothered counting now. It was obvious. Craters were everywhere except where the Japanese had aimed. Nothing was damaged, nothing was missing.

10

WELL, FAT MAN, WHAT NOW?

Lou Goodman leaned back in his office chair, rolling the frayed cigar stub from one side of his mouth to the other, trying to concentrate upon immediate and pressing problems. It was a hopeless task, for at unexpected intervals the mirth in his mind would bubble forth and he would chuckle and shake all through his bulk.

Those crazy bastards had pulled it off. They'd actually done it. It was a lunatic caper from the word go; impossible, stupid, without a chance of succeeding, and yet so incredibly outrageous in its concept and so perfect a manipulation of human fear and foibles that it had worked. Goodman still didn't believe it, but in his combination of shock and mirthful pride, he made certain the crates in which the machine guns were stored had "disappeared." No sooner had the trucks rolled back to Garbutt Field than they were driven to a remote part of the airbase, where men were waiting to tear open the crates and remove their contents. It was just as important that the crates themselves disappear, with their incriminating numbers and identification marks. The numbers were burned off with hot irons and chisels and the slats put to immediate use in improving the integrity and appearance of the officer's club. Within hours of the trucks rolling onto Garbutt Field there simply *weren't* any crates.

The machine guns were another matter. Here Lou Goodman put to good use his expertise in handling other machinery in his past — the filing down of serial numbers, the

changing of identification marks and the stamping of new
I.D.s onto the weapons. Bills of lading were manufactured
by his administrative staff, who somehow never quite
managed to wipe away the grins that kept returning to their
faces. The caper that crazy bastard Russel and his men
carried off had done more to boost the morale and spirit of
the entire field than anything else in the damned war.

Goodman turned to Whip. "You figure your schedule
yet?"

Whip sprawled in what had become "his" chair in the
colonel's office. "Uh huh." He hesitated. "The crews, Lou,
well, they sort of wanted me to, you know — "

"If I have a choice between thanks and a medal I'll take
two Iron Crosses with three clusters each for risking my
career."

Whip grinned. "Okay."

"Now, that schedule."

"How long you think the modifications will take?"

Goodman ran it through his head. "Working day and
night without a break, using your crews and my people,
anywhere from ten to eighteen days."

"*That* long?"

Goodman wanted to curse. "Jesus, Whip, use your head."

"We hadn't counted on being out for the rest of the war."

"The chaplain's on leave, son. Go tell it to Jesus."

"Okay, okay." Whip held up his hands. "If those are
your numbers I know they're the best."

"Believe it. They are."

"Well, I guess a couple of us will go upcountry then."

"You can't get much more upcountry in Australia than
where you are now."

"Not here. Papua. New Guinea."

"What the hell for? You that eager to get shot at again? I
thought you'd wait for your iron birds to be ready."

"We've got things to do. We're leaving most of the people

here, but Muhlfield is going with us. He's the key to the whole operation we've got in mind." Whip's eyes had narrowed and Goodman knew he was easing into, well, whatever it was that pulled him back to the combat zone.

"Care to fill me in?"

First Lieutenant Paul Muhlfield — Mule — nodded. "Ain't no way we can keep from telling this man what we're doing, Captain."

"Yeah." Whip turned back to Goodman. "I didn't say anything about what we've got cooking because I figured we put you into enough hot water as it is. Mule used to spend a lot of time in the hill country of New Guinea. Before the war, I mean. He did some flying there for the Dutch. Some old Junkers and Lockheeds up to the gold mines in the back country. He knows the place better than most of us know our own neighborhoods."

Goodman turned to look at the silver bar on Muhlfield's collar. "How much time you got?" he asked.

Muhlfield showed a thin smile. "Fourteen thousand hours, Colonel."

"You're how old?"

"Forty-three."

"What the hell are you doing being a first looie? Major or light colonel would be more like it." Goodman was surprised and he didn't bother hiding it.

The weathered face looked back at him from amazingly clear blue eyes. "They know how old I am," he said softly. "It's training command or flying some old clunker of a transport. So I lied and told them I was twenty-three and I wanted bombers."

"Mule, there ain't nobody ever believed you were twenty-three years old."

"Course not, sir. But the man sitting across the desk from me was an old pilot. Like myself. *He* lied."

"The whole goddamned war is being run by thieves and liars," Goodman murmured. He sat up straighter. "All right. Tell me what harebrained scheme you maniacs are working on."

Whip picked it up. "We're flying back to Seven-Mile Drome at Moresby because we want to see how Field X is coming along."

"Field who?"

"We call it Field X because no one's bothered naming it yet. Its up Kokoda way, but not near anything. Completely isolated. Look, Lou, we've been working on a special assignment. That's why its so important to get our airplanes modified into gunships, the way we've worked it out. The Japs are giving us their own special brand of hell because of all the fighter fields they've got along the northern coast of New Guinea. Salamaua, Lae, Buna, the whole lot of them. That's only part of the problem. The real nut is that they know every field *we've* got. They're able to keep track of just about everything we do."

Whip took a deep breath, let it out slowly. "You know the numbers, Lou. They've been knocking the crap out of our fields, they outnumber us, and well, I don't think you believe our press releases. General Smyth down at FEAF is going to let us take a crack at a project I've been selling him for some time. That's to get an outfit up in the middle of the combat zone, but without the Japanese knowing anything about what's happening. That way we can keep them guessing, hit them in a way they just don't expect. If we can get them off balance, and they don't know where we live, we can do them some damage."

"You're going to be living right in their back yard, Whip."

"I know, I know," Whip said, impatient with the explanation he had to offer. "Look, right now we've got the B–17s hitting Rabaul up on the far end of New Britain. Every once in a while we send some B–25s or B–26s along, but when you get right down to it all we're doing is squeezing pimples on the Japanese ass. We're not really hurting them because we can't hit them one shot after the other. The reason General Smyth is so willing to take the long shot with our outfit is that Intelligence is reasonably sure the Japs are going to make an all-out effort to push down from their positions along the north coast of New Guinea. A real hammer job and — "

"They'd have to cross the Owen Stanleys. That may be too tough even for the Japanese," Goodman observed.

"They haven't been stopped yet," Whip retorted. "Besides, it's not our people who are taking the worst of it in the jungles and mountains in New Guinea. It's the Aussies. They're having a bitch with it, Lou. A real bitch."

Muhlfield moved into the conversation. "Until you've seen it, Colonel, there's no way to appreciate the problems of moving along those mountains. The Japanese soldier has an advantage. He lives off what he carries and he forages in the field. He's the closest thing to a native you can find. If they're willing to spend the lives to do the job they *can* get across. Once they're on the way down the southern flanks of those mountains it may be too late to keep them back. And if that happens, we'll lose Port Moresby and that whole complex of airfields. I don't think I need to spell out what that means."

"No, you don't," Goodman said grimly. "We're next."

"Yes, sir."

"Go on, Mule."

"You see, sir, right now the Japanese can't do the job. Not yet, anyway, and it's a very big 'not yet.' The first thing they've got to do is increase, by a considerable margin, their flow of supplies into New Guinea. Supplies, and men."

"In the meantime," Whip broke in, *"we're* short of

everything. Men, supplies, aircraft. You name it and we've got a shortage for you."

Goodman grimaced. "Tell *me* about that."

"Well, there's no reason we've got to be short of ideas. That's why we're doing the job with the B–25s, and why we're going to set up an advance base in hill country."

Goodman rose to his feet, pacing slowly. "I've been thinking about that ever since you mentioned Kokoda. You don't really expect to get away with that lunatic idea. You *can't.*"

Whip didn't find the conversation amusing. "I don't think you understood us, Lou. We're not just getting away with it. We're doing it. We've already started."

"How the hell can you handle your supply situation, for God's sake! You know what it takes to run an outfit like yours! Ammo, fuel, parts, bombs — the whole package, Whip. There isn't enough manpower in all of New Guinea to do that kind of job. And I haven't said a word about the field. You'll have to carve out a runway for B–25s. In the mountains? Right under the noses of the Japs?"

"There's a way, Colonel."

Goodman turned to Muhlfield. "You'd better have your own brand of miracle, Lieutenant. I accept you know the country. You'd better accept *I* know logistics."

"Yes, sir, I understand. But we do have what you call a miracle."

"You're keeping an old man in suspense, Lieutenant."

"There's an old dry lake bed in the mountains, sir. It's completely off the beaten path. Not even that many natives know about it except by word of mouth. The ones that do — they're headhunters, by the way — are friendly to us. I even knew a few of them from the old days. The lake bed, well, the natives did us a favor. They dragged in bushes and spread them all over the field so that aerial reconnaissance

by the Japanese wouldn't show a thing. The lake bed is in
clouds quite a bit, but we can operate from it. We've got
about four thousand feet of runway and — "

"What we're planning," Whip broke in, "is to make sure
some old B–25s, even wrecks, are left in the dispersal areas
and on the flight line at Seven-Mile so the Japs will see them
there. Having all our airplanes disappear could be a tip-off
and we don't want to take any chances. But the 335th *will*
disappear. Hell, Lou, we've been stashing supplies up there
for weeks. The natives have been lugging them in for us. A
steady long pull. Every now and then, when we know the
Japs are occupied, we fly in whatever we can. We've been
using two C–47s and that old Lockheed 10."

"A what?"

The two men stared at one another. Once again it had
leaped into being. The old Lockheed 10. The same kind of
airplane in which Lou Goodman, for the first time, had taken
a kid named Whip Russel into the air.

Whip's eyes sparkled. "Hell of a thing, ain't it? Lou, why
don't you join up with us?" The words rushed from Whip as
if he were afraid he might not say them if this moment
passed. "I mean," he went on hurriedly, "running our
operation from the ground. Jesus, if anyone knows all the
answers, it's you. We need a man who can make iron
airplanes out of wood if he has to, and you're the best there
is!"

"Hold it, hold it," Goodman chuckled, but his laugh had a
touch of harshness to it. "I couldn't get my ass out of
Garbutt Field if I wanted to. And believe me, son, I *want*
to." He shook his head at himself. "Or do I? Hell, I don't
know. But this whole caper you people are putting together — "

Goodman turned to stare through his office window at the
heat-baked nothingness of Garbutt Field. "You've had some

crazies in your time, Whip, but this one takes the cake.
I — "

"I can bust you out of here," Whip said with sudden quiet.

"When did you make general?" Goodman demanded.

"I mean it," Whip said stubbornly. "All it takes is a phone
call. Our code name is Billygoat — "

"Appropriate. It stinks."

" — and we've got top priority on a secret basis."

Lou Goodman scratched his belly, came to a sudden
decision. "Tell you what, boy. Don't make any phone calls.
I can always break out of here to inspect Moresby if I say it's
necessary. Okay; suddenly it's necessary. I'll go along with
you crazies just to see how it all stacks up."

A crooked grin appeared on Whip's face. "On to other
things. You've got a B–25 here with long-range tanks, don't
you?"

Goodman nodded. "We do. Belongs to the 317th.
They're waiting for some special radios for it."

"We'll borrow it for a while."

A wary look crossed Goodman's face. "I don't think I'm
going to like this."

"It'll be a blast, Lou. Make your vital body fluids move
faster. I said we haven't used skip bombing against the
Japanese yet, that we were waiting until the whole outfit
was ready to go. But someone's tried it a few times. You
know Bill Kanaga?"

"Yeah, I know him. Hawaiian. He's almost as crazy as
you. B–17 driver. What about him?"

"He's going into Rabaul, into Simpson Harbor, tomorrow
night with his B–17."

"Night intruder run?"

"Uh uh, boss. I didn't say *over* Simpson Harbor. I said
into it, and we're going along with him. That's why we need
that 25 with the long-range tanks."

Goodman stared, speechless.

"And we'd like you to go along with us, see how the whole thing works."

Whip had never seen Lou Goodman turn dead white before. But the big man did it now. The blood drained from his face as he nodded his assent.

11

SEVEN-MILE DROME was still the same stinking, broiling, bug-infested, dusty, humid and pestilential outhouse Lou Goodman remembered. The best of the airfield facilities remained primitive, support operations were a ghastly joke, the fighter defenses an embarrassment. Only the Japanese remained adept as they made unannounced sweeps down the mountain slopes for target practice against the hapless occupants of Seven-Mile. Airfield defense here was a mockery; no siren, no radar, a pitifully few machine guns. The air-raid warning system comprised one sentry who, when alarmed by the sound or sight of approaching Japanese aircraft, fired three shots rapidly into the air. At least the system was foolproof. If you didn't hear the sentry firing off his alarm you were certain to hear enemy bombs exploding.

Shortly before they returned to Seven-Mile an additional warning system had been put into effect. The operations tower — a rickety assembly of logs — mounted a single pole over the structure, and if you heard shots *and* saw a red flag being run up the pole, and also saw the tower operators jumping or tumbling to the ground as fast as they could move — well, no one else came to visit except the Japanese.

Lou Goodman climbed down from the B–25 and surveyed the local sights with a sinking heart. God, Garbutt Field was bad. *This* stank. No revetments for the planes on the ground. If there came a warning of only a few minutes, standby crews kicked over the engines of their bombers and ran like hell to get into the air and away from the enemy bombs that would be whistling earthward at any moment. It was the only defense against the enemy, but it had its own perils of emergency takeoffs with cold engines, and, possibly running into a swarm of Zeros waiting for just this sort of marvelous opportunity to catch the bombers at the worst possible moment — staggering into the air, on the deck and at slow speed.

Goodman walked slowly along the soft and unpredictable runway — itself a matter of profanity and accidents. The more he ran through his mind the hellish conditions under which these men had to live, the more astonished he was with the dogged tenacity of these people to push themselves into combat.

Lou Goodman paused beneath the wing of a B–17, grateful for its shade, and looked with bleak thoughts at the mountains in the distance. It took a specific effort to remind himself that New Guinea was an island. *Island?* It was a mockery of the word, and the very use of that term, island, was what contributed so strongly to the misunderstanding, or lack of understanding, of what these men like Whip Russel had to face.

Greenland was the largest island in the world. New Guinea was the next largest, and who the hell even thought of New Guinea as a body of land just about sixteen hundred miles long and at least five hundred miles from north to south at its widest point? My God, thought Goodman, the bloody place is more than three hundred thousand square miles!

The single most dominating feature of New Guinea was the massive cordillera extending the length of the island. The huge upthrusting contained a number of parallel east-west mountain ranges that narrowed into the Owen Stanley Range in the Papuan Peninsula. You think of jungle and you imagine, at the most, high hills. *Not mountains that peaked 16,000 feet into the sky.* They compounded the normal and lethal everyday problems of combat air crews. Navigation under conditions of poor weather was a nightmare. Survival in such country could often be a happenstance; a man alone, trying to slog his way across this country — and there was so damned much of it! — faced grim odds.

But then, Muhlfield had an incalculable advantage in having been here, in this very territory, before the war began. During that period, faced with the stark reality of no roads or ports worthy of the name, the Australians had exploited air travel in the best of textbook fashions. Winged transportation had been almost solely responsible for developing and maintaining the gold fields of the Bulolo Valley in the mountains southwest of Salamaua. There had been other fields, but most especially there had been an effort in locating what might be bonanza finds. To do this the Australians had cut airstrips in many isolated areas and carried on their work by flying in machinery and materiel. This is how, of course, Muhlfield knew of that dry lake bed and its potential as a landing field.

If they could operate from their Field X, then Whip Russel's force of B–25 bombers had much more available to it than seclusion and shorter range to the Japanese airfields along the northern strip of eastern New Guinea. They would bring closer the vital Japanese targets that lay beyond. Across Vitiaz and Dampier straits from New Guinea's Huon Peninsula lay Cape Gloucester, the western tip of New Britain, which curved northeasterly to culminate in Gazelle Peninsula and Rabaul. New Ireland, long and narrow, paralleled the long axis of the Papuan peninsula of New Guinea so that New Ireland, the Admiralty Islands, part of New Guinea, and New Britain all enclosed the Bismarck Sea.

And that — *all* of it — was hostile territory.

Lou Goodman scuffed his boots in the dust of Seven-Mile Drome. For a strange moment, he might have been on a dusty California strip, walking idly, content to let his mind meander as he strolled along the runway. He treasured the moment, and he tried desperately to grasp onto the past, to warm himself with its friendly touch. But he could not shake the harsh reality of the New Guinea sun, the rumble of engines being tested, the distantly looming mountains that seemed suspended over the thick and dangerous jungle.

And beyond all that lay the ocean and the islands to the north, and at the far end of New Britain, the powerful Japanese bastion of Rabaul. Where they were flying that night, on a mission suicidal and impossible, but so brash in its concept it might work.

If it didn't, he would die before the next dawn. He was surprised that the threat of death was more curious than frightening. Lou Goodman walked just a bit more briskly after that astonishing thought.

Bill Kanaga smiled all the time. Or so it seemed to Goodman. He looked like the last choice Goodman would have made for the pilot of a four-engined bomber.

"I understand you've made out your last will and testament," Kanaga told him with startling cheeriness.

"You seem to have me on a griddle, Captain," Goodman said, still unsure of his own sense of this roly-poly killer.

"No offense, sir," came the bland reply. "I do."

Goodman smiled at him. "Your reasons should be interesting."

Kanaga nodded. "You seem sane enough, Colonel. What the hell are you doing with this bunch of thieves? Didn't they tell you what the odds were tonight?"

"I can figure those myself," Goodman said, a bit more gruff about it than he should have been.

"Nothing intended to offend, Colonel," came the bland retort. "But it's unusual tonight. I fly my missions alone. Nobody comes along. If I have to look out for someone tailing with me it messes up my concentration. A night strike like we're going on is safer with one plane than two."

"You mean we're dead weight," Goodman told him. No use in anything but straight from the shoulder.

"I mean you *could* be dead weight. It depends on many things."

"And if you decide we're a lead bucket, what then, Captain?"

The round face was unmoving. "Then, sir, you don't fly with me. Not you and not Whip Russel, who just happens to be the most natural pilot I've ever seen in my life."

"Then what's the beef?"

"You're a bird colonel. You really shouldn't be here. You're going along as a passenger. Maybe," Kanaga said slowly, "you might just saw some sharp edges in that B–25. Russel's going to be a very busy pilot and anything could interfere with — "

"Captain."

Kanaga went silent. His eyes were dark and flashing.

"Captain, I taught Whip Russel to fly. A very long time ago."

There was a moment's hesitation, then the round face broke out into an enormous smile, and Lou Goodman knew he'd sailed through the test. "Colonel, did you know you remind me of my favorite uncle?"

"No, I didn't, but I think I like the idea."

"You should, sir. He's a marvelous man. And, Colonel?"

"What is it, Captain?"

"I don't want to sound like a Dutch nephew, but you'd do well to get some shuteye."

Goodman didn't answer for a moment. "Yeah," he said finally, "I guess I would."

"See you tonight, Colonel. Bring your rubbers. You never know when its gonna rain."

12

THE DULL RED LIGHTS stretched away in narrowing lines and converged in a bowl of utter blackness. Good God Almighty, thought Colonel Lou Goodman. It's like a railroad tunnel out there. With both ends sealed off to make it as dark as it is.

The dull red lights were hooded flares spaced evenly along the runway of Seven-Mile. They could be seen only by the pilot of an aircraft moving in their direction, and the guidance they provided seemed pitiful. But the flight crews, and especially the pilots, Bill Kanaga and Mike Anderson in the B–17 and Whip Russel and Alex Bartimo in the B–25, had been under "red light only" for the last hour. To their night-acclimated vision the dull glows were beacon enough for the job at hand.

They had been waiting for one final word before starting engines, and Goodman knew it was "go" for the mission when he heard Whip and Alex beginning their checklist in the cockpit above and behind him. At the moment Lou Goodman was crammed into the plexiglas nose of the B–25, along with a fifty-caliber machine gun. Normally the bombardier would be in this position but Goodman had bounced him, because where they were going, and the manner of their visit, made the presence of a bombardier more than excess baggage. If someone was going along for the ride Goodman preferred it to be himself.

That presupposed a measure of insanity, Goodman mused with a crooked grin, but, what the hell . . .

The big engines kicked in with growling, coughing rumbles, then broke into their throaty roar. To one side Goodman knew the B–17 was also churning into life as the four engines wheezed and banged into motion. Goodman knew the message they'd waited so long to receive had to be positive. The Australians had a PBY out there in the darkness, far to the north, and it had sent back a code that the weather was acceptable.

"This is the pilot. Call off your stations. I want everyone strapped in tight. Colonel Goodman?"

Lou Goodman cinched his straps just a hair tighter. "Goodman here. All set." One by one the other crewmen called in. The radio operator, turret gunner, side gunner. Six men in all in the twin-engined raider.

Goodman felt the brakes released and the B–25 dipped gently on its nose shocks. He stared through a side panel and saw a ghostly movement: Kanaga's B–17, trundling slowly out to the edge of the runway and lining up. There'd be no radio contact between the two aircraft until *after* the mission was flown. If the Japanese did no more than intercept radio communication on the aircraft frequencies at this time of night they'd flash the word to all major stations that the Americans might be staging a night mission, and then every damned antiaircraft position at Rabaul would be waiting.

Then the B–25 came alive, shaking and shuddering through every metal fiber, groaning and rumbling as the pilots locked the brakes. In his mind Lou Goodman went through the checklist with them. Mags right and left, holding high r.p.m. on the props, coming back on the prop controls to check propeller blade angles, the sound whooshing and hissing as the blades shifted through fine and coarse pitch. Then it was all done. He leaned forward as the B–25 rolled slowly forward, shaking from side to side on the uneven surface beneath them. They came easily to a stop, waiting.

In the darkness, peering through the glass, Goodman saw the ghostly blue flames of the B–17 engine exhausts increase in brightness. Rich mixture, props all the way forward, Kanaga was running her up to full power before releasing his own brakes. A single dull white light showed from the tail. They'd need at least that for aircraft separation on their way upstairs.

The exhaust flame and the small white light seemed to flow away from them. Long moments later a green light flashed three times from the far end of the runway, the signal from an observer standing to one side that the B–17 was off clean and climbing out.

The B–25 rolled forward, jerked to a stop. The throttles were going forward, then they were at the stops and the airplane was straining at its leash. Whip didn't bother telling the crew when they were going to roll. There was no mistake about it as he and Alex came off the brakes and the airplane surged forward, responding to the howling engines and whirling propellers. The acceleration pulled Lou back in his seat and he leaned forward to compensate for the motion. Other sensations rushed upon him now as the bomber accelerated, picking up speed swiftly, and he felt Whip coming back on the yoke just a hair to get the nose wheel out of the soft runway.

At this moment Lou Goodman had fled the known world and was plunging through a surrealistic tunnel, the dull red lights to either side of him rushing faster and faster at him and then speeding away, out of his peripheral vision. Finally they became a blur. He knew Whip was holding the bomber down longer than necessary, getting some extra speed — money in the bank — because of the night takeoff. If he knew his man behind the yoke he knew also Whip saw nothing of what Lou Goodman was watching, for Alex Bartimo would be on the rudder pedals, holding the B–25 aligned exactly down the runway, while Whip himself was on the gauges. When Whip lifted the bomber from the ground it would be a thundering crash into darkness and he would be flying for a while strictly on his instruments, his entire world no more distant from him than the gauges that presented him with the sight of an artificial horizon, a dial to show him his air speed, another to indicate course, still another to show his rate of climb as the earth fell away below, another to show their increasing altitude. He would let Alex attend to the gauges that showed oil pressure and temperature, cylinder head temperature. Alex would come back on the throttles, ease off the whirling speed of the propellers, attend to fuel tanks, coolers, flows, pressures. He would be the priest attending the power flow and lifeblood of the machine. The flaps had come up slowly, the gear had thumped into its wells, the engines were pulled back to something less than hammering thunder. The B–25 was in her element now, running straight and true, flying the curving, invisible line that would bring them up and behind the heavier machine with Kanaga and Anderson at the controls.

Goodman loosened his belt and leaned forward, straining to see that dull white light. There was always the danger they might collide with the Flying Fortress, and a single mistake could be the final one for them all. "Colonel, you see anything?"

That was Whip calling from the cockpit, enlisting every eyeball available. Goodman strained to see. Almost at the same moment he felt the rolling lurch that went through the entire airplane. They were in the wake of the B–17, feeling the air that twisted back from the whirling propellers and the vortex spilling off the wingtips. Almost at the same time —

"I've got him, Whip. Just about eleven o'clock and slightly above us."

"Great, Lou. We're locked on."

Navigation lights, red on the left wingtip and green on the right, flicked into being. A moment later the same lights appeared ahead of them as Kanaga received word from his tail gunner that the B–25 was behind them and had given the signal. All lights save the dull white light at the very tail-end position of the B–17 went off now. From this point on Whip and Alex Bartimo would have to fly formation position, to the right and slightly behind the heavy bomber. There would be no conversation, no other signals, for with every passing moment they were getting deeper and deeper into Japanese territory.

The minutes settled down to routine. Goodman eased from his seat and went for the thermos jug to pass hot coffee to the two men in the cockpit. They were going for eight thousand feet, away from the islands, away from Japanese ground positions. Eight thousand at night wasn't too high; they wouldn't need oxygen and they were high enough to clear anything that might loom up out of the sea.

Then they were above scattered clouds. Goodman estimated their height below at three thousand feet beneath their own level. A half-moon came over the horizon, seeming to loft itself through the sky with a purpose. Moonlight scattered off the clouds and they were in a ghostly world of dull, snow-cold illumination. It helped enormously in their navigation, for even in that baleful glow reflecting from a barren world a quarter of a million miles away they saw the long silver on the ocean and the small islands providing reference points. It was an added bonus. Above them the stars crowded darkness, and in the B–17 the navigator was peering through his small plexiglas bubble, shooting the stars with his instruments. This was a blessing — the weather had broken right for them.

It was a long haul. In the blessed cool air of their altitude Goodman stacked his parachute against the side of the glassed-in nose, wedged his body as comfortably as noise and vibration and metal would allow and fell asleep.

The presence of another body in the nose compartment brought Goodman instantly awake. Opening his eyes he stared up at Alex. No words passed between them for a moment. The increased cry of the wind, the sound of the engines, the changing pressure told it all to the colonel. They were on the way down.

"Colonel, if you need to take a leak, now's a good time. We're going down pretty fast."

Goodman nodded. Alex was right. A full bladder during a night bombing run could get pretty hairy. As he relieved himself he had to brace his body against the side of the nose. They were picking up some turbulence as they dropped lower and lower. Goodman went back to his seat, belted himself in, leaving enough slack for easy movement.

"This is the pilot. Charge your guns."

Goodman felt a strange thrill sweeping through him. His blood ran faster and he knew he was breathing hard. Not, he was grateful to see, with too much fear, but with an abundance of growing excitement. Well ahead of them, in the now brighter moonlight, he could see the coastlines of both New Britain and New Ireland. They'd make a fast run on the deck due north through St. George's Channel and come around in a wide sweeping turn to the left, cutting to the east, to set up their punch into Simpson Harbor.

Everything happened now with a rush. Kanaga was pouring the coal to the Fortress, getting all the speed he could out of the big bomber without beating his engines half to death. The faster B–25 had no trouble staying with the B–17, but Whip began to ease his plane more to the right, giving greater clearance between them.

Then they were committed. The land to their left fell away as the shoreline curved sharply, rising hills and lower mountains barely silhouetted against that moonlit sky. Goodman watched the B–17. Everything would happen according to what Bill Kanaga did. This was his show, he was the seasoned veteran here, and Whip, for all he knew, was the student following the master.

The last curving edge of land fell away. Simpson Harbor lay between volcanic mounds and tree-lined shores, but no one looked any more at real estate. Ahead of them, metal reflecting dully under that God-blessed moon they hadn't expected, lay an enormous fleet of ships: cargo and troop-ships and destroyers and cruisers and barges and tankers and whatever else the Japanese had moved into the harbor.

Water seemed to flash in a terrifying blur directly before the B–25, and in the thundering, pounding rush only scant feet above the waves, Goodman marveled at the sight of the big Fortress with her propellers hurling back a stream of spray. Four running, rushing lines streaking the water as if an invisible brush were being dragged along the sea.

The Japanese came alive with a fury. One moment the world was dark, all blacked out, the ships clinging to the darkened mantle of the night. The next instant dazzling flares arced into the sky, pointing in the direction of the thunder rushing into the heart of Simpson Harbor. Yet, they had made their approach with little warning, and even in the light of those flares it would take the Japanese precious moments to galvanize into action the full fury of their massed antiaircraft weapons on the ships and along the shoreline.

The flare staggered Goodman, streaking across the entire harbor, highlighting the B–17 in an eerie silhouette, a strobe effect brought on by the propellers.

The fireflies came next. Goodman sucked in his breath, disbelieving the sight. Glowing coals, tiny spatters of lights, a fantasy of curving patterns drifting lazily upward from the forward darkness; spears and blobs and diamonds and teardrops and globs, glowing, burning brightly, and Goodman, both hands clutching the fifty-caliber machine gun, forced himself to understand that the weaving of glowing light was Death. They were the tracers of machine gun bullets, of cannon shells, of everything the Japanese had that could fire solid and explosive projectiles in their direction. The moment they —

The B–25 rocked sharply and Goodman felt a wild stab of fear. The helplessness of *his* own position, stuck there in the glass nose of this hurtling machine, with half of the goddamned Japanese navy shooting at *him* . . . it was almost too much. Here he was, surrounded by a greenhouse, horribly unsubstantial, and they were doing their best to kill *him. Screw everyone else,* he thought, as the sense of nakedness to death tore away even his psychological protection, *I'm the one who has to get out of this thing alive.*

He laughed suddenly at his own idiocy, even as he realized the sudden sharp rocking motion had been the airplane taking a hit in the right wing. Those glowing fireflies arcing so lazily toward them; the tracers had struck, smashed into the bomber, and Goodman had a fleeting fear of the fuel tanks erupting. He dismissed it from his mind even as he chided himself for stupidity; if the tanks had gone he wouldn't be thinking about it.

They swept forward with a howling rush that exhilarated him. Of a sudden Whip Russel and Alex Bartimo and everyone else in the B–25 was a million miles away, and Lou Goodman was alone in a great plastic bubble with a machine gun in his hands, hurtling forward into the teeth of a powerful armada, twisted in a world of darkness and eye-stabbing lights, and Death had become a happenstance stranger about whom he no longer gave a damn. Death was incidental, Death might or might not come, but sure as hell he wasn't invited to the party. If he crashed the gate, so be it.

Goodman hunched forward, fingers tighter on the handles of the machine gun, startled suddenly to realize he hadn't had a thing at which he might shoot. Almost as if reading his mind he heard Whip's voice in his earphones.

"Goodman, we're closing in. When we get within range of anything out there, hose 'em down."

"Yes, sir."

My God, here was the colonel saying "Yes, sir" to the captain. Well, who was top dog right now? It sure wasn't the fat colonel in the greenhouse, squeezing the firing handles just short of blazing away.

It didn't take long. It was all happening so fast it seemed unbelievable. The darkness and the shattering of all that black did that to you. Changed your sense of time reeling by. Whip took her down right above the waves, cutting the margin to the closest he dared. He'd have to pull up later but the lower they stayed right now the less of a target they made. He held the yoke in those gentle-strong fingers, his feet riding the rudder pedals. He watched the glowing lights, instinctively easing rudder, sliding the B–25 with surprising gentleness from one side to the other, trying to slip inside those curving fireballs to stay away from the mass of steel and lead and explosive he couldn't see. The movements were instinctive, automatic.

Faster and faster they raced over the waves, plunging down the ever-brightening tunnel of darkness. Now they saw the wild reflections in long yellow-quicksilver patterns on the water, following the wake thrown up by the propellers of the B–17, and then, on cue, it seemed, as Whip followed every move of Bill Kanaga in the big Fortress, they slid to the right. The signal was the sudden great shower of flaming sparks racing from and spearing ahead of the heavy bomber. Kanaga's top turret gunner, his nose gunner, and Kanaga himself, with three fixed machine guns in the nose of his airplane, had all opened fire at the same time as the targets rushed into range of their weapons. Whip skidded the B–25 well to the right, opening the distance, leaving room for both planes to make their attacks without one interfering with the other.

The world was spattering and sparkling and glowing. Searchlights were coming on along the ships as the Japanese tried to blind them, and this gave Kanaga's gunners the targets they wanted. Suddenly the B–25 vibrated, a series of steady, hammering blows. In that fiery maelstrom of churning fire and water the two pilots grinned at one another. The hammer banging within the B–25 was Lou Goodman, firing his fifty-caliber gun, aiming at searchlights and flaring muzzles of antiaircraft weapons at the same moment firing at them.

Time slowed to nothing, the targets coming up slowly, so goddamned slowly, and if the Japs would wait just long enough before depressing those flak guns . . . well, the harbor was filled with destroyers and cruisers, and those people were damned good gunners, and what had really saved them so far was that everyone was shooting well over them, shooting much too high, because who would expect two planes to be flown by madmen? Who would fly this low to the water *at night?* A single slip, a stab of vertigo to untwist the brain; anything would be the end.

Time is an enigma in battle; it is mercilessly brief or it is distressingly extended, and it all depends upon the viewer. To the Japanese the two bombers were rushing toward them so swiftly they had almost no time to get their major weapons depressed to fire at the planes assaulting them.

From within the bombers the entire world was unrolling ahead with dragging slowness. But now time began to accelerate, for as they drew closer to the ships they expanded in size, and viewpoint changed, faster and faster.

"Bomb bays open." The words slipped easily from Whip and Alex was ready, anticipating, his hand hitting the control almost as swiftly as Whip voiced the command. Moments later the doors were open and a new rumble filled the airplane, adding to the shaking and roaring and thunder of their passage. Moist air swept up through the bays and mixed with the stink of fuel and the acrid smell of gunpowder and changed the thrumming uproar of their flight.

Radio silence was behind them now. "Whip, I'm taking that cruiser dead ahead of me," Kanaga called, and even as his voice crackled in their earphones the B–17 eased upward, sliding in a smooth curve to just the altitude the pilot judged to be perfect, boring straight in.

"Got it," Whip came back. "We'll take the tin can over to the right." He eased the bomber in, a gentle control motion that set them directly on a line toward the destroyer he had selected as his target.

The world was blotchy with its dark and reds and yellows and glowing, burning things ripping the sky, reflecting eerily in the water. Whip was just starting to come up to altitude for the strike when he saw the sudden white spots on the water beneath the B–17, and he knew that Kanaga had dropped, spacing his 500-pounders exactly so, the touch of the artist, all of it by judgment and feel, and then to hell with the Fortress, the destroyer was rushing upon them, the decks twinkling and ablaze with antiaircraft, and Whip felt a touch of admiration for the fat man below and ahead of him in that nakedly exposed position, for tracers were streaming out ahead of the B–25 and in the distance they could see toy figures jerking spasmodically.

He cracked one bomb away, and then another, and if everything had been done right the bombs would be hitting the water flat, the nose and fins in perfect position, and they would bounce, skip back into the air, staying just above the water so that if everything was right they would arrow into the side of the warship and tear a savage hole where they struck. The B–25 seemed abruptly to stagger as an explosive shell erupted beneath the left wing. Whip corrected automatically, but the airplane was still in a near vertical bank as they shot over the destroyer, and the top turret gunner hammered away with his twin fifties, giving it everything he had. They were too fast and too low to take any return fire from their target, but other ships were tracking them now, and the world was another mass of glowing claws of destruction arcing and spinning in their direction.

"Let's take the tanker." The words came from Whip so casually he sounded almost laconic. "Lou, wake 'em up," he added to the colonel, and the fifty-caliber machine gun roared and bucked again as a great dark shape loomed out of the water, seeming to plunge toward them rather than their racing toward their new target.

Far to their left and behind them a terrible mushroom of fire sundered the night as it leaped upward. "Kanaga got a good one!" came the shout from Joe Leski in the top turret. "Cruiser! Looks like he got the engine room!"

Whip concentrated on the tanker swelling monstrously in size. He let the next two bombs go. Before he had time to think of the strike Leski shouted in near-hysteria. "The destroyer! We got the son of a bitch! Split 'em right in two! He's — "

Leski's voice cut off as the destroyer they had hit dead-on with two heavy bombs exploded violently. Dazzling flame shattered what remained of the night, a huge pulsation of ghastly flaming light as the warship tore itself apart.

They went rigid with shock. Not from the kill they had just scored. Not from what might happen with the tanker into which Whip had cracked his last two bombs.

It was Bill Kanaga. His last bomb had bounced across the water, a dense stone of finned metallic hell that tore into the side of another tanker. The Flying Fortress, with destroyers on each side of the tanker, lifted its nose and barely skimmed the masts of the Japanese ship. Kanaga was his usual skilled self, clearing the masts cleanly and only by scant feet. In the same instant the tanker exploded.

Had Kanaga gone for the safety of altitude from his skip bombing run he would have been exposed to withering antiaircraft fire from the warships and the long-range guns on shore. His best move was to stay low.

The best sometimes isn't enough. The tanker turned into a huge ball of dark red flame that enveloped the racing B–17 and even as Whip and the others in the B–25 watched, frozen with shock, everything a flickering screen of unreality before them, another brilliant flash speared the sky.

They knew it was the B–17.

They flew home silently. No one talked about the three, possibly four ships they had destroyed in those terrible minutes in Simpson Harbor. It didn't seem to matter very much.

13

It WAS NEVER quite the same again. At Seven-Mile Drome, they climbed wearily from the B–25, gaunt-eyed, troubled within themselves. The airplane was moved beneath trees and camouflaged and they lay under the wings and body as dawn brought with it heat and the pervading humidity of the nearby jungle.

They gathered that evening to discuss their next moves. "Mule will stay here with some of the other men," Whip told the small group. "He's more important coordinating the logistics than wandering off in the hill country." He laughed quietly at the expression on Muhlfield's face. "You'll be back in the hills soon enough, Mule. In the meantime, see what you can keep moving with those Gooney Birds and that Lockheed. We've got to get everything up to that field before the weather knocks us out or the Japs tumble to what's going on."

Whip turned to Bartimo. "I want you to spend some time with the Aussies here at Seven-Mile and down at Moresby. There's also the matter of working with the native bearers, see how they're coming along, and — "

"I hardly speak their language, old chap," Alex said with open distaste.

Whip didn't raise an eyebrow. "Tough shit. You're the brain in this outfit. You'll make out."

"You have an elegant way of expressing yourself," Alex murmured. Seeing the expression on his pilot's face, Alex threw up his hands in mock horror. "I know, I know. Go screw myself. You've told me enough times."

"It's about all the tail you're going to get," Muhlfield offered.

Alex turned with a bland expression to Colonel Lou Goodman. "You'll see how much good those silver eagles of yours do, Colonel. Whip doesn't seem to have learned how to recognize insignia. Now, if this were the Royal Australian Air Force, we would — "

"You'd be getting your ass shot off, that's what."

Alex shrugged. "True. Better without a bloody arse than be barbaric, however."

Muhlfield shook his head in dismay. "How the shit would you know?"

"Are you asking if I'm assless or barbaric?"

"Knock it off, you clowns," Whip growled. He turned to Lou Goodman. "I'm going upcountry. If you're going to run this outfit, Lou, I guess you'd better come along."

Goodman studied him for a moment. He scratched his leg to stall. He needed to have it straight, right out in front. "I'm glad you said that," he responded quietly.

"About running the show?"

"That's about the size of it."

"There never was any question." The expression on Whip's face told Goodman of the lack of guile in his remarks.

"All right," Goodman said. Russel studied him carefully. In a sudden fluid motion he was on his feet. "Let's take a walk, Lou."

They moved slowly along a path bordering the runway. Neither man paid attention to aircraft or vehicles. There wasn't that much they had to say to one another, but it would be vital in the coming weeks and months that the words came now.

"It's not like you to press about top dog, Lou," Whip said finally.

"Top dog has nothing to do with it," Goodman said, keeping it low key. "Neither does rank."

"You're still pushing, fat man."

Goodman smiled despite himself. Whip's use of his favorite name for the man he held in higher esteem than any other told Goodman what he needed to know. "I've got to push," he said, surprising Whip.

The pilot stopped in his tracks. He was into another of those moods that came upon him with explosive force. "But what the hell *for?*"

"You."

"Me?" The astonishment was genuine.

"Look, Whip. You run this outfit. You run it better than anyone I've ever seen. You've made these airplanes do everything but talk. We're building them into better weapons. Those people who fly for you will follow you anywhere." Goodman took a deep breath. "But you can't run your outfit in the air and operate the whole thing from the ground. You can't be two people at the same time and you can't be in two places at the same time. You — "

"Goddamnit, I know that."

"Do you really? Don't you see what I'm getting at?"

"Do it ABC, Lou."

"If I take over this special operation, Whip, then it's got to be all the way. *I* run the show."

"Shit, there's no argument there! I — "

"*You* take orders from *me.* Orders, Whip. Not counsel or advice of friends. *Orders.* From the colonel on down. There'll be times when you won't agree with me. I'm not going to screw with your combat operation and sure as God made little green apples I'm not going to see you embroiled in a fight with me. If that happens you lose something in the

air. I don't want that on my back. So it's got to be clean
between us. Not colonel and captain. It's got to be Goodman and Russel coming to that agreement, *now*. Just
between the two of us."

Whip chewed his lip, fighting with himself. Goodman
knew what chewed inside him as well. This whole affair
was Whip's from the very beginning. He'd fought to get this
operation going. He'd dragged it through channels and
risked official wrath by going over heads. It was his, body
and soul. Now this man was saying to him that he'd have to
step aside on a major part, perhaps even a critical part, of
what would be happening.

At the same time his respect for Goodman's expertise and
wisdom had no qualification. As for kicking over the traces
of his own absolute authority, Jesus, he'd have to go to Lou
to know what to do and — He shook his head, his brow
furrowed with his concentration. What it all boiled down to
was that this was a team effort. Period. He'd have to yield
the iron fist, he had to trust this man. A shudder seemed to
pass through his body and Lou Goodman knew the decision
had been reached. Whip turned to stare directly into his
eyes.

"Feels like we're back in that old Lockheed of yours, fat
man."

They clasped hands tightly.

"You call that goddamned thing an airplane? Jesus
Christ, it's a refugee from a rag factory!" Lou Goodman
looked with disdain at the battered Piper L–4, a single-en-
gined two-seater resting on old tires and a sagging tail
wheel. The yellow fabric had been patched more times than
could be counted, and half the wings and fuselage was
masking and electrical tape.

"I think it's something we were supposed to sell to the

Japanese before the war," offered Muhlfield, "but they gave it back."

"Do you blame them?" Goodman jerked a thumb at the weary liaison plane. "And we're supposed to land this thing in the high country?" he shot at Whip.

"The airplane has only one problem," Whip said.

"Yeah, I know," sneered Goodman. "It forgot how to fly."

"Uh uh. It's got a fat, loud passenger."

Goodman pressed his lips together. "Get in, you sawed-off bantam rooster. I cut my teeth on the old J–3 and I wouldn't trust you or anyone else in this . . . this travesty."

They grinned at one another. Goodman had to stuff himself within the narrow cabin. When finally he was wedged into the machine he could hardly move his shoulders. Whip took the front seat, fired up the rackety sixty-five horsepower engine, and taxied away from their position beneath the trees. He didn't bother with any routine. He simply pointed the old airplane down the runway and went to full power. The engine backfired and wheezed but the tail came up quickly enough and they lumbered into the air. The old Piper had one rule it demanded from its pilot and everything would be fine. You flew in slow motion. At seventy miles an hour, *if* the Piper felt like performing that day.

At first the weather was lousy, with scattered rain showers and broken clouds sometimes all the way down to the treetops. The longer they flew the higher the ground rose beneath them, so that they were climbing constantly in a confidence-shaking clatter of the engine, but the ground seemed always to be at the same distance beneath them. It was more than watching carefully for sudden hummocks or high trees. There were showers that almost wiped out visibility and that was a great way to fly into a hill. If they got caught in clouds or those heavy showers their instruments would do them little or no good, for the gauges in the clattering old fabric bird were strictly for blue-sky eyeball operation, and neither man relished whirling out of the sky because they couldn't tell which end was up.

But the weather was also perfect cover against any Japanese fighters that might have been on the prowl. A Zero would have eaten them alive, but no sane Japanese would be wandering down among the upsloping hills in clouds and rain.

There was yet another aspect to what was happening. The old Piper swayed and shook and bounced as they flew along in their circuitous ascent. They were doing more snaking than flying. The smell of gasoline, the banging sounds of turbulence, and the constant rocking of the wings and wallowing of the machine was its own brand of music to the two men.

"Hey, remember that first cross-country I gave you in one of these?" Goodman shouted.

Whip half turned from the front seat, the grin all across his face. "How could I forget? I got lost."

"Got lost? You skinny little bastard, you *never* knew where you were that day! You even missed the ocean!"

"Got any idea where we are now, fat man?"

"Shit, *no*. Except that I'm climbing into jungle country in an airplane that can barely rise as fast as the ground is coming up." Goodman sobered as he studied the trees through swirling mists. "More to the point, do *you* have any idea of where the hell we are?"

A greasy chart was pushed into the back of the cabin. Whip's finger stabbed against the paper. "See that ravine? There's a river crosses here from the northwest. It's about five miles ahead of us. We fly up the ravine and break through a mountain pass. The field we want is about fifteen miles northeast of there."

Goodman studied the chart. "You couldn't prove it by me," he muttered.

"Fat colonels got lousy eyesight. I read that in a magazine once."

"Turn around and pay attention to where the hell we're going."

A sudden downdraft dropped them like a rock and Whip skidded off to one side to avoid trees looming in their direction. The hard maneuvering was exhilaration to Goodman. For the moment it was flying in the old days again and the war was another place and another time.

Fighting rough air all the way they crossed the ravine-river checkpoint on the chart. What had been rough before became a tumbling invisible waterfall of air now as they eased into the ravine. Whip had no time now for idle chatter. He was fighting and flying the little airplane with constant attention. They bounced their way wildly through the ravine, broke out and headed across tumbled, tree-covered hills without a single reference along the ground. Yet Whip had been here before and he knew what he was doing. Suddenly Whip banked the Cub. Goodman looked to where he was pointing: three strange mounds arranged in pyramid fashion.

"That's it," Whip announced.

Goodman studied the surface. You really had to look hard to see the field. A light drizzle was falling and if you hadn't known just where to look for those three mounds you couldn't ever have known an airstrip was down there. Whip rocked the wings and brought the Cub around in a rolling dive toward a space just to the west of the three markers. Was he going to land in the middle of all that goddamn growth down there? The Cub bounced and jostled toward the earth, and at the last moment, as Goodman braced himself for what seemed an inevitable crunch with a tree, the bushes and trees directly before them melted away to the sides. Goodman had a glimpse of men hauling away foliage and a path was cleared magically. They rolled to a stop in less than six hundred feet, and by the time Goodman turned about to look behind him the foliage was replaced and any sign of an airstrip was gone. Moments later netting and tree fronds were heaped over the Piper and the airplane disappeared. Goodman was impressed.

He didn't waste any time. With Whip and two officers who'd been roughing it out here Goodman went on his own-style inspection. To one side of the old desert lake, hills reared steeply, and natural caves had been expanded to provide rough living and working quarters. It spoke well for the initial planning. Old parachutes, canvas, even woven grass gave good overhead security against rain and the elements, and also kept the inevitable insects from an inside-cave rain on the occupants. In its crude form it was all there. Roughhewn workbenches for armament and technical details. Radio sets sealed well against the rain, and antennae cleverly run up the trunks and upper branches of trees.

Along the airstrip proper the heavier and larger trees had been set up on rough rollers so they could be moved quickly out of the way of moving aircraft. Whip and his people had put together an ingenious system. Whether it would hold up under the pressure of operational flights and the oftentime downpour was something else again. Goodman had less than huzzahs for the lake bed. The natives had pounded it down but the water runoff was questionable. The consistency of the soil would hold a man, but what it would do under the weight and pressure of bomber wheels was something else again. He made a mental note to see about having the area of the lake bed that was used for the airstrip mounded along its center so that mud collection might be avoided.

In almost every direction there were hills and mountains,

thickly forested and carpeted with foliage. In every direction but the south, toward Australia. There the land fell away sharply, and it was in that direction the bombers must fly for takeoff and from which they must land. No matter in what direction the wind might be blowing. And the wind, if it was strong enough at certain times of operations, could be a killer — or stop a mission from taking off. It was for just such contingencies that Lou Goodman had been forced to have his showdown with Whip Russel. One day the little tiger would be wildly gung-ho to strike a certain target. The moment for the attack, in terms of the enemy, would be perfect — but such moments sooner or later must be accompanied by field or flight conditions begging for a disaster. The showdown would come then, and the only real strength Lou Goodman would have with Whip would be that handshake at Seven-Mile Drome.

Well, it's going to work, *if* . . . And God knew there was going to be an absolute avalanche of ifs, ands or buts when it came to running a combat strike outfit from this stone-age airstrip. But it *could* work, and the key would be in-the-field maintenance, being able to keep these machines ready for flight. The heaviest logistics — bombs, ammo, fuel — would be a running affair of supply from Seven-Mile, where the B–25s could stage, and then slip up to the dry lake bed. They could —

"How does it shape up, Lou?" Whip looked at him expectantly.

"It's impossible," came the reply. "It can't work, it won't work, but" — he shrugged, and on his face was that crazy grin Whip remembered from the old airfield days — "it's the only game in town. We'll give it a shot, little man."

Whip nodded. "Fat man, you've got a deal. Let's head back for Seven-Mile."

They cranked up the little L–4 and taxied into position,

the natives and other men waiting for the signal to move aside the brush and trees on their hidden rollers. Whip gave the signal and the takeoff run was suddenly clear. Just before he went forward on the throttle he saw it.

On one side of the strip. The sign that hadn't been there before, that read *Kanaga Field*.

"Why, you old bastard . . ." But the words were spoken to himself. Even after all these years that fat bastard behind him still knew how to keep his feelings bottled up. Well, almost.

They took off and rushed down the mountainside.

14

THIRTEEN DAYS after they flew back to Garbutt Field the job was finished. The B–25D bombers had been transformed into winged weapons the likes of which no one had ever seen before. No airplanes flying anywhere in the world had the punch of these machines. They had been patched and cleaned and if they lacked the new-shine gleam of bombers fresh from the production line, they were far more impressive with what had been done to them.

Whip spent several hours just *looking* at his own airplane. The B–25D he had known was no more. In its place was the killer of which he had long dreamed. The strike bomber which could carve a hole out of air or wood or water or metal or enemy guns as it bored in to its target.

Yet he must approach these new aircraft with caution, with exquisite attention to detail. The transformation went deeper than the eye. The manner of operation was altered. Tactics would be more severely demanding. They had to learn quickly, and they had to know these aircraft before they committed them to combat with the enemy. So Whip Russel and the other pilots and crew members were brought up short in their own enthusiasm. It was back to basics.

"You've got to know every last and small detail about these iron birds," Whip told his men. "You people will draw up new weight and balance charts. You will graph your c.g. down to the last digit. You will be required to answer any and all questions about these airplanes. *Before* you take them up for your first test flights you will know them inside and out. You will approach everything you're going to do as if you were seeing these airplanes for the very first time. *None* of you, and that includes me, has any experience in what we're going to be flying. And you will stay at it day and night. Any questions?"

The airplanes had started out in life as stock B–25C and B–25D models. Standard equipment, twin-engine medium bombers distinguished by tricycle gear and twin rudders. Squared lines, almost ungainly, but a sweetheart to fly, and without any vices to trap the man who wasn't constantly wary of what was going on about him every moment in the air. It was the kind of airplane the crews came to know well, and to trust, because if you knew the B–25 and achieved intimacy with the machine, then that symbiotic relationship between man and iron meant a pilot could perform in remarkable fashion. No single case could have more dramatically emphasized this point than the older B–25B models that were used for the first strike against the heart of Japan in April of 1942 from the wildly pitching deck of the aircraft carrier U.S.S. *Hornet.*

A bomber is, after all, a machine of clearly specified performance, and the B–25 calls for so many thousands of feet of racing down a runway, accelerating constantly, before it is able to drag itself with its fuel, crew, bombs and other weight into the air. The pilot's flight manual, the bible of all operations, spells out in no uncertain terms what you can do and what you should *never* try to do, because if you violate the tenets of the manual the odds are you'll kill yourself and prang some nice expensive metal that had been sculpted into the form of an airplane.

There was an old saw: Thou shalt maintain thy air speed, lest the ground reach up and smite thee.

Well, there were times to throw away the book, and when the need arose for a fast, long-ranging bomber on a navy carrier to rattle the homeland cages of the Empire, which had yet to experience high explosives going off in the front yard, about the only hardware around that could even be considered for the job was the B–25. At first blush the idea of using the Mitchell for the mission was laughable and ridiculous. Large medium bombers were not and are not made for carrier operations, and they take too long and too much runway to claw their way into the air. The people who occupied the conference table chairs in the Pentagon wanted an airplane that could haul a ton of bombs into the air and fly for a range of twenty-four hundred miles — but it must start this phase of its life from the deck of a carrier on the high seas.

There was an added fillip. The people who recommended the B–25B for this impossible task knew it was all the more impossible because the airplane, to meet the mission needs, would have to struggle into the air with a gross weight of 31,000 pounds. Pilots who had read the flight manuals and who were familiar with the flying characteristics of heavily overloaded airplanes hooted and made rude gestures. But the navy pilots, to whom a pitching wet carrier deck was home, were less rude about the idea. People who lived *every day* with the necessity of beginning flight in a manner that horrified ground-based aviators, considered "impossible takeoffs" from a carrier deck unacceptable profanity.

Navy pilots joined army pilots (who, strangely enough, were all spirited volunteers for what they were told was almost guaranteed to be a suicidal mission) in a remote Florida airfield, where they imparted their expertise to their landlocked friends. The impossible had been done before; Whip and his men could do no less now.

Whip planned to fly his strikes with a combat formation of eleven bombers. The magic of eleven emerged from studies of tactics and his own enormous experience. It was a number of aircraft sufficiently large to mount a murderous punch, yet not so large that the formation became unwieldy. It was also small enough so that each pilot would know what to expect from the other men; from the shared intimacy of long hours in the air they could function as one machine, skidding and sliding together when adversity called for such maneuvering, rather than rigid and even fanatical adherence to maintaining formation, as tactics had been taught them in the training schools, while the Zeros clawed them to shreds. And when everything was going to hell in a handbasket, the men who could *as a team* throw their machines wildly through the air, who violated the rules, sometimes, even often, got in a pause from enemy mauling, as well as the chance to get in their own licks.

The gull-winged spread of the B–25 spanned sixty-seven feet and six inches, and the airplane was just one inch short of fifty-three feet, although the length changed from one plane to the other, depending upon what Whip or his pilots did to it. At times those changes were drastic, and it was impossible to match one airplane exactly against another. On some machines heavy weapons protruded a greater distance from bulkheads than on others. On some B–25s the crews had hacked and cut and rebuilt the tail sections to take either fixed guns or to carve out a position for a tail gunner.

If aircraft length proved to be a sometime thing, the height was essentially the same at fifteen feet and nine inches. *Not* so the weight of each machine. Poundage was a factor critical to flight and even more critical to flying at the whim of the pilot. And it was ultracritical to fighting in the air. Which meant that knowing the weights and the balance of a bomber at any time, and under any conditions, dictated to an enormous degree what you could do with it and survive. If you knew you could stretch the rules a bit, you got more performance from the thing than the manuals promised. This meant certain end results — better pilots, better airplanes, better combat ability, and, last but not least, more survivors.

The factory had reckoned the empty weight of the B–25D models received by the 335th at just about 21,000 pounds, but everyone in the combat zone knew this was silly. Especially if you believed it. It was approximately or about or around 21,000 pounds, and approximation was a fact of life because if you had been modified with a new type of self-sealing fuel tank or had new radios installed, your empty weight changed. It changed all the damn time as the airplanes were modified with armor plating, weapons, ammo feed racks, survival gear, shackles, racks and the other assorted hardware people take with them to war.

What really mattered was the combat weight. Now, according to the book you flew the B–25 with a normal combat weight of anywhere from 25,000 to 30,000 pounds, but this was, once again, only a guideline. It all boiled down to the maximum weight with which you could get into the air and fly from the field on which your airplane rolled to heave itself into the air. *Period.*

The 335th rarely flew their missions at less than 32,000 pounds gross weight when starting engines. If they needed extra speed for a strike they flew with less. If the strike was an all-out mission calling for maximum range with maximum bomb load, they could fly with a weight of 40,000 pounds, perhaps even more. At such weight you had to beat your engines half to death, your wing loading soared and the otherwise responsive machine flew like a half-dead truck until you lost some of that weight first by burning off fuel, then ridding the machine of such specifically disposable items as bombs and ammunition. One of the keys to the success of the 335th was that except for crossing mountains, they could stay low. Long-range missions meant heavy loads and lead-in-the-arms feelings at takeoff, but they burned fuel steadily on the way to the target, and their weight when they arrived in the strike area was within the limits of throwing about the airplanes in wicked maneuvers.

If you tried those fancy sidesteps at high speed with an overloaded airplane the Japanese wouldn't even have to try to cut you out of the air. Overloaded airplanes flown with less than sensitive skill have a nasty habit of breaking their wings, and that can mess up your plans for a whole day.

The only real way to take the measure of their airplanes was to judge the effectiveness of delivering destruction to the enemy, as it balanced out to the best chances of returning from a raid. This translated into defensive armament and bomb load. The slide rule held great flexibility.

There was also the matter of the enemy. You had to get in tight to mix it up with those little people who had also come so far to fight a war. Now, by God, there was the means to do some mixing.

A fifty-caliber machine gun is an effective and lethal weapon, drilling out heavy slugs with a high rate of fire. The effectiveness of a gun is measured in its punch at the target. If one fifty is good, two is better, and four is even better than that, and — well, the trick was, as Whip saw it, to stuff as many heavy machine guns into and onto his airplanes as was feasible.

The first time Whip decided to transform desire into hardware he almost gave his chief of maintenance, Master Sergeant Archie Cernan, and his ordnance officer, First Lieutenant Dick Catledge, a joint heart attack.

Whip rested a hand on Cernan's shoulder. "Arch, you know what I want you to do with this airplane of mine?"

"Sure, Captain. Stick some more guns on it. Especially pointing in the same direction you're flying."

Whip shook his head. "Uh uh. You're going to tear the nose out of that airplane."

"Tear it out?" Cernan echoed. He remembered nothing of captain's silver bars or sergeant's stripes. "What the hell for?" he demanded.

"So we got more room in this tin can, Arch, that's what for. Tear it out. Bombardier's station, lights, oxygen lines, radios, intercom, *everything.*"

Cernan glanced at Lieutenant Catledge, then back to Whip Russel. "And then what?" he demanded.

"And then, sweetheart, you will fill that great big space with fifty calibers. You will mount stanchions and crossbars or whatever it takes to handle the recoil and the blowback and the gases and the shell cases and the heat, and you will put in ammo feed boxes that, goddamnit, work when they're supposed to. You will rig the gun tit for the whole shebang on the left yoke of this here airplane. Because when I fire those babies, Arch, I want to blow a hole clean through the side of a Jap destroyer, and without using one stinking bomb, to sink the son of a bitch. Got it?"

The end result of that conversation long ago was now "alive" before Whip Russel and his men at Garbutt Field.

Whip's airplane still had that same black finish, with patches and outbreaks of rash along its metal skin, and it still had two engines and a double tail and tricycle landing gear and — that was about it. Gone was the naked glass nose he had hated so long. Now it was solid, both in bulk and in the weapons it mounted. Protruding from the rounded nose were eight fifty-caliber machine guns, four sets of two powerful weapons each, arranged one above the other. A sledgehammer if ever there had been one.

There was more. On each side of the fuselage, down along the rounded lower flanks, Catledge had installed

package guns. Individual weapons in their own fairings,
two to each side, clamped and bolted to the airplane.
Pointing forward. All the machine guns controlled by one
small gun tit that rested beneath the thumb of Whip Russel.
My God . . . he thought about that. He had more
firepower under his thumb, now, than *all* the bombers in his
squadron had when they first flew into Garbutt Field. Yet it
was more than that. When he fired his weapons all twelve
screamed at once and the firepower was a massive buzz saw
churning in every direction wherever the river of steel-jacketed and incendiary slugs met. When his weapons howled,
the impact where they struck was the same as if someone
had set off a devastating explosion *that kept going.*

There were four more weapons to his airplane. Atop the
rear fuselage was the dorsal power turret with two guns
that provided defensive fire to the flanks and behind and, in
an upper arc, through three hundred and sixty degrees. Two
more weapons completed the basic armament. On each side
of the fuselage, just forward of the dorsal turret, was
another gun, and having weapons in these positions provided additional rearward flanking protection, and to some
extent against attacks from below. Whip gave the latter no
more than a passing thought. Formation positioning, and
fighting at minimum altitude, would keep belly attacks to
their minimum.

Not all the bombers were alike. They had been modified
according to a basic plan, but there were no similar tools for
all the aircraft, there were no drawings or blueprints nor
was there even experience for this sort of thing. Certain
design details had been left to the crews of individual
bombers. Three B–25s had been fitted with fixed guns in the
tail. Where there had been a plexiglas cone for observation
the men installed one or two fifty-caliber weapons. They
would be fired only when a fighter was making a dead-

astern attack, and the value was questionable, but a pilot's freedom to alter his airplane according to whim was a tenet of Whip Russel's. Four bombers had plexiglas sheets with cross-bracing in the belly, and at the center of the bracing a ball socket had been installed to hold a single machine gun, providing some defense against belly attacks.

There was, finally, the matter of the bombs. The bombs these machines would carry in combat were the end of the long line that had begun in a California factory and had now come to its realization in northeastern Australia. The ultimate purpose of a bomber is to function as a weapon, to deliver ordnance to the target.

The specifications for the original B–25 called for a machine to deliver one ton of bombs over a range of twelve hundred miles. To the Death's Head Brigade even the term "a ton of bombs" had no meaning unto itself. What was the mission? What were the targets? Were they after warships where deep penetration of decking and armor plate was necessary, so that they must use armor-piercing missiles? Were the ships thin-hulled destroyers or merchantmen where you wanted the bomb to go off as soon as the detonator struck *anything?* If the strike called to hit airfields you might want parafrags — fragmentation bombs lowered by small parachutes to get the drifting cluster effect you wanted, and the maximum blast wave and frag effect above the surface. A hundred other factors, small or vital, determined the ordnance loads.

The drastic alterations to the B–25s called for shuffling about the crew positions. The "book recommendations" no longer had meaning. No one sat up front any longer, of course, since the entire nose of the airplane was now a killing machine of weaponry. There were still the two pilots who shared the duties of flying the airplane, operating its systems, operating command radio and coordinating mis-

sion strikes. With the modified airplanes the pilot was now
the gunner and the bombardier, although most crews found
it expedient to have the pilot shout his command for bombs
away and the copilot, finger against the release, was able to
respond in a split second.

In the space immediately behind the cockpit sat the
navigator, tucked away within a tightly confined world. He
could watch all hell breaking loose from his compartment by
staring ahead between the pilots, or he might try to get into
the back of the airplane. Not a pleasant or easy task, for the
only way back was through a narrow crawl space atop the
bomb bays. Because a man in the navigator's compartment
could go crazy — being unable to *do* anything in combat
— Whip gave his men the option of installing a single
machine gun in a crossbar hatch by the navigator's dome.

This modification was performed on Whip's airplane by
his navigator, Second Lieutenant Ronald Gall. Whip's first
sight of the gun position was less than enthusiastic. "What
the hell are you going to do with that thing?" Whip asked
Gall. "You've hardly got any room as it is now, and your
field of fire, well — " He shrugged.

Ronald Gall snorted with something less than cheers for
his pilot's observations. "Tell you what, boss. Next time we
get into a fracas with the Emperor's favorite people, I'll fly
and you come back here and chew on your fingernails. I'm
fresh out."

Behind the bomb bay, just aft of the wing trailing edge,
was the rear fuselage area where the radio/operator gunner,
Staff Sergeant Joe Leski, operated the liaison radio equipment and fired the two waist guns. Corporal Bruce Coombs
completed the crew at five; he was flight engineer, worked
the dorsal power turret in combat and doubled in brass with
Leski to operate various fixed cameras in the fuselage.

Once again, crew designations were reflections of the

training bible. In Whip Russel's outfit it was mandatory for the crews to be cross-trained and adept in the tasks assigned "on paper" to the other men. It gave the bombers greater flexibility and reliability and imparted that intangible but critical level of shared self-confidence on the part of men who join one another in flight where death is only a garish fireball away from them all.

The men completed their inspections, test-fired their guns on the ground, turned dials, studied gauges, pulled levers and operated handles until every element of their airplanes had been moved and activated.

All but flight, and the 335th was ready when Whip Russel notified the crews to be on deck for takeoff the next morning at dawn.

15

IF YOU WENT by the book the B–25 — as the manuals listed the numbers — showed a maximum speed of 322 miles an hour, reflecting a flying weight of 27,000 pounds. But that weight itself had meaning only when you specified a specific altitude at which engine and aircraft performance was at its optimum. It was a sort of crossbreeding between weight, power settings, altitude, temperature and the angle at which the propeller blades were set to chew into the air. Then, the speed also was a direct reflection of just how clean an airplane might be — that is, without all the garbage that characterized the combat birds. They had the drag of the nose guns, package guns, wing racks, antennae and other equipment, all of which slowed any machine moving through a resisting medium such as the air. Combat airplanes also tend to be smeared and caked with oil and grease and dust, all of this complicated by such things as dents and dings. Everything considered, hauling between two and three thousand pounds of bombs, with the throttles hammered forward and the props whirling at top speed, the loaded airplanes turned in about 280 miles an hour.

You could always gain speed, a hell of a lot of it, by mixing gravity with your performance. The gravity ride was a favorite of Whip's because his initial strike on a mission could then be made with everything full out, and taking care of his engines, yet plunging toward the enemy at well over three hundred miles an hour.

And there was the matter of just how high the B–25 could climb. No one in the squadron, or no one any of the pilots knew, had ever flown the airplane to its listed service ceiling — that altitude where the B–25 could still climb at a rate of at least one hundred feet per minute. Out of curiosity and also his fervent desire to know just about everything there was to know about the machine in which he flew off to war, Whip took up his bird for a joust to high altitude. He carried only fuel and ammunition for his guns; no bombs.

The flight manual said the airplane would take off with a full load and climb steadily to a service ceiling of twenty-five thousand feet. The book proved right; they passed that height with a climbing rate of at least three hundred and eighty feet per minute. But —

"Captain, how much longer we going to keep up this crazy shit?" A pause, then: "sir," added grudgingly. The complaint was voiced by the flight engineer, Corporal Bruce Coombs.

"What's wrong back there?" Whip quipped. "You guys don't like clean air?"

"Skipper, how high are we now?" Coombs ignored the pilot's query.

"Twenty-nine thousand and we're still going."

"Let's go the other way, sir. Like, *down.*"

"Is that an official complaint, Coombs?"

"Shit, *yes,* sir! Captain, it's thirty-two degrees below zero in this here airplane and these clothes and blankets don't hack it. We're freezin' to death!"

His own enthusiasm had permitted enduring the cold. They'd dressed as best they could for the flight. All the clothes they could borrow, blankets, canvas; they looked like refugees running from a glacier. It worked only for a little while. The temperature went down steadily until the men *were* half-frozen. Alex Bartimo turned to Whip. "You can't see me because of this bloody oxygen mask, but my teeth are blue and my lips are yellow and my liver has curled up and died, and it is way past time to get the hell out of here." A spasm went through the Australian. "Whip, you're going to have a crew with frostbite. I don't know if you're laughing behind that gargoylish mask, but this is *serious.*"

Whip looked down on the earth nearly six miles below. He was enraptured with islands shrunk to tabletop relief models, the sun silvered and gleaming across a vast stretch of ocean, clouds blinding white on their tops and casting splotchy shadows below and —

He sighed, pulled the plug and started down.

Alex Bartimo had been right. Bruce Coombs had two frostbitten toes. The whole squadron came to visit him. It was a special occasion. The temperature at Garbutt Field was one hundred and twelve degrees above zero and they had a cursing gunner with frostbite.

"I'd like to see the face on the guy in the Pentagon who reads *that* medical report," murmured one pilot.

Whip sat on the hood of the jeep three quarters of the distance down the runway at Garbutt Field. Thunder snarled across the field and bounded along the desert. Dust flew wildly behind spinning props. The Death's Head Brigade was alive, testing its muscle, honing its skills, finding out just what it could do with the modified airplanes loaded to their limits. Whip had marked off runway distances so that he would *know* what his men could do. Every pilot in the squadron was going through takeoff tests. Here at Garbutt they had plenty of room. A man who didn't get off the ground in the distance allotted to him found his mistake wasn't irreversible. Plenty of room left. Once they got to Kanaga Field there wouldn't be any room. Not extra

feet, anyway. Here and now was the time to find the flaws.
At the far end of the runway a killer airplane rolled slowly
onto the active. It bobbed on its nose gear, coming gently to
a stop, the nose wheel aligned with the runway. Whip
grinned at the sight. Huge yellow fangs to each side of the
eight guns in the nose marked the number seven ship in
the squadron. First Lieutenant Octavio Jordan was at the
controls, with Duane Collins, another First, in the right seat.
The full crew was aboard, and the bomb bays were loaded
with bombs filled with sand.

Whip brought the radio microphone to his lips. "Seven,
how about it?"

"We're ready."

"You'd better be. What's your numbers?"

"Density altitude at just over five thousand feet, boss."

"You still think you can get that thing off in three?"

"You're my mother. I can do anything mom tells me I can
do."

No more time for conversation. Thunder rose from the
far end of the runway as Jordan went to flat pitch on
the props and brought the throttles steadily forward. The
airplane shook and trembled from the nearly four thousand
horsepower screaming through the engines. But they didn't
move yet. The pilots stood on the brakes, holding her back.
They'd move only when every gauge in that cockpit told
them they had it all going for them. Behind the bomber a
small sandstorm had leaped into being, hurled away from
those wildly thrashing propellers.

"Seven to control. We're, ah, go."

At almost the same moment Jordan called out brake
release Whip heard the change in propeller pitch, a clear
aural signal the airplane was moving, hacking great chunks
of air as it pulled forward. Gone now was the levity they'd
exchanged for several moments, for pounding along a dirt

runway in a bomber loaded with lead up to its ass was no game. Not when a single mistake could produce a blinding sheet of flame and five dead men.

The B–25 howled louder and louder as it sped down the runway. Whip watched Jordan's technique with the airplane and nodded his approval. The pilot had the nose wheel up slightly, preventing it from digging into the soft ground, decreasing his drag. It might add up to only a fraction of performance but fractions have a habit of getting together and producing major results.

Faster, faster, still faster, and Jordan would need every bit of speed he could squeeze from his airplane. The engine gauges were all the way around to max performance; manifold pressure and r.p.m. and fuel flow and the rest of it, everything in the green and at the stops, and a blast of thunder pounded Whip as the B–25 hurtled past him. He watched with hawk eyes. At two thousand seven hundred feet from starting his roll Jordan was coming back on the yoke. The airplane was heavy, God, she wallowed a bit in the heat, but the wings had their grip on air. Jordan was flying as if he were taking off from the airstrip in the New Guinea mountains he'd never yet seen, committing to what lay in the future, and as fast as he had the machine above the ground they were dragging up the gear, getting it out of the way, cleaning up the airplane.

"Not bad for a wetback," Whip said into his mike.

"It was all the help from the flies in the bays, boss. All them wings going for us."

"How did she feel?"

"Like the wings were made of lead." The B–25 was climbing out in a wide circle about the field as Jordan exchanged his observations with Whip on the jeep. "Funny thing, though. She acted like she *wanted* to fly. Had to hold her down a bit until we hit the marker at two-seven."

"Roger that."

"Don't think that mystery field of yours will be any problem, boss."

"Better not be," Whip said. "Okay, off you go to that target area. They'll be waiting for you."

"Roger. Seven out."

Jordan and his crew eased off to the west to join several other bombers already making practice runs against a target in the desert, a silhouette of a Japanese ship patched together from trees and brush.

Whip dismissed Jordan's airplane from his mind. Number Eight was moving into position. Whip looked down the runway. Captain Hoot Gibson in the left seat and First Lieutenant Ray Gordon to his right. No teeth or fangs on this bird. Dazzling orange lightning flashes marked the Number Eight airplane.

"Eight's ready to wind up," came the crackle in Whip's earphones.

"Okay, Kansas. Let her rip."

"Roger that, little man."

"Sound off when you kick loose."

"Right."

Number Eight went to the wall with power, another winged killer straining at the leash, and then she was on her way, pounding down the airstrip. At just that moment Hoot Gibson brought her off the deck the right engine faltered.

Number Eight and five men hovered on the brink of oblivion.

Gibson played it like the virtuoso he was. He didn't waste a second in getting the nose down again. They were going too fast and were too far down the runway to come to a stop; the B–25 would have gone screaming out into the boonies and torn herself to pieces. Everything had to be decided on a matter of split-second timing. Gibson put her

back on earth, *kept up full power.* The right engine banged
ominously, but Gibson was now gambling on that good left
engine and whatever power he could strain from the right.
At the last possible moment he hauled her into the air. It
was a total commitment. Gibson had well over the minimum flying speed necessary to fly her out on one engine, *if*
he hadn't been on gross overload. The B–25 boomed into
the air, grabbing for sky, the gear coming up. Her speed
was falling away swiftly and their time was fleeing with
terrible haste.

And then the bomb bay doors came open and Gibson
salvoed the full load of practice bombs. Two tons of dead
weight plunged from the airplane, lightened the load on the
wings, gave the good left engine the chance it needed. It had
all happened with terrifying speed and there hadn't been a
second to spare, for even as the bombs were falling the right
engine died completely and they were feathering the propeller blades knife-edge into the wind. Gibson brought her
around with only one fan running, still hot because of her
heavy fuel load, and put her down on a feather mattress.

Not until they were rolling on dirt did Whip Russel say a
word. "What the hell kind of takeoff was that?" he asked
the still shaken pilots.

"The best kind," came the response. He could hear
Gibson sucking in air. "We're back home."

"You think that thing is supposed to fly on one fan?"

"Practice makes perfect, boss."

"Consider yourself graduated. Good job, Hoot."

"I'll take three fingers. J and B on the rocks. Don't bother
with the ice."

Five days later Whip considered his men — and their
planes — ready to go. The bugs had been worked out of the
machinery and the men knew their machines. They gath-

ered on the fifth day, seated or sprawled by Whip's airplane.

"We've had a signal, as Alex would say," Whip announced, "from General Smyth. The long and short of it, gentlemen, is that we leave tomorrow morning for our new home. Takeoff at first light. You will load the aircraft tonight and have your ground crews aboard while it's still dark. We're going into Seven-Mile to refuel and then stage on up to Kanaga Field."

Chris Patterakis looked up at a threatening sky. "What's the weather for tomorrow?"

"Front's moving through. But it doesn't look too bad for what we want to do. Seven-Mile will lay on a diversionary strike somewhere to keep the Japs occupied and away from us when we come in and go out." He looked at his men. Lou Goodman stood behind him, by the nose of the airplane.

"Get your beauty rest tonight, troops. The general also passed on the word that the Emperor's best have started to make their move. The big push into New Guinea."

A murmuring rose from the men at his words. "Hold it," Whip added. "As soon as we land at Kanaga, we get ready to fly. Within two hours of landing, if we get the call."

16

THEY OBSERVED strict radio silence going into Seven-Mile. The tower handled the eleven bombers with light gun signals and brought in the B–25s hastily. On the ground the airplanes were rolled to one side and the fuel trucks driven to them. Some of the ground crews left the bombers here, to wait for another B–25 coming up from Garbutt Field, and two more still being worked on to provide replacements. There would be fourteen airplanes in all at Kanaga: eleven ships committed to missions, one always on standby, two more waiting in the wings to move out on call. There wasn't room for more.

They had a land line in by now between Seven-Mile and Kanaga and they could pass on the exact moment the bombers left the Moresby area so that the ground troops and the natives in the mountain field would be ready to roll the false barriers away from the airstrip. Whip's crews assembled on the ground, and Whip stepped away from center front. From this moment on it was Lou Goodman's show. That was their deal.

"You're all being issued sidearms," Goodman told the men, "and you will wear them at all times when you're at Kanaga. I'm going to repeat that. *At all times.* Flight and ground crews both. Just so no one makes any mistakes that's a direct order and there'll be a court martial for anyone who screws up." He let his eyes rove about the men as he spoke. They may as well understand *him* right from the word go.

"You're not just flying into an advance airfield," he went on. "You're going into territory that may have as many Japanese in the area as friendly troops and natives. You may have to defend that field at any time day or night. It's all down to the bare bones. When we land at Kanaga, everyone will move all belongings and other materiel from their aircraft. You'll do that before you walk six feet from your plane. Captain Russel has already told you we're to be on standby call, ready to roll, two hours after we hit Kanaga. I'm changing that."

He paused. Let them look at one another. Let Whip's eyebrows go up a notch or two at the same time. It'll do the little bastard good to know what side his bread's buttered on. "It's ninety minutes now, gentlemen. You'll need that half-hour for personal activities. Because when you get your first good look at Kanaga the first thing you're going to want to do is take a good crap. All right; load up."

They were ready, bombed and fueled, one hour and seven minutes after landing at Kanaga. Goodman didn't bother the crews. They knew what to do and didn't need anyone screwing up their well-drilled act of getting ready to fly and fight. He understood this kind of outfit. You had to be ramrod straight with them. The moment they even suspected you were playing soldier you'd lost them. They'd take orders but there'd be a wall of ice between the men and their commander so thick you could make iceberg sandwiches.

The two hours after landing came and went. Tension heightened as men's eyes kept returning to their watches. Idle conversation petered away. With the passing minutes they began to take stock of where they were, of what the hell Kanaga Field was all about. If was as if they were seeing for the first time the extent of the preparations, the hundred and forty Papuans who had to be ready at any one moment to roll trees and brush from the airstrip. If they screwed up the takeoff it was into the trees on the south side of the mountain and they'd kill only themselves. If an airplane got away from its pilots on a landing and ran loose there was only one place for it to go — straight into the caves where they lived.

At least the mechanics would do everything in their power to be sure all brakes on all airplanes worked . . .

Three hours now since landing. Whip had been right about the weather. Broken clouds and scattered showers. The wind picking up. Now they had scud and it swept low overhead, bands of gray sheep fleeing the wolf of wind. The clouds were barely five hundred feet above the ground.

First Lieutenant Paddy Shannon held down the left seat in the tenth aircraft. "The colonel was right." He stood up and stretched, looked into the ominous sky. "For sure we ain't about to be going anywhere on this day."

At chow that evening, a mixture of iron rations and local food the natives had brought in, Goodman gave them the latest poop. "General Smyth has laid on the mission for us. A PBY picked up a concentration of invasion barges working down from New Britain. They want us to hit them as early as possible. They're anxious to see how our fancy new guns work out. You'll roll out of the sack at zero four four five."

At three that morning the bottom fell out of the sky. They got it all. High winds, a cannonading of lightning and thunder, a downpour that would have done credit to a monsoon. Normal rain for New Guinea. No one slept well the rest of the night. Too many lingering thoughts about a soft, muddy runway.

Their first takeoff from Kanaga would have to wait. First light came clammy, cold and thick with fog. They were in the midst of clouds. The morning was gray and dismal and got worse. New Guinea mosquitoes haven't read the book of instructions. They like to do their work in rain or sun, and they followed the men everywhere.

The caves went from tolerable to damp, soggy, clammy, soaked with perspiration. Condensation ran down the walls. Strange insects swarmed to the caves simply because it was better than continued exposure to the relentless downpour. The men took to sleeping in the bombers. At least there they were free of water collecting about them. Parachutes and flying gear and personal equipment made up lumpy beds. Better than none.

It rained for three days and three nights and Kanaga Field disappeared under a layer of water. Goodman cursed his inability to put his drainage program into effect before the rains chained the 335th to the ground. The men grew listless, bored to frustration.

Headquarters didn't help matters any. The Japanese were already landing their forces along the northern coastline. Fighters had staged down from various fields, flying low, and were reinforcing the garrisons at Lae and Salamaua. A bunch came down to Moresby and turned Seven-Mile and two other fields into a shooting gallery. Thirty-two men were killed, eighty more wounded, four bombers destroyed and a dozen other airplanes shot up.

The 335th walked in mud and cursed.

The rains ended on the fourth day. Still no flying. The field was sticky mud. Pilots, crewmen, mechanics, natives, everyone worked to get the field ready. The sun came out to help them.

Not Moresby and not Seven-Mile. A flotilla of bombers came down from Rabaul and worked over the airfields and port with devastating effect. The plans to hammer the invasion barges had turned into a mockery. The killers of the Death's Head Brigade stayed on the ground, the reinforcements all got through where the Japanese had sent them, and the Americans were getting clobbered from all sides.

Goodman gave no orders to his men to be ready on their fifth morning at Kanaga. By four o'clock the crews were at the airplanes, running up engines in the dark, fretful, pissed off mightily at the whole world. At five o'clock Goodman got the new orders. Forget the barges; they were empty. But the pick of the Japanese fighter crop was now at Lae Airdrome.

"Your orders are simple," Goodman told the men. "Get Lae."

Whip was the first. He waited at the end of the strip, the big Cyclones ticking over. Dark outside, but the eastern sky showing the first signs of the earth rolling on its side to meet the sun. He glanced through his side window. Ten more bombers fanged, tusked, emblazoned; all ready to move.

Now or never. Enough light. He flashed his position lights. At the far end of the strip Lou Goodman caught the signal, answered with three flashes of green from a hand-held light gun.

Whip nudged the power, lined up, went on the brakes with Alex. He started forward on the power. "Thank God," Alex murmured. That's all he said, needed to say. They had begun to doubt their own justification for being.

Full power, everything full forward, and they were rolling. The ground was firmer than they'd hoped. Whip held back pressure on the yoke to keep the nose wheel light. The bomber accelerated steadily, wings rocking along the uneven ground. But the engines were sweet and he felt the wings grabbing air. He held her down until the air speed read eighty. With her continuing acceleration the takeoff was a piece of cake. She eased into the sky and the gear thumped into the wells and Jesus Christ but it felt good to have flight again at your fingertips. Whip flew a slow climbing circle, watched the ten other bombers rolling down Kanaga and easing into the air, forming up on his plane. By the time all eleven planes were in the air they had plenty of light.

This mission wouldn't take long. The distance between Seven-Mile and Lae was about one hundred and eighty miles, and they'd started a lot closer than that. Even if the Japanese had a sub off the southern coast, or watchers in the hills, they'd have no word of the takeoff from Kanaga. Surprise was going to be theirs.

They went up the slopes of the mountains in formation, holding it in tight, strict radio silence between the bombers. No one needed to talk anyway. Lae had become personal to them all.

Whip didn't waste any time making his approach. He could have come into Lae from the northwest, over land, but he wanted a first shot at the powerful Japanese field from over water. On the deck. That meant flying directly between Salamaua and Lae, but they'd be cutting it so close the Japanese wouldn't get more than the briefest warning. Just enough time to get some Sakae engines started in those Zeros. Whip grinned to himself. He liked that idea. Some of the fighters might even be clawing into the air by the time they boomed out of the southeast and came right down their single runway. That meant he could get in a few licks with that madhouse of firepower against a Zero that was flying. He needed some more flags on the side of his airplane, anyway.

They crested the mountain range and started running downhill, staying tight to the trees, twin-engined sharks knowing where their prey waited for them. Faster and

faster, taking the gravity ride down the slopes, and then a
sweeping, tight-formation turn over the waters of Huon
Gulf, and there was Lae waiting for them.

Probably the best antiaircraft crew the Japanese ever had
stood watch on the end of the Lae airstrip. They'd been
knocking the crap out of bombers and fighters for months.
They'd chewed up the 335th before. Everyone making a
strike into Lae always took a whack at the AA crew, but the
Japs were smart. They moved it around and they heaved
sandbags all around it, and the crew always managed to
zero in on the bombers coming into the Japanese field. No
one argued that this flak outfit was far and away the winner
in the competition between the AA gun and the attacking
planes.

Whip intended to change the game. The B–25s eased into
a strung-out formation, two planes to an element, spacing
themselves carefully for the most effective bomb drop. But
Whip wasn't playing the game according to the rules the
Japanese knew.

From the cockpit the water directly before the B–25
flashed with terrifying speed at the lead airplane. Far ahead,
Lae itself grew slowly in size, that slow-motion expansion of
things and space that was so contrary to the rushing speed
of a bomber down on the deck. Whip and Alex searched for
the flak gun. Lae swelled in size with tremendous speed
now and they found the flak position barely in time. The
Japs got off the first round. A mistake. Whip saw the flash,
eased in rudder. Behind and to his right Czaikowicz followed every move. The bomber plunged forward and Whip
had a fleeting thought as to what the Japanese might be
thinking.

The first shot was theirs; they never had time for a
second. Whip held the flak position in his sights. He opened
fire with a single burst to test his aim. Tracers flashed in

glowing blobs and sped away from the airplane. A touch of
rudder, a hint of pressure on the yoke. Then, a long burst. It
all poured directly into the antiaircraft position.

"My God . . ." That from Gall, watching behind them to
see what it would be like.

Twelve fifty-caliber machine guns were dead on their
target. The flak position *erupted.* A shattering swarm of
steel-jacketed and incendiary hornets tore into the gun, the
sandbags, the crew. The heavy gun itself was hurled from
its mounts. There was no need for a second burst.

They hardly dared believe what they saw. Zero fighters
everywhere. So many of them the Japanese hadn't been
able to disperse them all in revetments. At least thirty
fighters lined up on each side of the runway. Whip and
Psycho bored in, pounding out short bursts with their
batteries of machine guns. The bomb bays were open and
they let go with 250-pounders. Even as he was flashing by
Whip was changing his plans for the strike. He went to his
radio.

"Make it one pass only, troops," he called to his men.
"Break to the right and form up over the water. Kessler,
you take the lead and I'll pick up. Head straight down the
coastline and we'll pay those other people a visit. Over."

"Three to Leader. Wilco."

"Psycho, you read?"

"Roger from Two."

"You got the play?"

"Got it. I'll fall back a bit."

"Roger."

Czaikowicz already knew what had formed in his mind.
The first two bombers thundered low over Lae, their bombs
creating carnage behind them. Nine more B–25s sledgeham-
mered in their loads, the pilots snapping out short and
devastating bursts from their massive nose armament.

"Jesus, will you look at that . . ."

A long burst from one bomber slammed into a row of fighters. The first three airplanes whirled crazily into the air as the rivers of steel and incendiaries from the B–25s smashed into their midst.

The bombs walked along the runway, into revetments, plowed up trees and buildings and airplanes. The B–25s howled their song on the deck, too fast, too quick for the Japanese to do much about it. Nine airplanes broke right over the hills at the far end of the runway, going wide, out of range of what guns were still firing, easing out over the waters of the gulf, and taking up a heading to the south.

No one would ever fault the Japanese for not giving it everything they had. On the smoking, cratered runways and taxiway, four Zeros were doing their best to get into the sky. One went into a crater and cartwheeled out of control, snapping the gear. But three more made it into the air, and took up pursuit of the nine bombers.

Exactly as Whip wanted them to do.

The two B–25s, Whip leading, Psycho just the right distance behind, came out of the northwest, catching the Zeros racing away over water. Whip lined up his sights on the first fighter, still punching for speed. At this moment the B–25 had it all over the Zero, coming in from better altitude, the engines wide open, with an advantage of a hundred miles an hour. Whip pressed the gun tit from two hundred yards.

No more Zero. Whip and Alex gaped. The screaming hose of firepower from the bomber simply blasted its way *through* the Japanese fighter. One moment it was there, the next it was gone, and pieces of wreckage whirled through the air.

Whip walked rudder and skidded. The second fighter was in his sights but only for a moment. The Zero went up swiftly on one wing, the pilot ready to come down again in a beautiful arc and catch the speeding bomber as it went by.

It worked.

Except for Psycho who came in without warning. His slugs went into the fuel tanks and a ball of fire arced through the air, and began its death fall.

The third fighter pilot didn't know what was happening. His first reaction was that an unseen fighter escort was coming after them and he hauled back on the stick, horsing the Zero into a sudden zoom climb. It saved his life, for the two bombers raced away at full speed, fleeing to the south.

"Coming up behind you," Whip announced on his radio. By now Psycho was in tight, and the gunners of both planes were keeping that last Zero in sight. Still far behind them. A brave son of a bitch back there. He was alone and coming on like a tiger.

They ignored him. Directly ahead of the eleven-bomber force waited Salamaua. The auxiliary base was alive and Zeros were scrambling down the runway and into the air. "One pass only, troops," Whip ordered. "Spread out and pick your targets. Keep it straight and true. I don't want any turns."

They went through the Salamaua airstrip with blinding fury. No bombs, but everyone lining up targets on the ground. The last two bombers eased back to hold their Tail-End Charlie positions. A couple of fighters came around in steep banks to hit the B–25s as they went by, were baffled by the explosive punch of the bombers. Shannon in Number Ten picked off one Zero and Captain Dusty Rhodes in the last bomber damaged two more. He was too eager; no kills.

Salamaua disappeared behind them. More Zeros were in the air now, and Whip decided it was time to quit pressing their advantage. He eased into a steady climbing turn and they pushed into broken clouds. They stayed in the climb, the formation easing apart for more room, until they had enough altitude to clear any peaks below.

It was sheer jubilation all the way back. Not to Seven-Mile, where the Japanese might seek them out, but into Kanaga. Sixty seconds after they landed there was no sign of an airfield on the dry lake bed.

"Well, shee-yit, looka' *him*. A major, no less."

"Don't no one call him 'Boss' no more. It's *Majuh* from here on in."

"Does that mean we gotta call the little son of a bitch 'sir'?"

Whip grinned at his crews. They grinned back. General Smyth would have sent flowers if he could have managed it. Far East Air Forces was jubilant. The first strike with the 335th and its new bombers had flattened Lae. Twenty-four fighters destroyed on the ground or shot out of the air. Heavy casualties. Salamaua had lost another eight planes.

No B–25s lost. No wounded. No casualties. Just a few holes in two bombers.

Success beyond belief. And with the congratulations from the general had come another message. Whip Russel could shed his silver bars.

Lou Goodman pinned on the oak leaves. He'd carried them for two weeks, waiting for this moment.

17

"THE JAPANESE appear to be cooperating with us. The weather is holding and apparently they feel they didn't get in enough troops with their last run down from New Britain." Lou Goodman tapped the large map hung from rollers beneath the woven roof that served as his briefing "room." He turned back to the assembled flight crews. "We had a B–17 at high altitude in the area, and as of a few hours ago" — again the pointer tapped the map — "our little friends have put together a heavy concentration of troop barges at Wanigela. You people have been wanting a crack at just this sort of target and today you'll have your chance."

He waited for the inevitable murmuring among the men, brought it quickly to a halt. "FEAF wants those barges torn up. They're small, which means many barges with not too many men aboard each one. Made to order for us. Now, after what you people did at Lae and Salamaua the Japanese are edgy. You can expect them to protect those barges with everything they have."

He held the pointer in both hands, bending it slightly against his protruding middle. "Seven-Mile is laying on a harassing strike of Australian P–40s to tie up the Zeros at Lae and Salamaua, and six B–26s will go in against the fighters at Buna. Between those two strikes they ought to tie up most of the Zeros from the fields closest to us. However, you'd better expect some local cover at Wanigela sent down from Rabaul.

"Your favorite weather pundit has some good news for a change," Goodman added.

Hoots and jeers met Captain Paul Egli, who took the moment to bow ceremoniously to the crews. Finally he held up both hands. "All right, all right. What the colonel said is true. It's almost *too* good to be true. Scattered clouds at three thousand. Winds out of the northwest at twenty knots or better. That should make the surface choppy and give the Japs conniptions in handling their barges. It also means they'll have lousy gun platforms for any flak they have. The same weather pattern should hold for the rest of the day with some areas increasing to broken from scattered. But no significant changes. Colonel?"

Egli stepped aside and Goodman again faced the men. "Lieutenant Mercer in Number Two will take navigation lead on this mission. Any questions?"

They had them but not to be voiced then. Men looked around to find Ronald Gall and saw the lieutenant was as surprised as the rest of them. What the hell did the colonel mean by making Mercer lead nav? Shit, Gall was prime crew for Major Russel's airplane and —

Gall saw the colonel motioning him over for a private talk. He stood stiffly, puzzled and still uncomfortable. "I'm taking your place today, Lieutenant."

"Is, uh, anything wrong, sir?"

Goodman shook his head. "Hell, no, son. It's just that my job calls for me to go along on a few of these soirees and you happen to have the best seat in the house." Goodman studied the youngster before him. "You seem to be taking this personally, Lieutenant."

"Begging the colonel's pardon, I sure am."

"You don't like being left behind?"

"Hell . . . sorry, sir, but . . . but, goddamnit, Colonel, *that's my crew.*"

Goodman rubbed his chin, tried to hide his disbelief and pleasure. "Care to ride in the back, Ron?"

The grin was his answer. "Sure, sir. Leski and Coombs need someone to baby-sit them, anyway. And besides, we're going after those barges, right? What the hell can I shoot at with a gun that points only straight up? Thanks, Colonel. I just wouldn't feel right being left on the ground."

Goodman nodded. "See you aboard. Dismissed."

It was another first-light takeoff. The high winds left something to be desired, but the B–25s were well below maximum gross weight and the runway left them breathing space in getting off the ground. They formed up well south of the field in a long, wide turn. Thirteen planes were flying today. FEAF wanted every gun aimed at those barges.

The only thing that went right were the targets. If Egli could have found a place to skulk away he would have taken it. The forecast of scattered clouds fell apart within thirty miles of takeoff, although to Lou Goodman, watching directly ahead of the B–25 in which he was riding, looking between the shoulders of Whip and Bartimo, it was a rare moment of beauty. They were threading their way through broken clouds and unexpected towering cumulus, a fantasy of brilliant sun against white cloud flanks and deep shafts of light between cloud mountains. The bomber rocked gently in the climb and war seemed to be the game of the denizens of some other, unknown planet.

Reality came back to Lou. He leaned forward to tap Whip on his arm. "We going to have problems with this weather?"

"We already got 'em," came Whip's terse reply. "Climbing out ain't no problem but if this stuff closes in beneath us we've got no way to tell the cloud deck in the target area. And how the hell are we going to find Wanigela in this shit?"

"That's a neat question! How?"

"You waiting for me to say something smart, Colonel?"

"Yeah."

"Keep waiting."

But the clouds didn't pack in solid beneath them. Almost, but not quite. They had eight-tenths cloud coverage or better between their formation and the sea. Twenty percent, often only 10 percent, of the water surface was visible. Not the best way to go to war.

"There's a good question waiting around to be answered, sir," Alex offered to Goodman. "The Zeros. Will they be waiting for us above the clouds, or, below?"

Goodman looked at him in surprise as a thought came to him. "That could be the answer."

They shared the thought together. "Of course," Whip said slowly. "If the cloud deck is real low they'll —"

"Probably split their cover," Goodman finished for him. "Keep some people on top and the rest below."

"Which means that if they can fly down there —" began Whip.

"We can fly down there," finished Alex.

"I suggest," Whip said slowly, peering ahead, "that we stay awake. We've got to look for two things. Zeros, and a hole to go through in a hurry."

They cruised unusually high for their mission, at just over eight thousand feet, skimming the cloud battlements, silvered motes hurrying along the tumultuous growth beneath them. It didn't seem possible they'd have a chance to make their mission before the clouds —

Corporal Bruce Coombs saw them first. "Major, we got company," he called in from the top turret. "I make out at least a dozen fighters, two o'clock high. Looks like they're orbiting a target area, sir."

They looked up and slightly to their right. "Well, they did us a favor," Whip said. "Those barges have got to be somewhere beneath them."

"Major, Gall here in the back. That hole we just passed. I made out some pretty good wakes on the water."

The three men up front looked at one another. Wakes they could see from eight thousand feet? That would have to be the biggest damned barge ever built. And no one made them that big.

Whip made a sudden decision. He rolled the airplane into a steep left bank, the squadron following as if the move was rehearsed. "If we can keep that thunderhead between us and those Zeros," he told Alex and Lou Goodman, "there's every chance we can go downstairs without that top cover seeing us." Whip had debated breaking radio silence but their unknown presence could prove an enormous advantage. He'd trust to his well-disciplined troops coming through with him.

He came back on the power, far back, and the B–25 eased into a steep glide. Whip kept the bank steep, pulling the plug for a rapid descent. He fed in trim to ease off on the stick forces and let the bomber ride her way down at two thousand feet a minute. The lower they went the less chance that top escort of fighters would have to see them. They were taking a gamble by working downstairs through heavy cloud, flying eyeball on glimpses of the sea. And that ceiling between the ocean and the cloud bottoms had better give them some maneuvering room, or it would be flying out of here on the gauges. He was still wound up with the report of ship wakes. That meant something big down there. They'd screwed up on the weather for this show. Could Intelligence also have been so far off the mark they didn't even *know* of some big stuff mixing in with those barges?

At fifteen hundred feet he brought in power, easing the rate of descent, the world a mixture of flashing sunlight and sudden shadows and grays and pale glowing as they streaked from open sky into and through clouds, an eye-stabbing flicker of movement and —

The altimeter was just unwinding through eight hundred feet when they broke through. Whip held the formation tight up against the flattened cloud layers just above them. They'd be tough to spot and they still had to find what they were after. They curved around the edge of a local but sharp rainshower.

"There." Alex pointed. "The whole bloody lot of them. And it's a hell of a lot more than barges, I would say!"

"You would, would you?" Whip grinned at him.

Radio silence meant nothing now. Those people on those ships could hear them coming from miles off. But seconds were precious. Whip brought his radio to life. "All right, troops, the curtain's going up. We have barges, at least three destroyers for cover and two troopships, it looks like, out there waiting for us. Ten o'clock my position right now. Anybody see any fighters out there?"

Someone had caught a glimpse of a shaft of sunlight off metal. Jim Whitson in Number Six. "Six to Leader. About a dozen of 'em. Two o'clock and they're turning toward us. Take them a bit to make it here."

"We'll race 'em," Whip answered. "Last one in is a rotten egg. Okay, troops. Two through Six stay with me. Jordan, you take the rest of the people and go after those troopships and barges. We'll keep the tin cans busy. Break, *now*."

Time slowed, the world dragged. Propellers went into flat pitch, shrilling their thunder. Throttles followed. Full power. Guns charged. Belts cinched just a bit tighter. Eyes searching out the Zeros, increasing in size, coming after them with all the power *they* had. A race to the targets. Whip and five other planes would take a crack at the destroyers. With their heavy flak guns they could chew up a low-level strike like this. They had to be stopped, fast.

"Two through Six, fan out. Take 'em line abreast to my right."

Five B–25s eased into a long wing-to-wing line. Thousands of Japanese soldiers looked up, wondering, frightened, at one wave of six bombers howling toward the warships. And another wave of seven coming directly at them.

The opening run was a classic maneuver straight out of the textbook Whip still had in writing.

The long-range guns of the destroyers opened fire first. But they hadn't expected the attack, not with the weather, with the Zeros on top of and beneath the clouds to give them plenty of warning. In those precious few seconds it required to turn and track and depress and aim, the B–25s were on their runs. The initial fire from the destroyers was light and sporadic. It didn't stay that way long. The Japanese were good, their shipborne flak had always been deadly, and the trick was to get in there *fast*.

Fascinated, almost hypnotized, Lou Goodman stared ahead between the two pilots as a Japanese warship swelled impossibly in size, its side ablaze with twinkling lights.

There was a tremendous explosion. A huge orange flash erupted into being just before Goodman's eyes, and the whole B–25 bomber shook violently from the blow. *My God, we've been hit . . . we haven't even reached them and we've been hit. Jesus; Whip, Alex —*

Goodman stared in wide-eyed disbelief. The flaming blast was still there, the terrible shaking and banging was continuing, and Whip flew as if nothing had happened. It was only when Goodman looked beyond that flashing, stabbing light that he understood.

The deafening explosion, the continuing terrible glare, the hammering and vibrating . . . *was all from the fourteen machine guns firing.* Their own weapons — so violent in their life that to someone who had not experienced the awesome fury at the moment of firing, it seemed they had been dealt a mortal blow.

His focus went beyond the dazzling orange. He braced himself against the pounding that swept through the bomber. The first burst of fire from twelve machine guns had ripped the entire side of the destroyer's deck. Two gun platforms disappeared in a blurred slow-motion explosion. Metal crumpled like paper, bodies were torn to chunks, guns went flying.

Whip walked rudder, skidding just a bit. The twelve machine guns screamed their fury across the deck from right to left. Men exposed, behind gun tubs, behind railings, behind thin armor plate, were chewed and mangled along with steel. The deck of the warship was a horrendous center of howling wasps with death in every sting.

To their right, Psycho in Two was doing the same. He wiped out the gun positions along the center to the stern. Whip was low, holding her steady, the bays were open, and he triggered two 500-pounders.

They swept low over the destroyer and Joe Leski's jubilant voice banged in their headsets. "One hit and a miss!" he shouted. "You got one into the engine room, boss! She's busting in half!"

By now they were tensed for the hail of fire from the other two destroyers as they rushed into close gun range. But there were only a few tracers.

The gun positions had been shattered. Blood and pieces of body and smoking metal littered the warship decks.

Three five-hundred-pound bombs smashed into the lower hull and superstructure of the second destroyer. The entire warship lifted from the sea, breaking in half a dozen places, and fell back a mass of steaming, burning chunks disappearing beneath scalding spray.

Ted Ashley and Jim Whitson in Five and Six didn't sink their target. They got one bomb into the stern that tore away the rudder and probably the screws as well. Flames erupted from below decks. The ship seemed to stagger as it drifted to a halt, burning, covered with broken and dying men.

"Watch those Zeros," someone called.

"Second group, they're coming at you from seven o'clock."

"We got 'em."

The second group of seven bombers led by Octavio Jordan was chewing up great pieces of barges and the soldiers jam-packed onto the decks. It was a brief but terrible slaughter when the Zero fighters came swarming in. But they didn't have any room to dive, they couldn't come up from below and they were forced to make curving pursuit runs or slide in from dead astern.

"Jordan, bring your people around in a sharp left turn," Whip called.

"Gotcha." With the answer they saw seven bombers clawing around in near-vertical banks. It held the Zeros off for just enough time. As the fighters came whipping around to follow the bombers they were in long turns to which they were committed.

It was a perfect setup. Six B–25s with forty-eight machine guns were cutting in, and the effect was devastating. Three Zeros exploded as they ran into the howling buzz saws hurled at them. The sudden effect threw off the others, let their targets break free. But only for a moment. Seven Zeros hammered in, snapping out bursts. A B–25 trailed smoke.

"Muhlfield here. I'm dumping." He salvoed his remaining bombs. "Gotta shut down number two." He feathered the right prop. He was now meat on the table for the fighters.

"Dusty, salvo your goodies and stay with Mule."

"Wilco from Eleven."

Dusty Rhodes would ride it out with the crippled bomber. The clouds were now a break for Mule. Before the Zeros could get it all over him he'd cleaned up his airplane and was easing into the clouds so low above the water. Moments later they were gone and the easy pickings for the fighters had vanished.

Eleven bombers remained, with frustrated Zero pilots doing their best to break off the strikes.

"Jordan, keep your group tight. Don't form up on us. I want everybody to go after those troopships, but keep it in two groups. Jordan, you lead. Keep weaving until you're ready to drop. Everybody make your run at the same time."

"Roger that." Jordan acknowledging.

"Group One, stay tight on me. Let's scissor them, troops."

Ahead of Whip's plane, five B–25s in a tight bunch made their run on the two troopships. The Zeros snarled after them, holding with the bombers as they kept up a sliding maneuver to the left. As the fighters pressed home their attacks Whip's force of six bombers was in a slide to the right. The scissors maneuver baffled them. Without warning streams of tracers were all around the Zeros. They broke off their runs, turned into their new assailants, stumbled into massive firepower. One Zero cartwheeled wildly through the air, breaking up as it struck the water.

More important, Jordan's force was laying it right into the large ships filled with soldiers. Lou Goodman, able to turn his attention to whatever caught his eye, watched in fascination as dark shapes dropped neatly away from the five bombers. The splashes were stupidly neat and clean in this churning mixmaster of death. Skips appeared again as the bombs bounced. There was a third skip, a multiple series of splashes, and then Goodman was counting in rapid-fire fashion the enormous explosions that smashed the thin-hulled troopships. Ten bombs had been dropped and six hit home, two in the leading ship and four in the second. Lou Goodman never *saw* the second ship again; it went up in huge chunks and came down in smaller ones. The lead vessel was a torrent of flames from bow to stern. Men were leaping into the water.

The B-25 shook from a new sound. Smoke filled the cockpit and explosions roared around Goodman's head. Whip jinked wildly to throw off the Zero that had hit them.

"Watch it, Lead. Another coming in from five o'clock."

"We see 'em." A burst of roaring vibration as Bruce Coombs opened up in his turret. More firing; Leski and Gall were firing from the waist positions.

"Two more from six o'clock, troops."

"We see 'em."

"Got the bastard!"

"Yeah, a flamer."

"Watch it, you guys. They're coming in from — " The voice broke off. They didn't know who it was.

Alex was having fits in their own cockpit, coughing, dragging back the side windows on his side, hitting switches. Electrical fire. He was shutting down systems. He coughed out his words. "We're . . . all right. Stay with it."

"Hang in there, people," Whip told his crew. "No marshmallows yet."

More firing. The horizon tilted wildly. "Everybody go after the barges," Whip ordered. A good move; nothing left to hit in larger ships. That destroyer was still afloat, but drifting away from the action, a crippled hulk.

They kept off the Zeros without further loss to either side as everyone rolled into their firing runs. *God help them,* and Lou Goodman was amazed with his own thoughts. Suddenly the Japanese on those barges weren't enemy soldiers. They were men, helpless, pinned to the water as the bombers swept in upon them.

The air churned into a pink froth above the barges. The terrible fifties had swept entire decks clean of human beings.

18

"BLACK Fox to Brigade One. Come in. Over."

Whip looked up, startled. That was the call sign of a P–39 outfit at Seven-Mile.

"Brigade One to Black Fox. Where the hell are you?"

"Black Fox is coming in from the south. We're on the deck. Six Cobras. Sorry we're late. What's your situation?"

"We got plenty of company. How far out are you?"

"We'll be there in less than a minute."

"We can use you. We're to the west of that group of burning ships. We — "

"Have you in sight."

"Can you see our little friends?"

"Roger that. Looks like they're getting close."

"Close enough, Black Fox. Can you get to them before we come around again to the barges?"

"Tight, but we can do it."

"Good show. We'll concentrate on the barges."

"Glad to help out."

Whip still didn't know who had laid on six Airacobras as assistance in the low-level strike, but God bless him. Sending in the P–39s on the deck, where the Japanese would have to stay low, was a godsend for the American fighters, because once you got over a thousand feet in the 39 the pilot went into automatic nosebleed and the airplane turned into a lead brick.

Whip looked back, saw the six long-nosed fighters pounding to get into position to hit the Zeros from the side and take them off the American bombers. Great; they could wrap up the slaughter now just the way he —

"Oh, *shit.*" Someone called from the back of the plane, then screamed into the radio.

"Black Fox, Black Fox, *break, break!*"

The Japanese, damn them, couldn't have timed it better. That top cover of Zero fighters. Everyone had forgotten about them and all this time they'd been working their way down through thick clouds. Now they *were* down, and as the P–39s curved in for their attack against the Zeros pursuing the bombers, the second force of twelve Zeros came whistling in low over the sea.

If the P–39 pilots had broken, sharp left or right, when the frantic warning went to them, they would have slipped through the vise. But their leader hesitated instead of reacting instantly, as he should have done, for it was the *only* thing to do. *"Break, break!"* Again that call, now near-hysterical, because the bomber crews could see it all coming, what was going to happen, and that stupid son of a bitch in the lead fighter —

They broke, a sharp rolling motion to the right, but it was too late. They rolled right just in time to expose their cockpits and the tops of their fighters to the Zeros, who had stayed in tight formation, and it was duck soup for the Japanese. Just like that, before they blinked several times, cannon fire tore four of the American fighters into wreckage or red-blossoming fireballs, and the remaining two were trying wildly to save themselves.

"Brigade Leader to Black Fox. Get the hell out of there. Climb out, climb out."

The P–39s were worse than useless. Whip was even debating about going to *their* help. But they were almost onto the barges, they still had half their ammunition left and there were still hundreds of enemy troops, ripe for the kill, and that was his mission, his job, why they were here, why men were dying and others about to be killed.

By now there were sixteen or maybe eighteen or even twenty Zeros coming after them. Whip could have broken off the mission at that very moment, and half his men expected him to do just that. They'd broken the back of the Japanese force, killed more than half or even two thirds of all the men and they were still in good shape.

But Whip wasn't having any of it. It was time to find out just how they could hold their own in the kind of situation in which B–25s had classically gotten the shit kicked out of them. The Zeros were hard after them in a loose swarm, some coming in directly from behind, others in pursuit curves, so that their tight formation had bellied out and lost the advantage of concentrated firepower.

"Everybody close in on me," Whip ordered.

No need to answer. Pilots nudged throttles, slid in closer, moved in tight, arranged themselves in a clustered formation.

"Stay tight. Get those barges."

Lieutenant J.G. Masahiko Obama observed the American bombers grouping together. He laughed to himself in his cockpit. Like so many frightened sheep, bunching up, as if dying together could take away the fear.

Obama was mightily pleased with the sight. The B–25s must fly straight ahead. If they turned they only exposed themselves more to the pursuing Zero fighters. And the last time he had found this plump morsel before him Obama had personally shot down one bomber and shared another kill with Ariya Inokuchi.

It was already a beautiful day. Although he had not

thought it would be. They had circled around and around stupidly above the clouds while the smaller force stayed low over the ships and barges. How the B–25s had managed to make their terrible blows against the ships without the Zero fighters interfering was something to which Obama would attend when he was back at Lae. They had received the frantic calls for help, and Obama took his Zeros down through very bad turbulence. The sight that greeted the Japanese pilot stunned him. Burning ships, barges wrecked in all directions, men floating on the sea. And almost at the same moment he caught sight of the six Airacobras. The cows with long noses. Obama expected a brief and furious fight with the American fighters. The bombers could have gotten away in the clouds, but then the Americans did a stupid thing.

They *stayed* in their formation run against the smaller force of Zeros. Stayed in it! Surely someone in those fighters or the bombers must have seen Obama's force and called for them to break. Obama could not believe their air discipline was so lax, but against all his fears, the Americans had kept their wide turn, and when finally they did break, they were helpless.

Obama watched the lead fighter growing in his sights. Strange; for an airplane so beautiful in its design the enemy machine was a poor weapon. Its rate of turn made it an easy victim. Obama closed in, disdaining use of the two light machine guns, using only the cannon. He held his fire until the last moment. A short burst on the gun tit and cannon shells exploded in the wing root of the leading Airacobra. Under the pressure of that turn and the erupting power of the 20mm cannon shells the wing snapped off as if it were cardboard. Obama denied himself the luxury of watching the American tumble into the sea. He eased in rudder and the cockpit of the second plane was before him, and he watched his cannon shells rip through the plexiglas before they exploded. The Airacobra went straight in.

Two more of the American fighters exploded under the guns and cannon of the Japanese Zeros. Then the surviving Airacobras were gone. "Stay with me," Obama signaled the other men. It was not really necessary. Two more fighters were small game. Up ahead were those bombers. They were the real targets.

It was too late to prevent the terrible massacre among the barges. Obama had a question cross his mind fleetingly: how were the Americans doing so much damage with only their guns? He would think of it later. Right now they were moving into position and the American gunners had opened fire at long range. Masahiko Obama did not lightly dismiss the defensive firepower of the B–25. A fifty-caliber machine gun is an effective weapon. They were fortunate in that the Americans were usually poor marksmen.

The Zero rocked in the turbulent air trailed by the enemy bombers. Obama noticed the Americans were holding excellent formation. So! These were better than average. Glowing coals raced by his cockpit. Obama ignored the tracers. You do not pursue and catch your enemy by dodging fireflies. He kept pressing in. A good enemy only made the victory that was to come all the sweeter.

Obama glanced left and right and pumped his fist up and down to signal his men to close in to the attack. Then he concentrated on the last bomber on the right side of the enemy formation. Just a few seconds more and he would open fire with his cannon. He already had nine American flags on the side of his cockpit. The two kills of the Airacobras would make it eleven, and here was his chance to add even more.

*

"All right, troops, they're getting close. Stay in tight. No stragglers." Whip was calling out the signals like a man on the gridiron. They'd chewed what was left of the barges to a blood-soaked shambles and continued on their way. The other ten pilots wondered why they were still staying on the deck with those Zeros snapping at their heels. All they had to do was ease apart and come back on the yokes and they'd be in clouds too thick for the Japanese to do anything about it but curse. Well, Whip had his own way, whatever it was.

"Coombs, how far back are they?" Whip called his turret gunner.

Bruce Coombs looked through plexiglas down the trailing tube of fuselage, between the two rudders, watching the Zeros coming in like lithe sharks. "They're almost in range, Major." Coombs hesitated. "If we're gonna play that game of yours we better do it now, sir."

Even as the turret gunner called in the position of the Zeros he saw the first bright flashes along the wings as they opened up with their cannon.

"They're in range *now*," Coombs added hastily.

"Everybody split, *now!*" Whip barked, hands and feet mauling the controls.

It could not have been better. Masahiko Obama thought of the next flag on the side of his fighter, squinted through his eyepiece and squeezed the trigger on his stick. He felt the thudding recoil of the cannon as they fired, and —

His face was a mask. The bomber suddenly wasn't there! Cannon shells split empty air. Like two swarms of fast whales, the bombers had broken from their tight cluster, splitting their tight formation to the left and the right. Obama rocked his wings, furious, giving the signal for the fighters also to split, to take each pack with an equal division of Japanese planes. He eased in rudder, moved the stick. All the Yankees had done was to delay the inevitable. Strange, however. They could escape easily enough in those clouds just above. They —

His Zero hurtled toward the B–25s, closing with enormous speed. He banged down on the trigger, firing all guns and cannon, but his aim was off, far off.

A stream of tracers splashed across his vision as turret and waist gunners in the enemy bombers opened up with a deadly crossfire.

In the B–25s the pilots and copilots were flying as if each man had an extra set of arms and hands. Struggling to keep in tight both formations the pilots and the men to their right were working in unison, hauling back on throttles, banging down on gear handles, dropping the first notch of flaps. The airplanes shuddered with the sudden deceleration, gear and flaps throwing out tremendous drag, as if the bombers had slammed into invisible quicksand.

"Here they come!"

"Man, they didn't expect that!"

"Get that guy to the right! That's it; hose 'em!"

Four Zeros, startled, whipped beneath the bombers, skimming wavetops. Several started up and broke off the maneuver because of the clouds. One fighter disappeared into the overcast, forced to climb to avoid a collision. But in that moment of utter confusion most of the veteran Japanese reacted with instinctive skill, breaking even more sharply to the sides, keeping up their speed so they could roll back swiftly. It was a dangerous maneuver that exposed the fighter undersides to the enemy gunners. Obama cursed; a Zero had become a ball of fire. Another was disintegrating in the air.

It took only moments to roll sharply one way and then roll

back the other, following the reasoning that a withering strike into the midst of the bombers was still the best move to make. Obama saw the bomber he'd been following shedding pieces of metal and one propeller starting to slow as cannon shells found the engine, but he couldn't slow his fighter in time. He had to break off the attack, skidding sharply to avoid a collision.

The other Zeros followed his lead, moving in a loose swarm *between* the split formations of enemy bombers, because there was nowhere else to go. The fighters plunged between the bombers, gunners tracking, lacing the sides of the Zeros with streams of fifty calibers. But it was no more than a fleeting shot, really. The Japanese fighters were moving too fast, and they raced ahead of the bombers.

Which was everything Whip had been hoping for . . .

19

"CLEAN 'EM UP!" Whip whooped into his mike, snapping out the words, and even as he shouted the command the pilots had been expecting, he and Bartimo were bringing up the gear, dragging in the flaps, going to full power on the big Cyclones. Emergency power, the copilots now on the quadrants, handling the levers, leaving the pilots free to fly, to concentrate on the airplanes and flying and what they might yet do with that awesome firepower pointing forward from each bomber. The gunners called out the Zeros splitting, some down, a few up, two breaking away completely, but the big bunch ramrodding it directly between the bomber formations.

"Okay, everybody bring it in close. *Move,* you people! Come on, *come on!*" Whip's shouted words were unnecessary. As quickly as he'd called to clean up the B–25s everyone knew what to do, had done it and even now were bunching together again. But Whip was alive with a glorious fury, savagely intense, every muscle and nerve straining, and the words were needed expressions for the energy burning from him. The formations closed, nine bombers in tight —

"Lead from Twelve." That was Ben Patillo, flying one of the two planes added to the mission. "I've got one burning, trying to feather. I'm falling back."

"Lead, Shannon here. I'm staying with him."

"Okay, okay. The rest of you tighten it up, goddamnit, *tighten it up.*"

Lou Goodman studied Whip Russel. He'd already dismissed the crippled bomber from his mind —

Masahiko Obama felt the centipede with cold legs crawling down his neck. He hadn't had that feeling many times, but now he knew he was racing ahead of the bombers, and he would be exposed to the nose gunners. He shook off the feeling. Foolish man! he cursed himself. Those are not fighters back there. Bombers, with only a single gun in the nose of each airplane. He shook off the feeling, ready to come around and —

"Now!" He shouted the command to himself, and in a move of beautiful precision he had the stick hard over to the left, tramping left rudder, hammering the throttle full forward. No airplane in the world turned like the Zero; the machine came around in a beautiful tight curve. Fighting the strain of centrifugal force Obama looked up through his cockpit glass, keeping the enemy formation in sight, and —

His blood ran cold. He looked into the most terrible sight he had ever seen in his life. An immense black bullet surrounded with rippling, blazing fire, pointing straight at him, coming at him, and the Zero shuddered from nose to tail, staggered in its flight as a fury of enemy bullets slammed into the machine. The canopy cracked wide, air howled. Obama felt one slug in his leg, a knife of unbelievable pain. Another blazed into a shoulder, the instrument panel coming apart before him.

He had no time to think, there was no thinking. Gasping with the agony slicing through him he rolled level, horsed the stick back as hard as he could pull. The Zero leaped upward, a stupendous bursting climb. More blows; holes in the wings, metal flying away, and then he was into a world of gray, in the clouds, struggling to remain conscious, to

keep that back pressure, keep the airplane flying, keep going
through the loop he had started . . .

*That's right, you bastard . . . keep coming around, keep
coming . . .*

Whip was raw nerve, hunched forward, thumb caressing
the gun tit, waiting, waiting. The right moment, he wanted
that as he watched the Zero with two orange slashes
diagonally across the fuselage, one of their leaders, coming
around in that tight turn and —

Twelve machine guns roared. The stream of lead from the
B–25 caught the first Zero. Whip saw metal flying, the
cockpit tearing open and — *he was gone.* Whip gasped with
disbelief. He'd had him cold-cocked, right on the griddle,
and the son of a bitch had jerked his fighter out of the
way.

*Not you, you son of a bitch. Oh, no, not you. You're
mine . . .*

Obama's wingman, Petty Officer Kumao Tokunaga, had
stayed with his leader. He'd rolled level, started back on the
stick with Obama. But he was just behind the lead fighter,
and for Tokunaga there was no escape.

Whip gripped the yoke until his knuckles were white. The
second Zero was pinned to the wall. In an unbelievable
moment the fighter took the full brunt of his massed guns.
It took only a moment as the engine was smashed from its
mounts, the cockpit churned into bubbling flesh, the tanks
blown wide open and exploding and the Zero was no longer
there, only a mass of burning sputum coughed from the sky.

It was the opening play in instant disaster for the stunned
Japanese. One moment they had been the pursuers, the
wolves snapping at their fleeing prey, and in the next instant
the prey had become dragons spitting terrible fire. Psycho's
bomber rolled sharply, in a wild and punishing maneuver

that put him directly on the tail of a Zero just starting its turn, and the Mitsubishi before him literally shredded as he held down the gun tit for a long, overwhelming burst. He watched pieces of airplane flying into the air, flashing past his own cockpit. A distant banging sound told him they'd hit some of those pieces, and then the wings, both of them, snapped away from the Zero and the wreckage whipped violently into the sea.

In just those few awful seconds, five Zero fighters were burning or torn apart by the incredible firepower of the bombers. The others were fleeing wildly to escape, breaking away in shallow dives in the narrow airspace still left to them.

It was over. They might blow the bastards out of the air, but they couldn't pursue them. Whip grinned at Alex Bartimo and the grin was infectious. God*damn*, they'd done it.

Whip glanced off to one side and the grin froze on his face. Out of the cloud cover, trailing a long scarlet tongue of flame, came a single Zero, more flying wreckage than airplane. The fighter was on its back, coming out of a loop, and Whip glimpsed two diagonal orange slashes, the same fighter he had chewed up when he opened his attack that had escaped with the unbelievable roll and breakout in a loop into the clouds. Now he was coming back, it was impossible, what the hell kind of impossible pilot was in that airplane?

And then Whip Russel knew the terrible, awful thing that was about to happen and there was nothing he could do. He started to shout his warning, but even as the words formed in his throat, staring through his left window, he knew it was too late, and he didn't know if he was going to cry or scream because —

*

He was beyond pain now. His leg was useless, numb, his shoulder still sending traces of its agony through him. He gritted his teeth to stay conscious, just a bit longer, and in the misty gray of the clouds all about him he saw the sudden reflection of fire from the engine, felt the heat wash into the cockpit through the shattered glass, and he knew the end was here with him.

But if death is here, one does not fight it. It is to be embraced, so its final sweet moment may be lived to the full.

Masahiko Obama thought of his home in Osaka, the temple on the hill that always caught the morning sun. Clouds vanished before him as the Zero whipped beautifully through the final part of its arc and he sliced away from the clouds, and there was the American bomber before him, leaping upward, growing in size. Blood spurted from between his lips and Obama smiled.

Banzai.

Live ten thousand years.

Masahiko Obama held the stick steady and true in his dying hands. He went to join his ancestors with peace in his heart and a smile on his bloodied lips.

"My God! *It's Psycho!*"

The Zero came straight down. It tore into the second bomber in the formation like a silvered, burning dagger. The engine went into the wing root between the fuselage and the right engine, and the fuel tanks exploded, and in that last awesome moment the B–25 and its five men vanished in the angry fireball that filled the world.

The shock wave cracked outward and the pilots fought to keep from one another, to avoid the collision that the roiling air threatened. Then small burning pieces fell away into the ocean and it was gone.

Alex Bartimo glanced at Whip. He was frozen, still

looking behind him. Alex saw their slow drift to the left. He
brought in rudder, held them straight.

"Lead, Shannon here."

They waited for Whip Russel to answer. But he was just
turning his head forward. He didn't seem to have heard.
Alex thumbed the transmit button.

"Lead here. Go ahead."

"Patillo can't make it back if he has to climb. He's on one
fan and the other may go any moment. His panel is shot out
and he hasn't any gauges. We're going to have to make an
end run around the island along the coast and hope we can
make it into Seven-Mile."

Still no answer from Whip.

Alex took it. "Everybody from Lead. Throttle back so
Patillo can come up to us. We'll go back together."

20

IT WAS a long and wearying flight down the northern coastline of New Guinea. After the intense fighting against the warships and barges, and then the hammering exchange with the Zero fighters, the men were exhausted. The loss of Psycho and his whole crew had been another drain of emotional and physical energy. Two bombers had flown from the combat area earlier, Dusty Rhodes escorting Muhlfield home on his one good engine. Psycho was gone and that left ten bombers out of the thirteen that had started, now making the circuitous trip back.

The two surviving Airacobra pilots had elected to stay with the bombers as long as their fuel would permit. Also, neither fighter pilot relished climbing out on the gauges, and to make it back to Seven-Mile overland meant flight through towering clouds.

What kept everyone on the edge, as well, was that remaining engine in Ben Patillo's airplane. He'd extinguished the fire in one, but the second power plant was acting up. The cylinder head temperature gauge was closing in on the red zone and no one knew if the thing would hold together.

To compound matters they couldn't fly directly along the coastline, but had to veer out to sea. They could barely make out Cape Ward Hunt far to their right, and they had quiet prayers for the rain showers between their slow-moving formation and the land, for southeast of Cape Ward

Hunt, along that coast, lay the Japanese airfield at Buna, and another slightly inland at Dobodura. Finally the extension of land containing Oro Bay came into sight and they found their first break in the clouds. Broken clouds, about seven-tenths. With the engine of Patillo's airplane still marginal, Whip, who had finally emerged from his stupor, elected to take a run due south, climbing steadily, where the Owen Stanley Range offered a shallow cut in the high mountains.

"Buck, you think it will help to dump some weight?" Whip called to Number Twelve.

"Ah, roger, Lead. We've been doing just that. Throwing everything over the side. It might help."

"Good deal, Buck. Let us know if anything changes."

A short burst of laughter. "You bet your sweet ass we will. Twelve out."

The Japanese had done more damage than they'd realized. In Number Five both Ted Ashley and Barney Page, the pilots, had been wounded, and their navigator, for Christ's sake, was doing the flying. Then, again, that wasn't so bad. Pop Yaffe was an old-time flier who could no longer pass the medical exams to qualify as a pilot, but he had more time than anyone else in the squadron with the possible exception of Muhlfield.

Jim Whitson in Number Six had a gunner more dead than alive, and there was no question but that both airplanes would have to go into Seven-Mile to get medical attention for their wounded. As for Buck Patillo there wasn't any doubt where he'd be landing with only one engine, and that was at Seven-Mile, with its longer runway and lower altitude.

They took moderate chop going through the clouds as they climbed, but even the crippled airplane under Patillo's control had it made. Somehow his engine was holding, giving him the power he needed to climb high enough to cross the ridge. Once he'd flown through that saddleback it was downhill the rest of the way.

The clouds thinned out beyond the southern flanks of the Owen Stanleys. It was a matter of clasping all the luck the men could gather to themselves and just hope they didn't run into any Zeros as they straggled for home.

Then they had Seven-Mile in sight, and everybody eased aside to give Buck Patillo all the room he needed. "I don't know if she'll hold together long enough to make it in," he radioed to Whip. "She's cutting in and out. I've got the field in sight and we're hanging in there."

Lou Goodman tapped Whip on the shoulder. "Can he bail out his crew?" Whip passed on the question to Patillo.

"Negative. My turret gunner's got a busted leg. He took a slug back there." Patillo paused. "The other troops have decided to stick with it. If one guy can't go, they say no one goes."

Goodman had listened to the exchange. "Damnit, *order* the other men to bail!"

Whip turned slightly in his seat. "They won't go, Lou."

Goodman's face was stricken. "I know, I know," he said quietly, as much to himself as to the other man. He loosened his belt, then threw it off entirely, half standing between Whip and Alex to get a clear view of what was happening.

He saw the first two bombers well ahead of them. Buck Patillo was playing it by the numbers, exercising every option available to him. A high, steep approach. All the extra air speed he could get to go along with the one faltering engine. Gear down as late as possible, keeping up the flaps until the last moment.

Pop Yaffe in Number Six was holding well behind Patillo. The old man with two wounded pilots on his hands was flying as well as anyone else in the outfit, and he too was playing it by the numbers, watching Buck Patillo ahead of him, giving him plenty of room, but in position to land at once to get medical attention for his wounded.

On the long final with one engine, in a crippled airplane, Buck Patillo lost his remaining engine. Lost it. Just like that. No one knew how or why or what were the reasons, for there might have been ten out of a hundred *why* it went. Something died inside that engine, or tore loose, or exploded, or flamed. No one knew and no one would ever know all the other things that might have happened because it happened too fast, when Buck was too low.

Pop Yaffe thought he saw a puff of smoke from the running engine, but he wasn't sure about that. It could have been something breaking away from the airplane, a piece of wreckage hanging on until that moment and letting go. Whatever. It didn't matter.

The bomber fell off on one wing, a great metal bird mortally wounded, bereft of its ability to remain in the sky. It whirled about crazily, only once, and then it smashed into the ground and exploded.

That was all. Just that sharp drop of the wing, the wild whirling tumble, and the huge ball of flame and wreckage geysering outward in all directions. There was nowhere else for Pop Yaffe to go, so he kept boring in, and the shock wave of the blast rocked the B–25 as it passed overhead and everyone inside had that gruesome moment of smelling the upwelling smoke and fumes from the airplane that was even at that instant incinerating their close friends.

Pop Yaffe brought in the B–25, fighting back tears, his leathery old face working fiercely as it sought to contain his emotions. He swallowed hard and rode the bomber down to earth, the wheels rocking gently on the soft runway. By the time he shut down the engines the meat wagon was waiting to remove Ashley and Page. By the looks of the two pilots there hadn't been a moment to lose.

Or to win. First Lieutenant Ted Ashley died twenty minutes later.

Pop Yaffe went off somewhere to cry it out.

"Don't tell *me* how to fight my goddamned war! We did everything we were supposed to do out there today, damn you . . . We were told we'd find barges and we found three destroyers and two troopships and . . . and, you fat son of a bitch, we sank those troopships and we sank two of their goddamned destroyers and left the other son of a bitch a hulk and —"

Whip Russel sucked in air, his eyes blazing, the muscles in his cheeks twitching. He was possessed of maniacal anger, throwing his arms about, gesturing constantly, his body trembling with the rage that seemed to fill him as quickly as it burst free. He glared at Colonel Lou Goodman who stood by the mouth of the cave they used for operational headquarters on Kanaga Field. The men were off to mess or sleeping or just sitting and staring vacantly into space. Except these two, and they were hammer and tongs at one another.

"You know, I just don't believe you. I mean, what the hell has got into you? Lou Goodman, the man with the smarts, the genius in creating new airplanes out of wreckage. The man who *understands*, for good Jesus' sake!" Whip stopped in midstride, almost stumbling, his own inertia threatening to carry his body forward despite his stopping. The blazing glare was still there in his eyes. He was furious and puzzled and angry and upset, and everything that had happened today was bad enough, I mean, Jesus, what happened with Psycho, and *then* with Buck Patillo and his whole crew, and, and now *this* . . .

"You sound just like you've come from MacArthur's headquarters," Whip said, trying to scowl and sneer at the

same time. It came out in an angry, defiant mask that
seemed a stranger to Lou Goodman. "I mean, for Christ's
sake, you *flew* the mission out there today! You *know* what
we did."

He pointed to the paper Lou held by his side. "That's your
message from FEAF, isn't it? Shit, yes, don't show it to me, I
know what the hell it says. Twenty-two out of thirty barges,
right?"

Goodman nodded.

"And it has a couple of things to say about those enemy
troops out there, doesn't it?" He sucked in air. "Well,
doesn't it, *goddamnit!*"

Goodman gestured idly with the paper. "You know it
does, Whip, but —"

"Don't *but* me! Think of what that paper says that your
message boy copied down. *Think* about it! Intelligence
estimates, what, Lou? The Japs had four to five thousand
troops on the water today, right? And we sank their
troopships and we sank twenty-two barges and we killed
somewhere between two and four thousand people and sank
four ships and . . . and" — he forced himself to slow
down — "and how many fighters? How many Zeros, Lou?
Fourteen? Or maybe it was fifteen or even more because we
shot the shit out of a couple of them that might never make
it home again, right?"

Again that lunging motion, that sudden sweep, the unexpected turnaround, like a ball bouncing off an invisible wall
in the middle of the cave. Energy rampant, turning the very
air blue and crackling all about him. Then, with shocking
effect, the shouting evaporated, the voice under control, but
much more intense than before. If a snake could talk it
would have this coiled intensity, the words stabbing air like
a flicking, forked tongue.

"Think about more than the numbers on that paper, Lou.

Do you know, do you have *any* idea, what a couple thousand troops means when you're trying to kill them *on the ground?* What the hell is it with you? *Really,* I mean." The ferocity began building up again in his eyes. "Aren't you even going to answer me, for shit's sake!"

"Yes," Goodman said, nodding. "I'm going to answer you, and I have a few things of my own to say. Your job is to go after the major targets. Ships, large groups of men, ground installations, airfields; whatever. It is not to make a grandstand play and fight Zeros. Because sooner or later the Japs will tumble to you, they'll know we're a high-button outfit. For quite some time we're liable to be one of a kind. We're now the deadliest force this part of the world has ever seen. And we can hurt the Japanese and hurt him bad, so long as you're stopped short of going crazy and fighting him on his own terms, just the way he'd like you to fight him. Every time you take on his bully boys in those Zeros, Whip, you're playing into his hands. If you shoot down thirty Zeros for every bomber you lose, and you lose six airplanes, you've given the enemy a tremendous victory, because losing those six B–25s might just let most of a convoy get through to where it was going in the first place. And those kinds of odds, Major, they *stink.*"

Whip pursed his lips and stared up at the colonel. "You, ah, think it would have been better if we'd run today? From the Zeros, I mean?"

"Better, *and* a hell of a lot smarter. All you had to do was pull up into the clouds. The Zeros could never have touched us. And we wouldn't have lost two planes and their crews."

"Don't you think I feel inside me what happened today to Psycho, to — "

"*That isn't the goddamned issue and I'll thank you to stay the hell off it, Major.*"

Whip threw up both hands and shrugged. "Okay, okay.

Let's cut the deck, then. I take it you don't want me or this outfit taking on the fighters?"

"That's the size of it. You cut your way through them if you have to, but you don't play tin soldier games when you *don't* have to."

"I don't buy it, Lou."

A silence hung heavily between them. "I could make it a direct order, Whip."

"Uh huh. You could. But I don't think you will."

"You never know."

"You *do* know where you can stick that kind of order, don't you?"

Lou Goodman's face was rock solid. Nothing showed, no sign, no clue. His eyes were dark glass. Finally he shook off the cold anger that had gripped him. "There's always something else."

Whip's voice was flat, toneless. "Would you really do that, Lou? Go to General Smyth or maybe even Whitehead, or beyond him, say, all the way to MacArthur? You could do that, I know. Go to the top man and make him choose between me and thee?"

"Shit, no, Major. I don't play the game that way and you know it."

Whip faced him. "Then how would you play it, Colonel?"

"I could always remind you of the man with whom I shook hands, the man who gave me his word."

Goodman threw the message to the cave floor and walked out.

21

THEY FLEW three missions with no more than eight bombers going out each time. The B–25s needed rebuilding to some extent, repairs almost everywhere. Waiting for the desired strike force of at least eleven bombers, which met the carefully prepared combat maneuvers of Major Whip Russel, would have meant no missions at all.

Each combat strike drew Whip further from the intensity that had lashed the 335th into shape as the best bomber force of its size or kind in the southwest Pacific. There had been the overwhelmingly successful victory against the enemy attempt to land heavy troop reinforcements in New Guinea. Then, his falling out with Lou Goodman, the delayed but inevitable crunch of *knowing* that Psycho was gone forever and finally the delays in getting his treasured strike force back into the air as a single team; all these brought on a slow metamorphosis from vibrant combat leader to a man who brooded more than his pilots could remember. He had lost none of that vital driving force, none of his fierce living of life. Lou Goodman had typed him weeks before: *wolverine.* But open ferocity was giving way to smoldering anger.

Only Lou Goodman saw the fretful chaining of psychic energy within the man about whom all their lives turned. Fortunately, they had not had to cross swords again on the matter of tactics of the Death's Head Brigade. It took two days for the outfit to lick its wounds, and the same weather front that gave such low ceilings over their last combat area now offered its reprieve in heavy rain over their home base. It gave Goodman the opportunity to prove that his runway draining at Kanaga Field worked, and they knew that they would no longer be operating from a quagmire. Whip managed a Silver Star for Psycho, but even he fretted over what he called a tinsel epitaph for so dear a friend.

When they finally returned to action, they teamed up with several A–20 light bombers out of the Moresby area and went out against enemy airfields at Madang. The mission proved a contest between enemy antiaircraft positions on the ground and the low-flying bombers. One A–20 took a direct hit and exploded off to their left. Their own force of eight bombers, dropping on high-speed level passes, took light damage with only one man wounded.

"It stinks," Whip told Goodman later that day. "I think we blew up two shithouses and killed a cow, or whatever it was that had four legs and horns."

Goodman nodded agreement. It was hardly the kind of mission for the special talents of the 335th. "They're laying low," Goodman offered by way of explanation. "Probably still trying to figure out what hit them the time before."

Whip shrugged. All he wanted was the call to get into the thick of it. Another mission, this time with nine B–25s to Wewak, offered slight recompense for the effort. They struck the enemy airfield hard, but the flak was heavy and gave them fits because it was so well concealed. Whip came back to Kanaga with over two hundred holes in his airplane, but his last moments at Wewak had proven eminently satisfying. Four Japanese bombers on the ground burned after a wild, jinking, scraping-the-trees strafing run.

Then they got the word. Stand down for two days, get all your planes ready.

Whip leaned over Goodman's "desk" in the cave. "What's the word?"

Goodman looked up. "This would scare the pants off anyone but you."

"That good or bad?"

"Depends on your point of view. FEAF is laying on a strike into Simpson Harbor at Rabaul." He took a deep breath. "A dusk strike, right at sunset."

Whip didn't say anything for a while. Then a smile tugged at the corners of his mouth and grew into the grin Goodman hadn't seen for a while. "Lou, I'll tell you something. Ain't nobody else I would say this to." He chuckled. "I don't know whether to be glad — or just plain scared."

Goodman kept a straight face. "I think maybe I ought to go along. I might even fly copilot for one of the troops."

Whip sobered. "Don't be so quick. This one's going to be a bitch. We're talking about *Rabaul*, remember?"

"Yeah, I remember. I'd still like you to think about it."

Whip studied him. "Fat man, why the hell do you want to go?"

"Someone's gotta look after you, kid. The navy is setting up a big scrap with the Japanese. They're probing, trying to find out everything they can before they get into it. They do know the Japanese outnumber us, and badly, in some respects. They want very much to cut down those odds. So we're supposed to go after warships."

They went into the target area with the engines screaming out all their power. Speed was everything and they stayed as low as the airplanes could fly, leaving long disturbed trails in the water behind them. They had made the flight far out to sea, using dead reckoning to navigate, and swung wide to come into their target. They would race over a thin neck of land that would hardly slow them down.

In the lead airplane Whip held her steady, engines to maximum power, watching the world racing at him, their closeness to the water turning it into a sea of burnished gold. To one side their long shadow leaped wildly across the waves, a grotesque ghost flashing along with them. Their timing was perfect, with the large orange disc of the sun about to touch the distant horizon. Then they were upon the northwest beach and they hurtled over the few dwellings, catching the antiaircraft positions completely by surprise. Whip caressed the firing button, held off. No use wasting ammunition here, now. In a few seconds he'd need every bullet he had.

They raced by trees and Whip held the slight altitude he'd gained to cross the neck of land. Before them Simpson Harbor spread far and wide, huddled beneath volcanic peaks on several sides. There were ships everywhere.

"Jesus, I didn't know there were that many ships in the whole world," Alex said.

"Do you see those cruisers?"

"Righto. Other end of the place; damn. Everybody gets a crack at us, it seems."

Whip grinned. "Gotta be fair, Lieutenant."

Alex gestured. "Bomb bays coming open." The airplane trembled as the doors gaped.

Fire rippled along the side of the warship. *That* crew wasn't asleep at the switch. The first of the tracers lifted at them, drifted and raced by. But they wouldn't have to worry about geysers. Too many ships in their way for the Japanese to depress their guns that low. They'd be shooting each other to pieces.

But this destroyer was right in line with their approach and he could be trouble for the planes following. All he had to do was keep firing and he was bound to snare one of them.

"This is Lead. Numbers Two and Three, take a crack at that tin can as you go over."

Whip brought in rudder, aimed at dead center of the destroyer from maximum range and opened up for a long burst. As the guns crashed before them and the terrible orange light flared, he walked the rudders from side to side. The murderous scythe of his twelve heavy machine guns raked the enemy warship in a tornado of gunfire. Half the flak positions went silent. Whip banked to clear the destroyer masts.

He heard Bruce McCamish on the radio; Mac had taken the Number Two slot from Psycho. "Kessler, I'll hit 'em left, you take them right."

"Okay, Mac."

The destroyer died. By the time the fourth bomber raced into direct line of its antiaircraft not a gun remained firing. Dead and broken bodies were strewn across the decks. The B–25s swept on.

The world turned slow motion, an erratic film, unreal, impossible, insane. Bombers tore through the harbor, working toward the three heavy warships that were their targets. By now all Simpson Harbor was ablaze with light and glowing coals. Hundreds of guns were firing, guns of all sizes and calibers, clawing into the air at the American raiders that had struck with such audacity. The bottom of the sun had slipped beneath the horizon and in the remaining half-light the flickering bursts of orange and red and yellow made the harbor a garish scene of strobe lights. As guns flashed and shells erupted about them, shadows became reality and real objects mere retinal images. A flashing, flickering world that threatened vertigo. There was not a single instant in which to do other than concentrate; stay high enough to clear those masts, watch out for that ship, FIRE! HIT THAT FLAK POSITION . . . warn the planes following. It was threading, working yoke and rudder, punching through the shock waves of exploding shells,

ignoring the thudding impacts into the airplane of enemy
bullets and shells striking home. And through it all, somewhere in the back of a man's mind, was that still greater
insanity, that if your plane was struck, if fuel turned into
flame, if metal broke and aerodynamic lines yielded to
greater forces, then it was better to die than to be a survivor.

"*There!* See it? Three cruisers. That big mother to the
left . . . that's our baby . . ."

Whip chanted his call of the target approaching, hidden
behind a line of waspish flame of antiaircraft guns. He
squeezed the tit with his thumb and his fifties roared and
bucked and exploded, and even as he poured in toward the
enemy warship he was walking rudder, and now he banked
sharply, kicked the rudder pedal, skidding, slewing wildly,
giving them no target to hang onto.

"Kessler! I'm going to drop straight into the bastard!" he
shouted into his microphone.

"Roger." That was all from Arnie in the second bomber.
They knew what to expect from one another. Whip hurled
the bomber about like a wild man and then he was only a
moment from position, he was ready to do what a man could
do only from feel and experience, and a terrible glare filled
his eyes as a shell exploded directly before them. Something
struck the windscreen with a terrible bang, but he ignored it,
he *had* to ignore it, and he was ready. He yelled *"Drop!"* to
Alex and his copilot cut away that fat 2000-pounder in their
belly and the B–25 jumped from the release of the weight.
No skipping of bombs this time — Whip had aimed so that
his missile would arc through the air along its ballistic
trajectory and if he had aimed right the goddamned thing
should hit that mothering cruiser at just about the waterline.
To his right Arnie Kessler, with the colonel aboard as
observer, the poor son of a bitch, was skipping his bomb
into the warship. Whip raced beyond the high mast and

hammered on the throttles, full emergency power, everything she could give, the engines howling at the world, they
could take only so much of this but to hell with that, it had
to be all the way and they cleared the cruiser and back in the
turret Coombs like to have torn their ears off with his
screech.

"*Bullseye!* We got the son of a bitch! Right in the
goddamned belly, we got the son of a b — " His voice died
away in a gurgle and they didn't know if he was busy or
something had happened to him, because there was no time
to ask. They swerved sharply and it was a game again;
jinking, bobbing, weaving, a wild run through the enemy
defenses of fire and steel, but they were punching through
and there were those volcanic peaks, they had their position
down clearly, and tomorrow, *all* of tomorrow and all the
days beyond that, lay in getting the hell out of this place.
Whip fired at anything and everything that lay before them.
His airplane was a dervish, a maddened thing flinging itself
through the sky, but he picked his targets, little toy dolls of
men and their guns, and he hammered out burst after burst,
because these same sons of bitches below could wipe out the
bombers that were coming behind.

One B–25 was hammered by a shell blast and missed its
target. The bomb was aboard and there was no way, no
hope, of ever going *back* into that charnel house of flak, and
the pilot saw a big ship before him, transport or merchantman, he didn't know and didn't care, he lined up and heaved
that fat bomb out of his innards, and the plane following
saw the whole incredible sight of the heavy bomb smashing
through the sides of the ship as if it were paper, going clean
through and coming out the other side, ripping through the
air straight into the side of a destroyer and blowing that son
of a bitch clean above the surface, and that's all they saw,
except the turret gunner, who was cursing and laughing at

the same time, reported a sheet of flame from where the destroyer had been hit and they figured they had that sucker wiped out.

And then they heard the heartrending sound that froze every man in the bombers . . .

"This is Jordan. We've been hit." He was calling in the blind, not to one man but to all, and they knew what that meant.

"Jordan!" Whip was shouting into his mike. "How bad . . . can you make it out?"

"No way, my friend." How could a man's voice go soft and gentle in the midst of all this hell? But . . . they say when a man knows it's all over, that his last seconds are trickling away like the final grains of sand in the emptying hourglass, there's no need for fear, no need to panic. That's all behind you.

That's what they say.

Whatever; Jordan's last seconds were trickling, fast. For Octavio Jordan and his copilot, Duane Collins, and his navigator, Ray Blair, and their radioman/gunner, Tim Bailey, and their flight engineer, Bud Marion, for all five men. The other crews saw the flames tearing at the bomber, gouging through metal, shrieking free of fuel tanks and ruptured lines as it thundered over the harbor, a dazzling beacon, a fireball reflecting a garish glow over the water, and they all wondered the same thing, how in the name of God was Octavio staying at the controls, still flying, working at it, controlling and directing his blazing meteor of an airplane, because they all knew the heat was *inside*, the cockpit was an inferno.

They were burning alive inside that son of a bitch, and every man prayed and hoped and shouted for Jordan to put her in, to smash her into the water and end it all.

But he didn't. He stayed with it, whatever of his flesh was

bubbling, and with agony tearing at him, and his skin flaying
off him and his lungs seared and choking. He stayed with
his dying airplane. Long enough to reach Lakunai Airdrome
where, to everyone's astonishment, they saw Zeros racing
along the runway, taking off to intercept them even as they
raced from the harbor, and with just enough light left to
work over the bombers no longer in formation.

Hell would have raked their ranks, except for Octavio
Jordan, who for all they knew was by now shrieking in
mortal agony, because there was more fire than metal, but
the huge spearhead of flame came across the runway right
on the deck, straight into the path of the enemy fighters just
breaking ground.

The dying man, the dying men, took out four Zeros just
getting airborne, and the now exploding bomber with what
everyone hoped were dead men smashed into parked
fighters at the far end of the field. Maybe a dozen more
Zeros went up and their pilots died in their cockpits as
twelve tons of blazing, exploding bomber erupted in their
midst.

One Zero made it off the ground, sallied forth into the air,
made a desultory pass at a B–25 and flew away.

They really didn't pay the fighter that much attention. In
the closing darkness, as they sped away for their own
survival, they kept thinking the same thing. A man knows
he's going to die.

What makes him live long enough to burn to death?

Someone said love of the men he knew, with whom he
flew, with whom he shared life and death every day.

Could a man love so strongly?

That was tougher to face than the enemy.

22

"IT'S NOT *my* idea. Read the orders yourself. FEAF is calling the shots. They want the fighter bases torn up, as many Zeros as we can get wiped out on the ground. Don't look to *me*, Lou. Go talk to headquarters." Before Lou Goodman could respond Whip was at it again. "Know why they're in such a sweat? Because the Japanese shot down seven out of twelve B–17s on one mission. The Fortress herself, the big invincible iron bird that's been giving the Japs so much shit all these months." Whip grinned wolfishly, enjoying the moment, watching Lou Goodman eating the words he had thrown in such heat and with such finesse not too long ago at him. Because headquarters wanted those fighter fields chewed up, and they had a new weapon with which to do the job.

Parafrags.

Oh, they were nasty little critters, all right. You take one twenty-three-pound bomb, stick an instantaneous fuze on the nasty end and hang the critter from a small chute. Pack the chute and the fragmentation bomb into a neat package, hang the packages from honeycomb racks inside a bomb bay, and one B–25 can dump more than a hundred of the things in a sweeping pass down an enemy runway.

The Japanese had never seen them before. There was something very special about a new weapon; its effect could be overwhelming, because if you didn't know what was coming you had no protection against it.

"I want the mission to Lae," Whip announced suddenly.

"Your job is to — "

"*I want that mission.*"

"Your job is to follow orders."

"Then *order* me to go."

"You — "

"You've got to send *somebody*, Colonel. You can't duck it. Somebody has to go out there and ring their goddamned bell."

Goodman turned slowly. "Yes, they do. But I don't want my men emotionally involved. And you're emotionally — "

"It's *my* pick, Lou."

"What makes that so?"

Whip threw out his arm. "This whole goddamned show has been mine from the beginning, remember? Special orders. Go out and kill Japs. Tear 'em limb from limb. The idea of a war is to *kill.* Well, I'm the best killer you got, Colonel Goodman, and if you send in any other outfit except the best, then *you* become the killer. One way or the other I get that mission. With you or without you, and if I have to I'll eat you alive and go straight to Smyth or Whitehead or — "

"You've got it."

"Smart."

"Yes, but not the way you think."

"Oh?"

"If you weren't the best outfit, Major, and if you didn't have the best chance of pulling it off and getting your people home, I might have been a bit more than you could eat alive or any other way."

Whip whooped with laughter and slapped Goodman on the shoulder. "You're a tough old bastard, you know that, Lou?"

"You little son of a bitch, get out of here."

"Not yet. When are you making contact with the Australian commandos?"

Goodman showed his surprise. "I don't understand."

"You will. *After* I have a little chat with them, that is."

Goodman glanced at his watch. "About two hours from now. Regular schedule. They could be late, of course."

"Of course. They could be dead. Tomorrow we could all be dead, right? I'll be there in an hour forty-five, Lou. Right in the radio shack."

Whip might have been fanatical, even crazy. But he wasn't stupid. He knew his airplanes had chewed up fighters, where other bombers had gone down like flies, but he was also aware that they'd had surprise by the ton that innovation and surprise and enormous firepower had been on their side. All the factors necessary to get the cutting edge and keep it. But by now the Japs had tumbled to their act. They could still take on the average Japanese fighter and give him a hell of a run for his money, but in the long-distance running, especially if the fighter jocks were sharp, you had to put your money on the Zero fighters. Because sooner or later they'd win. They were made to fight in the air and the B–25 wasn't and when it was all said and done, the odds lay heavily in their favor.

So the kicker was simple. Don't fight the sons of heaven on *their* terms. Hit 'em when they don't expect it and hit 'em in a way they wouldn't dream. That way they might not have their chance to shoot you out of the sky, before the Zeros clawed their way to altitude and built up speed. The B–25 flew on the deck and the kicker was to keep the Zeros *below* them.

Two days, the Australians had said. It would take two days to get into position, to set it up. But it would have to be timed perfectly, the coordination had to be exact. Whip would leave nothing to chance. He had to know down to a block of thirty seconds, no longer, the exact time needed to make his climb-out, the cross-country to get into position, the run onto the target.

And to brief his own men. They were going to have to fly and fight in a way none of them had ever done before.

But it would by God be worth it.

23

Two WINGED SPECKS in the sky approached from the east. The antiaircraft gunners at Lae airdrome relaxed when they recognized the airplanes as Zeros. Now they watched with professional interest. They had seen thousands of landings and they had become experts. They nodded to one another. They approved. These were some of the better pilots. You could tell the way the fighters rushed overhead, from the muted sound of the Sakae engines, the manner in which the men in each machine eased around to land. Ah! The gear, the flaps, the machines held so perfectly, fragile butterflys floating down from their cushions of air.

Commander Gaishi Naogaka felt his wheels touch gently. He had no need to look to his right and slightly behind, for even on the narrow runway of Lae he knew Tanin Yamaya would be in perfect position. Naogaka was the Wing Leader of Lae, and also the leader of the 1st Squadron. He had selected Yamaya to take his place when he, Naogaka, had to remain on the ground, as he did much too often.

Tanin Yamaya had been with him in China, and in the Philippines and in the Dutch East Indies when the fighting centered about Java. Yamaya had been his wingman then and he had scored twenty-three kills since early 1940. A good man. Skilled, utterly loyal, fearless.

And like most of the other pilots in the Lae Wing he was confused, beset with doubts. Things were not going well. That was the purpose of Commander Gaishi Naogaka's flight to area headquarters at Rabaul. To decide upon a course of action to counter the strange turn of events with the Americans.

Naogaka parked his fighter at the far end of the field and climbed down from the wing. He talked briefly with Yamaya. "You will say nothing to the other men. Commander Terauchi will be the one to speak."

"Yes, sir."

"After you have reported in, you will eat. Then wait for me in my quarters."

"Yes, sir."

Naogaka shed himself of his parachute and flight jacket. At altitude on the way back from Rabaul the temperature had been down to only fifteen degrees. Now it was again well above one hundred, and he had not reached the ground from his wing before the perspiration broke out on his body. He stood for a moment; that timeless stretch when the pilot makes the mental transition after the physical to compensate for his once again being chained to the earth. He looked about him.

Bah. He did not like this place. Perhaps he had never really thought of it before. They called this an airfield? This filthy hellhole? An airfield, without hangars or maintenance sheds or even a control tower? Lae was an insult to the meaning of airfield. One dirty, small runway no more than three thousand feet in length. It could have been a swamp. On three sides of the runway, in the immediate distance, there towered the rugged mountains of the Papuan peninsula. The fourth side, the open end of the runway, stretched almost to the ocean.

The runway ran at a right angle from a mountain slope to near the water. Adjacent to the beach lay what was left of a small aircraft hangar, battered and ripped with shrapnel and bullet holes. Made by both Japanese and American weapons, thought Naogaka. Months before three Australian transport planes had been shattered by bomb blasts and they still lay now where they had then, tumbled, rusting wreckage. Demolished equipment and debris littered the area beyond. There was no time here at Lae to spend in cleaning the grounds.

Naogaka wondered what it had been like here before the war, when the Australians had used this field to airlift supplies to and gold ore from the Kokoda Mine. Even then it could only have been miserable. Even then the seaport could have been no better than now. A joke, really. One primitive pier, and in the harbor mud, its stern and mast jutting from the water, a single small merchantman of five hundred tons. Australian. Sunk when the Japanese first struck, left where it sank into the gripping muck. It was the worst airfield Naogaka had *ever* seen.

How did they manage to handle seventy Zero fighters without hangars, wondered Naogaka. But they did, and their in-commission rate was so high it was astonishing. All the more so when one considered that the maintenance crews worked no matter what the weather. Improvised shelters of mats and canvas were enough.

For months Lae airfield had not even enjoyed the status of a control tower. Finally the pilots got together on their own and used logs and sawn timber to create an ugly but workable structure for the ground teams.

There were exactly two hundred and seven sailors at Lae and in the surrounding territory to man all the flak guns. These two hundred and seven men made up the *entire* air and ground defense of the base. Another one hundred and sixty-four men comprised the entire maintenance and ground support crews. There were seventy pilots and no more than a dozen other officers to handle weather, communications, medical and other needs. Lae was austerity at its ultimate.

The men lived twenty-three to a shack, laughably known

as a billet. Its size covered six by ten yards and that was *all*. Cots stood in tight rows. One center table was enough for eating, working, writing letters, reading. Illumination came from candles.

Yet men do amazing things when there is need and their spirit is high. Empty fuel drums had been cut into impromptu bathtubs, and no pilot ever went more than one night without bathing. Other fuel drums had been cut and bent and shaped into washbasins and used for cooking and mess facilities.

Lae was a potential pesthole, needing only a very slight edge to drag its human inhabitants down with disease or rot or whatever. Every man washed his underclothes, *every* day. It must be so.

Naogaka glanced at the billets. They were only five hundred yards from the airstrip. Dangerously close for a field subjected to so many enemy strikes. But the men had gouged their own dugouts from the ground, reinforced them with logs. Though crude, they were effective shelters.

Their living conditions were primitive, their food monotonous and unvarying, the airfield itself out of the stone age, and their morale unexcelled. Commander Gaishi Naogaka took singular pride in that morale. And their achievements. Among the thirty lead pilots of the Lae Wing, no less than fourteen men were aces, and several, he reminded himself, were aces several times over.

Yet they were disturbed. Their rules, to which they adhered with iron discipline, were being twisted and broken before their eyes. They still did not believe that Masahiko Obama had lost his life to bombers. Obama was too wise, too skilled, a man of too much experience to die at the hands of a bomber crew!

Yet it *had* happened. And more than a dozen other men went down in their Zeros. Something had changed drastically. The B–25 was not so difficult an adversary. Yet these same airplanes with which they had had so little trouble were now smashing their way through fighter opposition. And what they did to shipping . . . Naogaka had flown over the debacle of landing barges and destroyed troopships and destroyers. He had refused to believe what he saw, that only twelve or thirteen B–25s could have wreaked such havoc. But it was true. The pilots swore it was so.

And then, the strike in Simpson Harbor. That was why he had been called to headquarters in Rabaul. First the devastated troop convoy, and then the powerful blow in the heart of the strongest naval base in that part of the world. Again by only a dozen of those strange B–25s! They had lost one of their force, it was true, but only one, and the pilot — in the best Japanese tradition, it must be noted — had taken his flaming airplane into the runway of Lakunai Airdrome and he had destroyed sixteen airplanes and killed more than eighty men as the American machine exploded in a long gout of flame and debris.

Gaishi Naogaka had taken a while to relax in the presence of Wing Commander Eisuke Terauchi. It is not an easy thing to do, to bring a critical note from higher headquarters to the same man who is your commanding officer. But Terauchi understood. For whatever headquarters had to say, however sharp the tone of its message, it was true. The Lae Wing had been assigned to protect with aerial cover the troop movement of barges and shipping. It had failed to carry out its assignment. Thousands of soldiers and much equipment had been lost. The entire New Guinea campaign was jeopardized because of that loss. And all because of about a dozen American bombers. It had not taken the Japanese that long to understand the changes made in the B–25s. Somehow each plane had been given the firepower of an entire squadron. Getting in front of one of these new machines was fatal. Ships and flak positions and surviving pilots could attest to that.

So far the Americans had enjoyed the strength of innovation and surprise. No more. It was not to be so.

"Headquarters insists we must break the spirit and the back of this new group," Gaishi Naogaka said carefully to his commander. "We are to make a special effort to do so."

Terauchi waved a hand easily. "We will dispense with the special efforts," he smiled. He was free in the private company of his old friend. "We *will* deal with the Americans."

"Yes," Naogaka nodded. "We will institute the wolf-pack tactics. When we encounter these airplanes we will concentrate on one or two of them. Our men must cut those machines away from the herd and destroy them."

"Of course," agreed the Lae Wing commander. "But there is something else, Gaishi."

"Sir?"

"Why do we not have any reconnaissance photographs of this new group?"

Naogaka thought swiftly. Of course! "Sir, it had not occurred to me . . . but all the pictures, all of them, of the airfields near Moresby . . ." He nodded. "They have never been there."

"Yet there is no other airdrome from which they could operate, is there?" Eisuke Terauchi was speaking with a thin smile.

"None, sir. None that we know of."

"Ah. That is so."

"Then there is another field of which we know nothing. But it cannot be too far away." Commander Gaishi Naogaka rose to his feet.

"With your permission, sir, tomorrow morning we will

begin our campaign. We are at full strength again. We will hunt down the B–25s at their home field, wherever it may be. If we cannot catch these devils in the air then we shall destroy them on the ground."

"You will be pleased, then," Terauchi spoke softly, "to know there are other orders from Rabaul." He tapped the papers before him. "Indeed, commencing as of tomorrow morning, Rabaul has laid on a heavy bomber force to strike at the airfields at Moresby. Seventy-four bombers, and the Lae Wing will provide escort with forty-eight fighters. We will catch them on the ground *and* in the air. And you, Gaishi, shall lead the attack."

24

"Aн! I see the chef from the Imperial Hotel in Tokyo is visiting us once again." Petty Officer Masao Wada slipped behind the table in his billet and nodded to the meal before him. "Good morning, breakfast! I wonder which one of us will survive this encounter — you, or my stomach." The other pilots laughed at Wada. His was a daily routine. But it helped the sameness of food every day, of breakfast that was always a dish of rice, soybean-paste soup with dried vegetables, and pickles. At least they had given up on the barley. That twisted a man's innards.

They ate quickly and went directly to their planes. The last man to leave the billet blew out the candles on the table. First light was just streaking the eastern horizon. They would be flying soon. Rabaul was sending down a powerful bomber force for them to escort and they wanted the strike to take place directly after sunrise.

Six fighters were pulled from the line, pilots by the wing or in their cockpits. The emergency standby force, engines always ready to turn over instantly. The men waved to one another as they went to their individual Zeros. They looked toward the fighter with diagonal stripes, closest to the runway. Commander Gaishi Naogaka would personally lead this mission.

It would be a good strike. Once the bombers had hit, the fighter pilots were free to go to the deck, to shoot at whatever targets presented themselves on the ground. They would flush out the rabbits today!

A strange sound. That whistling; eerie. Bombs? They scanned the sky. Nothing in the growing light. A few birds, but that was all.

Standing on his wing, his face showing his puzzlement, it was Gaishi Naogaka who at the last moment recognized the terrible cry. "Take cover! Take cover!" he shouted, waving his arms furiously. "Everybody *get down!*"

Mortar shells. It was impossible, but as quickly as the realization came, the first shells erupted in spurts of dark red flame. One after the other the shells fell, arcing down from the sky with their awful whistling shriek. A Zero went up in a huge blast of fire, another spun around, breaking its gear and crumpling a wing. Even under the barrage Naogaka saw that it was a random shelling, intended to hit anywhere along the runway or the parked planes. No one could tell where the shells would land next. The Japanese commander cursed soundly — there are no Japanese troops out there in the jungle growth! He looked at the antiaircraft units; they were depressing their weapons to fire into the underbrush but could see no targets. The fools — Naogaka shouted orders and two squads of sailors with rifles in their hands ran from the field to the growth. The first squad began to crumple like rag dolls. But not from mortar shells. Naogaka saw the puffs of dirt where machine-gun bullets were striking about the men.

A cluster of shells ripped along the runway and the terrible truth dawned suddenly. He clambered back atop his wing where the others could see him. "Start your engines!" he screamed, turning about to repeat his orders so that all might hear despite the staccato bursts of the shells. "Start your engines! Take off at once!" He ducked as a nearby blast smashed against his body, rocking his airplane. Quickly, now. Into the cockpit. Good; the mechanics were still there, awaiting his orders. He gave the signal to start the engine. The rest would follow his example. He glanced up. A fuel truck vanished in a blinding flash. Smoke poured into the sky. Above the din he heard muffled explosions; more shells, perhaps grenades. The popping of light machine guns drifted across the field. Three more fighters were burning or broken and still they had not seen their assailants.

Gaishi Naogaka had a terrible feeling and the sound of sirens howling, two sirens, one at each end of the field, cut through him like a knife. Enemy air attack . . . and Naogaka *knew*, he knew by whatever deep instinct runs through men like him, that it would be those same damned B-25s that have been giving them so much trouble. Frantic, he cursed and shouted for the engine to start —

"Okay, we're coming up on Lae now. Everybody start spreading out. We're going into them Indian file. Look sharp, troops."

Whip Russel glanced left and right. The formation of B-25s was easing apart, sliding into six elements of two bombers each. They flew just above the waters of Huon Gulf, the sun directly behind them, just breaking the horizon. It was a beautiful cocoon of light.

"We'll hold this course until we're ready to break to the left," Whip said to Alex Bartimo.

"Righto. Wonder how our friend from down under is doing. He should be — aha!" Alex pointed far off to their left. "You can just make it out. There; see the smoke? Drifting just above the horizon." Alex pressed his transmit button. "Group from Lead. Our jungle friends have made contact. Lae is taking its beating. We have drifting smoke in sight. They should be rather unhappy with what's going on, so stay sharp."

They flew on, the coastline to their left growing larger as they edged shoreward, angling toward the land, setting up their approach so that visual contact with the Lae runway would come only at the last moment. "Okay. About two minutes from now," Whip called. "Break left on my turn. I'll go in first to wake 'em up, and you people carry on in your elements."

"Yes, teacher."

"Who's the wise-ass?"

"*Him*," came a chorus of voices.

The Sakae engine finally burst into the sweet thunder Gaishi Naogaka knew so well. His mechanic was signaling the all clear to him. Naogaka looked behind at other pilots with engines turning over. His fist pumped up and down in the unmistakable signal to scramble. Emergency takeoff. Get into the air as quickly as possible.

He turned to taxi to the runway, looking ahead to clear his path. In that moment his blood froze. What he saw was insane. And he knew that this was likely the last thing he would ever see in this world.

Off the end of the runway, great propellers flashing to either side of those enormous white teeth was an American bomber — *and the landing gear was extending into the wind.*

Even as he watched, the nose of the machine vanished in a dazzling glare of orange light. Well ahead of the Yankee devil dust erupted on the ground and Naogaka knew the main antiaircraft position had just been torn apart.

Wild for release, Naogaka rammed forward on the throttle. The Zero responded instantly, jerking forward, starting to roll, its pilot staring in continued disbelief before him.

Were the Americans crazy? Did they intend to *land* here in the midst of this attack? He stared and in that instant, as other bombers drifted into view in a long line, Gaishi Naogaka knew what his enemy was doing. He understood,

and despite the moment, and the overwhelming power
about to descend upon him, he was filled with admiration, a
respect for his opponent, for what he was doing. All this
time the Zero had been darting forward, grabbing for speed.
Did he have enough speed to fly? Could the machine get
into the air? It was his only chance and he snatched at it,
pulling up the gear even before he came back on the stick,
and he felt the Zero lurch, *but it was flying* . . .

"Look at that son of a bitch in front, willya?"
"The bloke's trying, I'll say that."
"If he gets up he could be trouble."
"One Zero? We'll eat him alive."
Whip had a touch of contempt in his voice. "I hate the
bastards, Alex, but I don't sell them short. And that one's in
perfect position to ram. We've got to nail him right *now*."
Alex never failed to amaze him. The flak guns to either
side of the runway were reaching out for them and they
were taking hits, shudders they felt through metal, and in a
singsong voice, finger and thumb cocked like a gun, Alex
was half singing to the Zero directly before them, "Bye-bye,
baby."

Naogaka was just about to turn, to make a desperate
attempt to flick-roll the Zero from before the path of the
devilship coming straight at him. The wing of his fighter
lifted and he was kicking heavy rudder when through his
windscreen he again saw that great flash of orange light.
The entire front of the bomber vanished in the sudden glare
and Gaishi Naogaka knew what was happening.
He had only that one instant as the eight heavy machine
guns in the nose and the four guns slabbed onto the fuselage
fired. A thunderbolt of flame lashed out and caressed the
Zero. Naogaka's last thoughts, befitting the warrior, were

of what was happening. He understood fully now what the Americans were doing, that with their gear down and the propellers in fine pitch the bombers had become rock-stable gun platforms. Speed was less important here than accuracy, and the Yankees could hazard their slow flying because the mortar attack had so thoroughly disrupted the Lae warning system and its defenses. It was a daring and a brilliant gamble.

But then Naogaka thought no more.

The climbing Zero was stopped — literally — in midair. The mass of bullets under high velocity represented an enormous force and the impact was as if two locomotives had crashed head-on. In a single timeless moment that seemed to last forever the Sakae engine pulped, tore away and the Zero began a wild cartwheel that never ended, because by the time it had completed only the first half of its gyration the wings were gone, and only burning, scattering wreckage remained in the air, falling in a blazing spray back toward the runway.

A short burst and the second Zero to make it into the air lost its left wing, spinning away like a sheet of paper in the wind, sending the Zero through the air in a berserk flat-wheeling of destruction. It pancaked into the runway and the torn fuel tanks let go and the fighter vanished within the great rose blossom of flame.

"Let 'em go!"

The bombs began spilling away. "Coombs, what the hell have we got back there?" Whip shouted into his microphone.

"Good release! Jesus Christ, it's like it's snowing back here! Those chutes are everywhere!"

The first element was coming over the end of the runway, and at the far end, the inland side, Whip had the gear coming up and his speed building rapidly. "Watch that flak gun to the north. The son of a bitch is hot."

"Got 'em, boss. We'll hose him down a bit." A long burst from the third B–25. Leaves, tree trunks, sandbags, antiaircraft gun and men exploded from the strafing pass.

The bombers were dumping their loads into the air. Lae appeared to have been covered with a mass of confetti. Then the parafrags began to hit.

Whip had made a high-speed climbing turn on the land side of the airstrip and as he brought the nose around and down to gain speed he and Alex had a perfect view of the airfield. Lae looked all the world like a pinball game gone mad. Every bursting parafrag exploded with a dazzling flash, and from the thirteen bombers there were thirteen hundred bombs raining down.

It was carnage, pure and simple. The parafrags burst at ground level, sending their blast and shrapnel horizontally instead of wasting energy digging deep holes in the ground. Zero fighters had been hit all along the runway, and flames and smoke poured into the sky.

"Stay right, stay right," Whip chanted to the last bombers still pounding over the field, raking the planes and men on the ground with their awesome firepower. Side gunners and turret gunners were hammering out bursts from their positions, and Whip came screaming back down the runway, in the opposite direction now, pouring savage bursts of fire into any target that appeared before them.

It was impossible but the Japanese managed to get seven fighters into the air. If they were great on other occasions they were maddened now and pressed their attacks home to pointblank range, disdaining the defensive fire of the turret gunners.

A Zero took on the row of bombers in a long head-on pass. Kessler in Number Two horsed back on the yoke to get a heavy burst into the fighter, but the Japanese pilot was throwing his Zero about in maneuvers that were bordering on the hysterical. He bored in to the center of the line and his heavy cannon shells smashed into the cockpit of Jim Whitson's bomber. Whitson and Second Lieutenant Allan Hillbrink died instantly.

There was no fire, but in a convulsive spasm of death, the pilot must have jerked the yoke full back. The stricken B–25 leaped skyward, rolling slowly, until the speed fell away, and then the nose whipped around and the airplane, still under full power, dove into the jungle off to the side of the runway and exploded.

One Zero went up in a ball of flame, but the bombers were taking heavy damage from the fierce attacks. "Close it up! Close it up!" Whip shouted into his radio. The B–25s scrambled together, joining their defensive firepower. It threw off the aim of the fanatically attacking Zeros, and the Americans were more afraid of deliberate ramming than of holding off the enemy fighters. Hoot Gibson lost his left engine but hung in with the formation, beating his right engine half to death on emergency overboost.

Heavy rain showers were hugging the upper slopes of the Owen Stanley Range and Whip Russel chose discretion.

"Let's go home, troops," he sang out to the other pilots. "Haney and McCamish, you take Hoot home the long way around."

"Roger that," Haney called back. "*Any* way home is the best way."

25

"SORRY, WHIP."

Lou Goodman showed him the orders. A strike against a protected beach area in the Admiralty Islands. Right off Los Negros.

Whip Russel looked up with disbelief. "But that's more than sixteen hundred miles when you figure screwing around for formations, the rendezvous; hell, more than that, maybe."

"I know."

"But it's crazy!"

Lou Goodman sighed. He was in complete sympathy with Whip. The reactions he was hearing now were merely a forecast of how the crews would also react. But there was no way out of it.

"Somebody in headquarters has a report, I guess they got a photo recce up there, that the place is lousy with landing barges. They want them hit as soon as possible and FEAF is laying on a coordinated strike. B–17s from twenty-five thousand feet and — "

"I know, *I know!* It says we're to bomb from eighteen."

Goodman looked miserable. "Yeah."

"What the hell are we going to hit with our guns from more than three miles up!"

"The orders call for a strike with a bombing pattern."

"Do you know how long it's been since anyone in my outfit used a Norden sight?" Whip's expression was total disbelief. "They're crazier than bedbugs, Lou." His voice trailed away. He wasn't going to fight city hall from this stinking field in New Guinea.

They flew the mission. It was a disaster. Sixteen B–25s from another outfit and eleven of their own. Nine B–17s went in ten minutes before they did. The B–17s beat the absolute living shit out of a beach. That sand would never be the same again. They didn't touch the barges.

The other B–25 outfit did pretty good and laid their pattern where it chewed up barges and hurt people. The 335th with Whip leading turned in a lousy performance. Three of his airplanes had already turned back. Their oxygen systems were riddled with fungus and jungle growth and men were turning blue. The eight planes that went into the target at Los Negros stayed in a tight cluster. If one B–25 was off it seemed obvious the rest of them would be. They killed a lot of fish. Maybe. No one would ever know.

The raid up to Los Negros was the first shock wave in the changing pattern of the air war. Something was breaking at a place called Guadalcanal and the navy and marines were having a hellacious time in the Solomons. The Japs had pulled a lot of their punch from other areas to deal with what they probably felt was insurrection on the part of the Americans. Either way, the targets that had been dangerous but juicy plums for the Death's Head Brigade began to evaporate.

Infuriated is too mild a word to describe how Whip and his pilots reacted to the shift in operations. Until now, because of General Smyth's ramrodding of special missions, the 335th had gone after the targets that had given head-quarters its own special brand of fits. The big push of the Japanese to heavily reinforce their army on New Guinea had twice been blunted. But with Guadalcanal commanding center stage, the Japanese went to low profile. They kept up a trickle of reinforcements rather than going to a solid move to get men and materiel onto New Guinea. The ripe targets withered away. Two or three ships, no more, would sail together, following weather as much as possible, to reach their unloading areas.

The big push, the final attempt, was yet to come. But in the meantime the special missions simply faded.

Fighting headquarters was like trying to kick a ghost in the groin. They were still laying on missions but their methods and procedures, and their reasons, were that special kind of insanity that so enrages men on the firing line. Orders would come in to hit Finschhafen. No one was told *what* they were supposed to bomb. No one specified fighters or bombers or fuel depots or ammunition dumps or shipping or what. Just hit the target. Which was stupid to the point of criminal conduct. Whip and his men had learned, and the other outfits were getting their education fast, that tearing up runways never really bothered the Japanese. Most of their fields were dirt or gravel or grass. They didn't have to resurface the material or pour cement. Men with shovels and bare hands could do the job, and they did, and their fighters were always clawing into the air against bombers without specific targets.

That was the worst of it. The Death's Head Brigade was the finest cutting edge the newly formed Fifth Air Force had at its disposal. Here were men experienced in knifing through to the most difficult targets, in fighting the Jap on his own terms, in doing damage that a force ten times their number couldn't manage — and doing so without the appalling losses other outfits were taking. Half the bombing squadrons and groups in the area were losing planes faster than they could be replaced, and new airplanes *were* coming into the southwest Pacific now in more than a trickle.

It had become a war of attrition. The 335th was ordered to join with the pack. Go out with the other bombers.

"Don't they ever *learn* anything in their ivory tower?
Jesus Christ, we've just spent the last couple months
proving what we can do! If they brought the rest of those
goddamned planes down to the deck like we fly they'd — "
And usually the anger came to its own brick wall of
realization. You follow orders. You go after targets even
when you know there's no justification for those targets.

You give the enemy some damned fine target practice.
You're the target.

They went back to Rabaul and Lae and Madang and
Finschhafen and Wewak and Hollandia and Aitape and
other targets. They followed their orders to bomb from this
towering level or that, and when the bombs had been
dropped and the orders had been followed, Whip held up his
middle finger, extended rigidly, on which all of headquarters
might seat themselves for proper insertion, and he took the
Death's Head Brigade back to the deck. Where they knew
how to fight, where they could destroy, where they could
kill, and do it all with unmatched ferocity and results.

What they did not know, but soon came to understand,
was that the ghost of Commander Gaishi Naogaka waited
for them. The Lae Wing had been whipped by a baker's
dozen of bombers with seventy Zero fighters on the ground.
The same Yankee devils had destroyed a convoy of barges
and troopships. They had smashed into the heart of Rabaul.
The fighter pilots had their signals out. Watch for the
special group. The B–25s with the sting in the nose. The
airplanes with the sharks' teeth, with fangs. Led by a black
B–25 with a death's head — and nearly twenty Japanese
flags — painted on each side of the fuselage beneath the
cockpit.

The combination began to chew into the fiber of the 335th.
Headquarters kept sending them out to strike targets which
weren't worth a single bomb. Headquarters insisted some
of their missions be flown in concert with other groups so as

to amass a large number of aircraft over target. It made great public relations copy, and it added up to a lot of bombs, but it really wasn't doing that much damage to the people on the ground. If they had gone after those fighter fields with the hammer-and-anvil tactics developed to such a fine pitch by the Death's Head Brigade they could have broken the back of Japanese fighter strength in the New Guinea area.

But they didn't have the chance. Not yet. There was a new general coming into the business. Now that the Fifth Air Force had been formed from the wreckage of a half-dozen old organizations, George Kenney was taking the helm. He was a no-nonsense, cock-of-the-walk pilot who knew how to get in low and fast and mix it up in an old-fashioned brawl. But George Kenney was still on his way. Lou Goodman swore to Whip he'd badger the old man before Kenney's ass could warm his seat. Until then the 335th could only grit its teeth and go to war. Wastefully, sometimes; stupidly, often. But they went.

Whip made two combat strikes out of almost every mission. If they went after a target at high altitude, he broke from the formation on the way home to hit an airfield as they raced back to Kanaga. That meant coming in on the deck, shooting up everything in sight. The massed guns of the B–25s were still terrifyingly effective. It was the hammer-and-anvil, but before many weeks the crews began to realize *they* also were on the anvil. Whip Russel was squeezing blood out of stones.

They bombed Arawe on the bottom coast of New Britain Island from fourteen thousand feet. The big formation flew almost due south over the Solomon Sea to return home, avoiding Japanese fighters on the way back. Eleven bombers slid from formation and began the gravity ride to

Finschhafen in Whip's favorite strike — on the deck from across the water. They beat up the Japanese field, and when they came around to regroup the Zeros hit them like a swarm of wasps.

"Close it up! Get together, you people!" Whip shouted in the familiar call to bunch together and bring their heavy firepower into a tight cluster of sky. The pilots skidded and climbed and dove and the formation pulled itself into defensive posture. The Zeros stayed away from head-on attacks. Suicide with all that firepower up front. They didn't come after the bombers in trail or a long file. Six fighters went after one bomber at a time.

The Zeros closed in to pointblank range, concentrating on the one B–25, and it didn't take long to smash the dorsal turret and shoot out the waist guns, and the Zeros ignored other turrets, despite taking damage and losses on their own. They stayed in there, tight, eyeball to eyeball, and they shot the bejesus out of the airplane they were after.

The first gang fight like that killed Paddy Shannon in his cockpit. The airplane was burning and Shannon drove for altitude with his life bubbling in a red stream from his throat. He got high enough for his crew to bail. There was always a chance a PBY could come back in and pick up the men on their small rubber rafts.

The PBY never had the chance. The Zeros killed one man in his chute on the way down, and they circled low and slow over the water while the three remaining survivors climbed into their rafts, and then they pumped streams of bullets and exploding cannon shells until the water was boiling.

Three days later Fifth Air Force sent out a total of sixty-two B–25s and fourteen A–20 bombers, with sixteen B–17 heavies going in first from high altitude, against Madang. The Zeros rose up in a great loose swarm like wasps climbing for altitude. Twenty-seven fighters in all.

There were P–40s flying escort at fourteen thousand feet and they went downstairs in a hurry to bounce the enemy fighters. The Japanese climbed up through them, exchanging a few shots on the way, and kept boring upstairs until they reached the level of the twin-engines.

All twenty-seven Zeros went after the thirteen bombers from the Death's Head Brigade. It was a bitter, savage fight. None of the other bombers was touched that day. Only the 335th was forced to take it. They did, but they shot down six Zeros, losing only one of their number. A nice kid named Matt Barber. They hadn't had time yet to remember the names of the other crewmen.

They rolled away from their bomb runs, their number cut to twelve. Arnie Kessler eased from the formation with his airplane showing gaping tears and holes. Smoke streamed from his right engine. Whip hit his radio. "White Fox, White Fox, you read?"

The P–40 leader called back at once. "White Fox. Go."

"Blue Goose. We've got a cripple and he's tailing smoke. Can you have some of your people take him home?"

"Wilco. Fox Seven and Eight, you have that thing in sight?"

"Roger."

"Got 'em."

"Give the boys some company going home."

Two P–40s peeled off and took up escort position with Kessler's battered airplane. They were high enough for him to go straight through a saddleback of the Owen Stanleys without any great turns. High enough to get across the worst of the mountains on only one engine.

The other bombers went for their home fields. Whip took the 335th still flying in a long descending circle. He wasn't through this day. Not yet, not yet.

Muhlfield called in. You could tell his worries from the

tone of his voice. "I got two people shot up pretty bad,
Lead."

"Go home then, Mule."

Quiet consternation in that bomber. "Ah, stand by one."
Muhlfield came back a few moments later. "We've had a
little caucus here. The troops say they don't mind bleeding a
bit longer." A pause. "Ah, Lead, are you thinking what I
think you're thinking? Over."

Whip burst out laughing. He grinned at Alex before
thumbing his transmit button. "Ah, that's affirmative,
Mule."

"Okay, boss. We go where you go."

Whip timed it with the touch of the master. He stayed at
four thousand feet and in the far distance, along the
coastline of New Guinea, he saw the tiny reflections of
sunlight in the low sky. "That's them. They won't be
expecting company now," he told Alex. He went to transmit. "Okay, everybody, down we go."

The old gravity train ride, the B–25s trembling with the
fury of air pounding past them, screaming through bullet
and shell holes, the coastline expanding steadily in sight,
and a slow-turning nest of moths in the sky.

Zero fighters in the landing pattern at Lae, speed low,
gear down, flaps down. Partridges plump and ripe, and the
335th came across the water with everything forward,
throttles wide open, light in weight, their speed high, and the
Japanese pilots had no more than a few seconds' warning
when the bombers struck.

One hundred thirty-two machine guns bucked and roared
as the bombers hit the stunned fighter pilots in a wide
sweep. It was a one-pass deal only but it was savagely
effective. Four fighters burned and exploded in the air.
Several more were hit heavily and, for all they knew, went
down with dead pilots. It would have been perfect except

that one Zero pilot, confused, turned and climbed in a
graceful sweep, and only three or four seconds after he died
from being pulped, his lifeless form fell forward on the stick
and rammed the fighter down, and it fell swiftly from the
sky to put its heavy engine directly into the cockpit with
Muhlfield and Russ Trotman.

That caucus hadn't lasted long. Mule's men did bleed
only "a bit longer."

The bombers tore away over jungle. The Zeros were low
on fuel and didn't follow.

It was a pattern that dogged their steps on almost every
mission. Their losses were brutal. More than half the men
with whom Whip had taken the newly formed 335th into
combat with its new killer airplanes were dead.

The word spread down the line. Impossible not to have
that happen. It went all the way to headquarters, Fifth Air
Force. Pilots talked because a legend was being created.
The Japanese wanted the Death's Head Brigade.

General George Kenney called in Smyth to ask him what
the hell was going on with this special outfit at Kanaga
Field. And where the hell was Kanaga? It wasn't even on
the charts. Smyth filled in the new air force commanding
general. Kenney was slow to react. He liked the idea of
special outfits. Their morale, their spirit, could be the
driving force of far vaster bodies of men. Yet, those reports
were disturbing. Kenney understood the hammer and the
anvil. He'd been around.

"Go up to their field," he told Smyth. "Find out what's
happening with your own ears and eyes and use your own
mind."

Smyth nodded. "What do you want me to do then, sir?"

A face leathered from years of flying — decades of flying
— looked steadily back at Smyth. "Whatever has to be
done, of course."

*

Smyth didn't believe it when he saw Kanaga Field. He landed at Seven-Mile where Alex Bartimo was waiting for him. "With all due respect, sir, I do think it would be better if I took the ship into Kanaga." Smyth thought the whole thing was ridiculous, but he had enough savvy to save his arguments for later. There weren't any. His pucker factor was going clear out of sight as Bartimo drove the light bomber straight toward the trees. Not until the last moment, the last *possible* moment, did the trees melt away so that the A–20 could slip onto the airstrip that had appeared as if by magic.

Smyth didn't waste time with amenities. He explained his mission and was thankful, after a burning study by the pilots about him, that it was he, Smyth, who'd been supporting this outfit all the way. It helped. My God, it almost felt like being in an enemy camp.

He listened to Whip Russel and he listened to Lou Goodman and he surprised them both by nodding agreement with their gripes. "Everything you say has merit to it," he admitted.

"Then what the devil gives, sir?"

"It may be," Smyth said carefully to both men, "that the 335th has outlived its usefulness as a separate and distinct entity. The Japanese are concentrating so hard against you that it's only a matter of time before they wipe out this whole outfit. We've gotten some of their communications, Major, and what I've said is fact. They're out to destroy you and your men."

Whip's response was a mixture of a growl and snarl. "Let the bastards come, General. That's why we're here."

"No, it isn't. You've lost fourteen crews in all when you count your replacements. That's a mortality factor exceeding one hundred percent."

"That's our job. You take losses in this work. No one promised anyone else a gravy train."

"You take losses," Smyth corrected him quietly, "only when those losses are unavoidable, or, you get a proper return for what you lose. What's happening with the 335th has gone beyond that point." Smyth walked slowly about the cave. "Let me explain something to you both. The colonel, here, may already be aware of it." Smyth turned to face Whip Russel. "You see, you've proven yourself right. You already know that. But General Kenney has decided that what you started with this outfit and its gunships is the way to go in this theater. Starting as of yesterday, every B–25 and A–20 that comes into this area goes to Garbutt Field, and several more centers we're setting up, for retrofit to heavy armament like your airplanes. The low-level strike with massed firepower is the way we're going to fight this war. If you never flew again, Major, you've done more to win this war than a thousand men could ever accomplish."

Smyth lit a cigarette. They watched him like two stone hawks, waiting. "In fact, although this is a bit premature, Major, you've been put in for the DSC."

"Screw the goddamned medal," came the rasping answer. "I'm not flying for any piece of tin on my shirt. I —"

"Major, you have a mission only five hours from now. You need some sleep." Lou Goodman was stopping this shit *right now.*

"Goddamnit, Lou, I —"

"That's a goddamned order!"

Whip studied him through half-closed eyes. He left without saying another word.

Smyth looked at Goodman with open relief. "Thanks, Colonel."

"What happens now, General?"

"You have an opinion, Colonel?"

"Keep me out of it. I was his friend a long time ago."

"And you still are."

"I am."

"Whip Russel has become a living legend. We've got to think of the big picture."

"I'm not sure I like what comes next."

The general smiled. "Not what you think. We want Whip Russel alive and we want to keep him alive. I can't tell him but I can tell you. He's a hero and we need heroes. Very badly, I might add. What Russel has learned and what he's done is more important than anything else. Skip bombing is now going to be the Fifth Air Force's standard form of attack. The factories will soon be rolling out airplanes like those of the 335th you modified. We're even bringing out a model with a seventy-five millimeter cannon in the nose."

"I'll buy a bond if I don't have to fly it."

Smyth crossed his arms. He was coming to a decision. One way or the other. "Times have changed, and it's time for more changes. Whip can teach other men to fight, teach them to fight the way he learned. And we have a better chance of letting the legend live longer."

Goodman studied his fingers. "He won't like that."

"Then, Colonel, as his friend, and, as you say, you've been friends a very long time, it's going to be up to you to make Major Russel understand what I'm talking about will do more than any one-man war."

26

THEY CAME BACK from the mission chewed to pieces. They had flown a loitering top cover for two hours. Below them an Australian force was trying to batter a Japanese stronghold. If they took the stronghold they had a good shot at major objectives beyond. The Aussies were squeezing, trying to punch through in strength along the New Guinea trails so they might establish a meaningful threat to the Japanese airfields along the northern coast. The B–25s stayed overhead, flying wide circles, trying to hit positions pinpointed for them by the Australians. But at best it was a kind of frustrating blindman's buff, shooting up targets concealed by heavy growth. No one knew if the Japanese were really being hurt by all the lead thrown at them.

It was also an appalling violation of plain common sense, because the key defense of these bombers was either tight formation, or a slashing attack when the enemy wasn't ready for that sort of maneuver. Now all that had been thrown away. The Aussies had a handful of Wirraways, airplanes that were nothing more than souped-up trainers, to drop smoke bombs and mark the targets. So all the B–25 pilots had to hit, really, were plumes of smoke shredding upward in the wind. It became a matter of throwing ordnance loads or making a strafing pass into an area where you hoped the Japanese had been caught — *if* they really were there to begin with, and *if* the Wirraway had been accurate in his smoke marker drop.

They stooged around for two hours and dropped their 300-pounders on cue from the spiraling smoke, and went in to shoot up waving bushes, and never really knew if they were doing anybody a damned bit of good. And they were nervous. They were so uptight their nerves were snapping, because to do this kind of mission, where your speed is low and your altitude is zilch, you need top cover.

They didn't have any, and they were getting headaches from squinting and shooting at shadows, and trying to judge the wind drop for their bombs, and shouting at the Aussies with radios that barely worked. It was a day of broken clouds, but there were plenty of holes, and the visibility was appalling, what with the uneven ground speckled and mixed with shadows and sunlight and you couldn't see for crap in the thickening haze and smoke, and everybody was trying everything he could to wax the Japanese on the ground and to keep from running into one another in the air, and always having one eyeball peeled above and behind, because they were in a perfect position to get bounced. And it happened.

The Zeros came whistling through the broken clouds and anviled them. It was that simple.

It was murder.

They had almost no chance to fight off the barracudas that were suddenly in their midst, darting and twisting and slashing in for attacks at pointblank range. The Japanese nailed three bombers at once, flying too low, too slow, out of formation. They were wide open to be hit and three B–25s went into the jungle burning and exploding, and their own heavy firepower managed, in the short and savage melee, to nail just one fighter.

Another bomber crashed trying to make it into Seven-Mile. The hydraulic system was shot out and the crew was badly wounded. They were a mess, and the gear snapped on landing, and when it was over only the two gunners in the back of the fuselage survived.

General Smyth listened in silence as it spilled from Whip in jerky, staccato phrases, the pilot's facial muscles twitching visibly with barely controlled rage. "It was the worst kind of waste, of good men and good airplanes, and the results were shit. Nothing more than that."

"The Australians might feel differently," the general replied. "They needed your help, and — "

"They didn't get our help," Whip broke in. He didn't see the star on Smyth's shoulder. Only the man. The figurehead for the stupid decision that had cost him four bombers. "Don't any of you people *understand?* We never saw a Jap. We never saw a gun. All we saw were trees and smoke and we bombed blind and we strafed blind. *Blind.* We didn't help the Aussies. General, you do not kill people by shooting with your eyes closed. And worst of all is that we had to leave ourselves wide open because we were ordered to fly a stupid mission by stupid people and that under the best of circumstances still wouldn't have been worth a tinker's damn. If we flew the way we've developed our tactics we wouldn't have been caught the way we were and I wouldn't have lost four planes and eighteen men dead and two more so broken up they'll never fight again."

Lou Goodman shifted uncomfortably in his chair. Whip was leaning too heavy on the man with the star. Oh, to be sure he was right. He was so right it was painful, and he knew it and Goodman knew it *and so did Smyth.* But all Whip was doing was raking the general over the coals and *he* hadn't ordered the strike. Goodman was grateful to the general for understanding. Otherwise he could just as well have dropped the boom on Whip Russel, right here and now, and rid himself of what was swiftly becoming a class A headache.

"You have my word we'll look into it," Smyth said finally. It wasn't much but then all the words in the world couldn't undo what had happened.

Whip dismissed the presence of the general in a way that hovered between preoccupation and insubordination. He didn't answer, he made no facial expressions. He didn't do anything except to ignore what he'd heard. He turned from the general to Lou Goodman. "What about replacements?" he queried.

"They'll be in this afternoon. I've set up Arnie Kessler to brief them. But the airplanes are glass, Whip."

He took that in slowly. The old glass-nose jobs. One stinking gun. "How the hell are we supposed to operate with those things?" he demanded.

"You bomb from twelve thousand tomorrow."

"That's one way to avoid an issue."

"Goddamnit, Whip, the other planes aren't ready yet! What the hell do you want me to do? Apologize because we don't have exactly the ships *you* want?"

Whip looked at him for several moments. "There was a time you'd never have said that. You would have made sure the planes were here when we needed them." A crooked smile tugged at the side of his mouth. "If you'll excuse me, sir? We have a mission to set up." He left without speaking further.

"No matter what he says," Smyth sighed, "we've laid on what we think is the most effective strike for tomorrow morning. A PBY picked up a big mess of barges. Looks like fuel. Maybe the Japanese are running low and maybe they're just stocking up for the big push against our fields here. It doesn't matter. We're going to hit them with as many airplanes as we can fly. And the 335th goes in with everybody else for the pattern."

Goodman nodded slowly. "On the deck," he said quietly, "this outfit could do as much damage as a hundred other aircraft."

"Not now they couldn't," Smyth retorted. "How many gunships do you have in commission?"

"Five. Four more will be ready the day after tomorrow."

"That's two days away. It's not tomorrow."

"Yeah." Goodman saw the strained look on Smyth's face. "I think I can hear a speech coming."

Smyth laughed. He sprawled on a bench. "Not really a speech. How would a pep talk go with you?"

"I don't believe it."

"Neither do I. But those barges, Goodman, are a clear indication of what we've been waiting for. We're positive they're stocking up for the big push against Moresby. So we want to stop their fuel supply before it gets here. That way we can force their hand. They might get jumpy because of Guadalcanal. They may even try an all-out assault against Milne Bay. Who knows? They've done some pretty daring things before. They could hit all the way into Moresby."

"General, you sound suspiciously like a man who *wants* the Japanese to come after us in force."

"That's what General Kenney wants, Goodman. It's precisely what he wants. To draw them out. Their reserves are getting thin. They won't waste them in small lots. They'll have to commit to the gamble. And we'd rather have a shot at them on the open seas than going into Rabaul."

But the general was on his feet. "I'm flying to Seven-Mile to have a meeting with General Spaulding. He flew in this morning from Kenney's office. I'd like you to come along with me. There's a hell of a lot more at stake than the 335th, Colonel, but I'm not ignoring this problem either. We're going to have to bring this whole mess to a head."

"General, it sounds like you're going to ask me to break

up this outfit. Jesus, sir, Whip and I have been friends a long —"

"I'd rather you didn't go any further with that line of thinking, Colonel. There's more to it than what we've talked about. I've spent some time with your flight surgeon. About Whip. He's getting close. . Did you know that? Much more of this and —"

"He's a hell of a lot tougher than any of you people could dream of, General."

Smyth ignored the remark. "I know how long you've been friends," he said with a tone of finality. "I wouldn't ask you to do anything of the sort, what you just said before." He paused. "So, I'm not asking. I'm giving you a direct order, Colonel Goodman. And I'm going to let you figure out the best and the easiest way."

"If it helps, General, I could always shoot him."

Smyth showed his first flash of anger. "My God, are you *all* insubordinate up here?"

"You could always shoot *me*, then."

"I've thought of it, Lou. Let's go."

27

THE JAPANESE hadn't waited for the bombers. Under cover of first darkness that same night the loose convoy of barges slipped from a sheltered cove along the north edge of Cape Gloucester on New Britain Island and started south within the Dampier Strait. This reduced their passage in the open sea to its minimum and kept them close enough to the northern coastline of New Guinea at daybreak to enjoy the patrolling protection of some two dozen Zero fighters.

General Smyth was right; Fifth Air Force had laid on a heavy strike. Sixteen B–17s crisscrossed the convoy from twenty-two thousand feet. It was like shooting at gnats with a shotgun. They never hit a barge, but the tumultuous wave action from the exploding bombs apparently upended one of the clumsy vessels and sent it to the bottom. The Zeros were still climbing as the Flying Fortresses dropped, and the heavies would have been in for a rough time except that the second wave was coming in. The big force of B–25s got a good bomb pattern and a half-dozen barges went up in blinding sheets of flame as the fuel stores let go.

Now the Zeros had the advantage of diving on the bombers well below them, and a massacre was averted only by the presence of sixteen P–40 fighters. They did less damage to the Zeros than they'd liked to have done but they did accomplish their mission in drawing off the fighters. It was one of those nip-and-tuck situations. There were enough Zeros to have rudely shoved aside the P–40s and still

worked over the B–25s, but the Japanese leader had his
orders to protect the barges. Three P–40s and two Zeros
went down and the Japanese broke off the attack and went
back to their elephantine charges crawling along the sea.

It should have ended there. But on the way back to
Kanaga Field Whip saw a dream come true. He stabbed the
air with his finger. "Alex, do you see them? Down there
. . . ten o'clock low, and they're going in our direction."

Alex Bartimo looked and his grin might never have
stopped if he hadn't wanted to talk. "Luvverly, luvverly.
How many you make out?"

Whip studied the air below them. At what he guessed
was five thousand feet at least eighteen enemy bombers.
"They look like Bettys," Whip said.

"You have just passed your aircraft recognition test, old
fellow."

Whip looked at the other aircraft in their formation. "I
don't think anyone's tumbled to our friends down there."

"The bloody P–40s are asleep."

"Leave 'em be. I think we ought to go downstairs."

"Wouldn't be right not to say hello. Besides, they're on
their way to Moresby from the looks of things."

Whip switched to squadron frequency. "Heads up,
troops. Kessler, Hoot, Mac, Dusty. You read?"

The answers came back immediately; they were listening.
Only those four bombers held Whip's interest. Only those
four planes and his own were gunships. The other B–25s
were mosquitoes.

"Okay, and this is only for the four people I just called.
All other aircraft stay with the main formation. You other
troops, look below."

"Whoo-ee."

"Eighteen fat goldfish."

"I think the boss man's got an idea."

"If we make our move now we can set 'em up."

"Okay, okay," Whip called in impatiently. "*Just* you four. Slide off to the right and form up on me."

Whip's bomber eased off to the side and began losing altitude. The Japanese in all likelihood had seen the bigger American formation and they'd be paying strict attention to the fighters. The odds were they wouldn't think twice about a few bombers easing from the main formation. Why bother? They were no threat.

The B–25s were light without their bomb loads and they had plenty of height, and there was all that beautiful altitude to use in the long dive. Whip started down the gravity train, the other bombers holding precision formation. He stayed well behind the Mitsubishi bombers, building up tremendous speed, and came up behind the enemy formation about a thousand feet *below* their altitude. Then they came back on the yokes and the five gunships arrowed upward, still with tremendous speed, directly through the blind spot of the Japanese bombers.

"I'll start at the left," Whip sang out.

"Gotcha, boss," Arnie Kessler called in. "We'll work it from left to right."

The Betty bombers swelled in their sights, expanding swiftly.

The engines thundered sweetly and the gunships sailed upward on a smooth curve, and then Whip was able to make out details of engines and hatches and exhaust patterns back from the stacks, and he kept closing, right in to pointblank range, and he had his sights dead-center on the belly of the ship to the far left of the enemy bomber, and finally he squeezed the gun tit.

Twelve fifty-calibers shattered the sky. In an instant the tornado of bullets smashed into the bomber. One moment it flew serenely, its crew oblivious of the death climbing up beneath the airplane, and in the next instant the tanks were a mass of flames and the right wing had exploded clean away from the fuselage and the bomber twisted up and over in a maddened cartwheel that took it tumbling toward the other bombers.

Everything seemed to happen at the same time. Whip saw his first target plunge into the bomber to its immediate right and he knew there would be a hell of a collision. He got out of the way fast, skidding well over to the right and he brought his guns to bear on the third enemy aircraft. As he started to fire the bomber exploded. One instant it was there and the next it was gone, and he heard Arnie Kessler's triumphant cry in his earphones.

"Got the son of a bitch!"

Whip wasted no time, breaking away to the left and grabbing for altitude. The other four gunships were like killer whales in the midst of an enemy, hammering death blows from their terrible massed weapons. In those first few seconds of battle, steaming up from behind and below, Whip's first long burst had destroyed one bomber, which smashed into a second airplane. That made two. Arnie Kessler exploded the third. Hoot Gibson and MacIntosh each nailed one. The sixth target trailed smoke and Dusty Rhodes didn't wait around to see what happened but poured a long burst into another Mitsubishi.

The Japanese, hanging doggedly to their formation, rear gunners firing desperately, went forward and down to build up speed. The Betty was powerful and she was fast and the Japanese pilots, once they'd gotten over the shock of what had happened to them, were taking the best way out — diving away from the American bombers. The B–25s went after them in hot pursuit, the pilots shouting wildly to one another. Dusty Rhodes and Kessler teamed up on one bomber lagging behind and literally shot it to pieces in the

air. Pieces of airplane kept breaking away, flashing past
them, and suddenly the enemy bomber was in an uncon-
trolled spin, plunging for the ocean.

They ignored that one and went to emergency power to
run down the fleeing bombers. But not for long. The voice
that came over the common channel chilled every man in
the B–25s.

"Blue Goose, Blue Goose from Rosebud —"

"Rosebud?" Alex Bartimo echoed the call sign. "Those
are fighters. What the hell are —"

"Read you, Rosebud."

"Then start a long curve to the left *and start it now.*
You've got about thirty Zeros closing on you. Break left,
break left. We're right behind the Zeros and you can bring
them closer to us."

Whip heard Coombs's voice on the intercom. "Jesus
Christ, Major, he ain't kidding . . . there's at least thirty of
them back there —" Coombs's voice faded away as his
turret guns opened up with a shaking roar.

The Zeros were almost on them in a beautiful bounce.
They knew what had happened. Those thirty fighters were
escort for the Betty bombers and the B–25s had moved in
just before their rendezvous for the final run into Port
Moresby.

Now the Zeros were after the B–25s.

And they had them.

Except for Rosebud. Whoever the hell it was up there.
Without that warning call . . .

The Zeros were just coming within range when Rosebud
hit.

"*I don't believe it! I don't believe it!*" They could hardly
recognize Coombs's voice from the screeching.

"What the hell's going on back there, Coombs?" Whip
demanded.

"*P–38s. It's P–38s, Major! God, they're beautiful!* I don't
believe it, I see them, but I don't — *look at them go!*"

Whip nearly broke his neck twisting around in the
cockpit, looking back through his side window. My God, it
was impossible, but there they were, eight silvery twin-
boomed fighters, coming downstairs faster than a man's
eyes could believe, and they sliced into the pack of Zeros
with devastating effect. Before the Japanese were really
aware of what was happening, at least seven were goners —
burning, wings torn away, pilots pulped in their cockpits.
The remaining Zeros broke wildly, twisting and corkscrew-
ing in dizzying maneuvers to escape what had exploded in
their midst. Several Zeros streaked past the B–25s, and the
gunners had a brief but ineffectual blast at them as they
went by.

Whip and Alex were pounding one another on the neck
and shoulders, and the same pandemonium swept the other
B–25s. They watched in wonder as the big fighters eased
alongside. "Hey, Rosebud, you guys came along just in
time. Thanks."

"Roger. You people weren't doing so bad yourself. Didn't
anyone let you know you're not flying fighters? We counted
eight bombers going down back there."

"Just funnin', that's all."

"You must have a hell of a sense of humor. You want a
ride back home?"

"Negative, Rosebud. And thanks. I think those other
people have called it a day. Hey, where'd you people come
from, anyway?"

"Forty-ninth. We've been laying low until now. This was
our first mission. Sayonara, you all."

The big Lockheeds went for altitude, the crewmen in the
B–25s watching with wonder. There was no effort, no
gasping engines struggling. The P–38s swept upward with a

grace and speed almost impossible to believe. Whip set course for Kanaga Field. Suddenly he pulled his hands from the yoke. "Take it," he told Alex.

Alex watched as Whip slid back his seat, fishing in a pocket for a cigarette. Damn . . . he was into one of his blue funks again. The man's mood changed so swiftly. Elation one moment and this sudden depression the next. Whip had unexpectedly rounded a corner in his own mind and stumbled headlong into himself. After the first flush of excitement about the P–38s showing up, he had resented their presence. Oh, Jesus, was it really that bad? Had there been something kind, restrained in the way Lou Goodman had fought with him? Whip had fought his air war, *his* air war for so very long now that the resentment he'd felt at fighters that no doubt had saved the lives of most of the people in their formation was, well, it was goddamned irrational thinking. And unspeakably stupid, he reminded himself.

In the bomber holding course for New Guinea, now growing on the horizon, safe within his own element of flight, feeling the solid throb of the airplane beneath and all about him, Whip Russel began some uncomfortable soul-searching. That flash of resentment was still a physical shock to his system, and he wondered how long he had really been thinking this way. Lou Goodman had been trying to reach him, to tell him *something*, but the fat man had been walking on eggs and, *oh shit, Lou, I think I'm beginning to understand, to see —*

The anger charged him with electric shock. Was it really so? Had Lou been trying to help? Or was this resentment he had felt toward Lou justified? Those P–38s out there, when they —

He drew up short in his mind. Good God, now he was trying to justify *not* being grateful because those fighters had snatched them from the brink of oblivion! Sure, his people would follow him anywhere, even to hell, *but did he have to take them there?* He sat back in his mind to take a long look at himself and he was disturbed. He knew what it was for a man to look at events with the tunnel vision that comes when you've got the only chair in town. As if the goddamned war had to be fought his own way.

"Hey, boss, we got troubles."

A glance through his window. Arnie Kessler's bomber. Even as he watched he saw the propeller blades of the right engine slowing, the blades knifing into the wind as Arnie feathered the system.

"How bad is it, Arnie?"

"The left fan is doing fine. I can make it to Kanaga okay."

"Maybe we'd better go for Seven-Mile."

"Nah. As that kangaroo with you would say, it's a piece of cake. We're pretty light, boss. Kanaga's fine."

"Okay." He didn't need to tell anyone else to modify their power to stay with Kessler. They rode it back together, pushing over a saddleback in the Owen Stanleys with no sweat. But they would be landing at four thousand feet and it wasn't going to be easy. Whip had second thoughts about Arnie going into Kanaga but he brushed them away.

They went down-slope and it was easy and they had the dry lake bed in sight, and everybody pulled back to give Arnie all the room he needed. Arnie played it by the book, coming down with gear and flaps only when he had everything made, holding a steep approach so that only one engine gave him plenty of room for modifying the approach.

The trees and brush were already out of the way. Damn, they're getting good down there, mused Whip, watching Arnie's B–25 sliding down the groove. Arnie took her in neat and they saw the dust spurt back from the tires. Down safe and rolling and —

Kessler's voice was almost a scream. *"Don't land! Don't land! Japs! Japs! They're all over the field! They're —"*

The frantic warning died away as a spear of flame shot skyward from the field where Japanese troops poured fire into the helpless bomber on the ground. Whip was already on his own final, number two in the slot, and his hands were a blur as he went hammering forward on the throttles. "Clean her up!" he shouted to Alex, but the copilot's hands were already hauling up the gear and pulling in the flaps and then through the long cut in the trees he saw them, swarms of little figures firing into the blazing B–25, others turning their weapons up at the approaching bombers, and the windshield took a round and cracked, and something screamed past his head. He felt a stinging sensation, but he didn't give a damn, he'd charged the guns and he accelerated now, engines thundering, and then the weapons were alive, the fourteen machine guns ripping into the suddenly scrambling figures. He walked rudder, sweeping the massed fire of his weapons from side to side in a terrible scythe, and heard himself shouting into his mike, *"Break! Break! The field's lousy with Japs!"* They knew that already, of course, they'd heard Arnie's frantic scream to warn them and they saw the B–25 mushrooming into the air in great blazing chunks because the tanks had let go, and he was still firing when the guns bucked and chattered into silence. Out of ammo. He'd never called off his men before but he did now. "Pull up," he ordered. "Form up on me. We're going to Seven-Mile."

He didn't look behind him because he was already sick thinking of the mechanics and ground support people and the pilots who hadn't flown. He wondered how a Japanese force had managed to work its way through the jungle, escaping detection, but obviously they had known where they were going, and they had come to kill.

Arnie Kessler and his crew were simply the last ones to die on the field, and he wondered —

It hit him so violently he thought he would vomit. *Lou! My God, Lou* . . .

He squeezed his eyes shut, a fierce, painful gesture, and then he remembered. Lou Goodman had left late yesterday with Smyth to fly down to Seven-Mile.

28

"WE'RE PACKING IT IN, Major Russel. As of right now, and you may consider this official, we are standing down the special mission of the 335th. The aircraft and the crews will be brought into the 48th Bomb Group. However, all those men who were with you when you started your outfit are being returned to the States for leave." General Smyth paused. He was rushing his words, trying to get everything out as quickly as he could. The news of what had happened at Kanaga had unnerved him, as it had Lou Goodman. But in a way it had solved their problems. There was no more special field for the Death's Head Brigade. There were no more arguments about the 335th still flying as lone wolves away from the larger pack. Smyth took a deep breath and hurried on.

"As you may have anticipated, Whip, you're grounded from combat. That's an order." He tried to smile but it came out crooked. "What goes with that order isn't so bad. You're in for lieutenant colonel and —"

Whip shrugged off the news. "Save it for the press, General." His lips were tight, cold. "Is there anything else?" After a bare pause, he added, "sir."

"No."

Whip glanced at Lou Goodman, started from the room. Then he stopped, and the chip on his shoulder was gone. "General?"

"Yes, Major Russel?"

"There's no way I can talk you out of this, is there?"

"Strangely enough, Whip, I'm sorry that there isn't. I know what —"

Whip had a half-scowl, half-smile on his face. "Strangely enough, General, I know you're a good man."

Lou Goodman found him an hour later in the tents assigned to transient crews. He pushed aside the flap. Whip, Hoot Gibson, MacIntosh and Dusty Rhodes looked up at him. "You allow officers in this joint?" Goodman asked.

Dusty gestured for him to take a seat. "Why not? This is supposed to be a wake but no one can play a fiddle." Dusty gestured again. "You break your arm, Colonel?"

They saw that Goodman had been holding one arm behind him. "No. I was just prepared to bribe my way in," he said, holding forth the bottle of Scotch.

"Jesus, Joseph, Mary and the Emperor himself," Dusty breathed quietly. "Will you look at that."

Hoot Gibson took the bottle, cradled it carefully. "Lock the door. Kill the next son of a bitch who comes in here. No matter who he is."

"Who's got a glass?"

"What's a glass?"

"Round and round the mulberry bush. Who's first?"

"The fat man said he was an officer. It's first dibs for him."

Lou Goodman started it off with a long pull. He smacked his lips and blinked rapidly. "Now I know what we're fighting for."

Dusty took seconds. "I heard something once about Mom's apple pie."

"Screw Mom."

"I tried but her old man walked in on us. That's how I came to be a hero in the air force."

The bottle reached Whip. He brought it to his lips, hesitated. He looked at all of them; together, then one by one. He held up the bottle.

"To a bunch of very great people," he said quietly. "May they have smooth skies all the way west."

He never again mentioned the 335th.

Lou Goodman and Whip walked along the side of the runway. They weren't accustomed to a cool breeze and a moon sliding between silvered clouds. The darkness pushed the war away.

"You know, I'm supposed to pack," Whip said to break the silence. "But I can't."

Goodman came up short. "Why not?"

Whip's chuckle came out of the gloom. "Because I haven't *got* anything to pack. Everything I own in the world is on my back."

"I'll take care of it. They got supplies up the ass in Melbourne. Uniforms, equipment, personal gear. Smyth is signing the chit. Take everything you want."

"What time do I leave, Lou?"

"Zero eight hundred. B–17's going down. You have a seat."

"I've forgotten how to be a passenger."

"I'll be there with you in the morning."

"Hell, I knew that."

"It's late. I better get some sleep."

"Okay."

Goodman tried to make out his face in the dark shadows of the moon. "How about you, Whip?"

"No way, Lou, no way," he said softly. "I couldn't sleep tonight."

"What are you going to do?"

"It's the last time. I think I'll go talk to my airplane."

*

They had parked the four surviving bombers of the old
335th at the far end of the field, off to one side in a clump of
trees. Whip stayed with the ship. He sat in the cockpit. He
could almost see the ghostly form of Alex next to him. Then
he climbed down and sat on the ground by the nose wheel.
He fell asleep that way.

A big engine grinding around slowly, the starter screeching at the world, brought him out of his sweat-soaked
stupor. A hand shook him roughly and he opened his eyes
to look up at Lou Goodman.

"Wake up, kid. Goddamnit, snap out of it."

He shook his head, rubbed his eyes. "Jesus, is it morning
already? I — "

"It's all off, Whip. Your going back. It's off. For a while,
anyway."

He was awake now, alert. "What the hell's going on?"
Even as he asked the question he heard more engines
rumbling and coughing to life.

"Someone's pulled out the plug. A reconnaissance plane
just got in. There's a big Japanese convoy coming this way.
A whole invasion fleet, for Christ's sake. They're coming in
from the Admiralties and Kavieng and Rabaul, and, there's
just a whole goddamned ocean full of them."

They started for the operations tent. "It's what we've
been looking for, waiting for. Intelligence figures they'll
work their way down between here and New Britain and
then come around from the south. Land at Milne Bay, land
here at Moresby."

"How many?"

"Don't know yet. Troopships and destroyers up the ass
from the looks of it. We don't know about any heavy stuff
yet."

Whip's mind was back in its old groove. "How about
navy? Carriers?"

"The Japanese timed it perfectly. There's nothing in the

area that can move in here in time. Oh, we have one carrier that could have made it, but —"

"Could have?"

"It took a couple of tin fish during the night. Still afloat but out of action."

"Neat."

"More than you think. They've launched heavy attacks on Guadalcanal. The marines are in it up to their necks. Every plane the navy and marines have in that area is tied up. Same goes for the army stuff there."

Whip slowed to a halt. "The picture gets clearer every second. It's up to us, isn't it?"

"Yep. The glorious Fifth. And whatever the Aussies can get together." He slapped Whip on the shoulder. "Let's move, kid. You're due in operations."

"Wait." Whip grasped him by the arm. "How many gunships do we have in commission?"

"Your four. The other four we were working on. Three more came in. We've also got a bunch of A–20s with four-gun noses. And you'll have about a dozen Beaufighters."

Whip ran them through his head. The Aussie Beaufighters, stumpy twin-engined jobs, would do well. Four cannon and six machine guns each. A good wallop to that ship.

"Whip, for Christ's sake, *come on.*"

General Harry Spaulding wore two stars on each shoulder, walked with a cane, showed the world a bristling mustache and was as tough as two wildcats in heat. He didn't have to tell anyone in the emergency briefing that this one was for keeps.

"Our information leaves much to be desired," he told the hastily assembled pilots. "At least fourteen troopships, a dozen destroyers, maybe twice that many. They were making rendezvous from several points so our final reports need updating. But you can count on at least two to three dozen vessels out there."

He looked around the tent, crusty, not needing to say he wanted to fly this one himself. "We're sure they're going for speed. That means modern troopships, not some old clunkers. They'll be fast and you can expect very heavy flak. The same for their tin cans. Speed and firepower. We can't let them get those troops ashore. The Japanese have been throwing heavy attacks all along the Owen Stanleys since yesterday morning. They've infiltrated with heavy forces deep behind our own lines. If they succeed in landing men from those ships, then we'll be squeezed badly.

"Get my message, gentlemen. You've got to keep those troops from getting on land."

He turned and the cane tapped the situation map. "You're going to have lots of company in the air. At least seventy, more likely about a hundred and fifty Zeros for escort, all the way from the deck on up. Also, we expect them to try to hit us with some pretty heavy bombing raids, starting at any moment from now.

"You will take off as soon as we get some light. We're throwing in every airplane that can fly. If you have any extra space, take bricks with you. Anything.

"Get the bastards. That's all, gentlemen."

29

EVERYTHING THAT COULD CARRY a bomb or a machine gun was prepared for flight. New ships with gleaming aluminum skin and old clunkers with leprosy on the wings; if it could fly it was committed to the mission. The Fifth Air Force managed to get 112 bombers into the air. If you weren't too strict in what you called a bomber. The navy sent down four lumbering PBY flying boats that clunked through the sky at 105 miles an hour. But each of the battered old Catalinas had some very brave men behind the controls and each carried two torpedoes. Their only hope of survival was that there'd be some fighters to punch a way through the Zeros for them. And that would take some exquisite timing. The fighters couldn't slow down enough to stay with the PBYs. If they tried they'd fall out of the sky. So while the land-based bomber crews were still being briefed the night air echoed with the deep droning bass of the Catalinas heading off to the north.

They would make their torpedo runs with first horizon light. That way the Japanese would have poor targets, but theirs would be unmistakable ship silhouettes on the horizon. If the Japanese had Zeros in the air — and no one doubted they would — then the fighters would try to cut a swath for the Catalinas. Timing, gloom and courage. They all had to come together at the same moment.

Six Lockheed Hudsons of the Royal Australian Air Force spent most of the night flying up to the Port Moresby area.

The exhausted crews wolfed down breakfast, left their twin-engined light bombers to be fueled and bombed, got their briefings and were scheduled as latecomers in the attack so the men might sleep for two or three hours.

Twenty-two B–17 heavy bombers were made available for the raid. Their orders called for a high-level strike. Major General Harry Spaulding pulled the plug on that one. "I want you people to hit something this time," he told them unkindly. "Because if you don't then the real estate you're sitting on could be Japanese next week." The pilots shifted uncomfortably under his glare. "You've been bombing from eighteen to twenty-five thousand feet. You will not do that today. You will bomb from no higher than ten thousand."

The pilots stirred and uneasy murmurs ran through the room. "Gentlemen, you will do a hell of a lot better today than you have ever done before. Or you will all learn how to use a rifle. You are going out against destroyers and troopships. The same Zero fighters that go after the other aircraft may have a crack at you as well. But you will *hit* your targets. Dismissed."

The Fifth Air Force scraped together thirty-seven B–25s, to be led into their targets by the eleven bombers — the gunships — that would fly under the command of Major Whip Russel.

Whip did the briefing. "It's a clean mission," he told the assembled crews. "We go in on the deck. Your attack will be skip-bombing. We go after the transports. I'll take lead with the gunships. If we know what we're doing there won't be many flak positions left by the time you glass-noses get there. One more thing. You're not going to like this but you will do it. Once you've dropped your bombs you do *not* leave the area. You come around again and you run decoy for the people who still have bombs. We're not out to score today, gentlemen. We're out to sink ships and if running

246 WHIP

decoy is one way of doing it, that's the name of the game."
Twenty-nine Havocs, the light twin-engined bombers, would make their own runs on the deck. None of the pilots had been trained to skip his bombs across the water. But they were experts at low-level strikes. They boasted they'd hit more ships' masts than any other outfit in the air force. They were right.

There were still fourteen B–26 Marauders with the 22nd Bomb Group. They'd make level-bombing runs from four thousand feet. They were veterans and they were good.

No one knew just when the Australian Hudsons would make their move. But six more bombers in the right place at the right time could tip the scales.

Every fighter that could fly *would* fly. The powerful Bristol Beaufighters, no adversaries for the agile Zeros, would go in on the deck before the A–20s for flak-suppression runs.

All in all the Fifth Air Force assembled a grab bag of twenty-six P–40 Kittyhawks, fourteen P–39 Airacobras and above all else, twenty-two of the twin-boomed P–38 Lightnings. Without the P–38s there'd be no top cover. With those big fighters they could sandwich the Zeros from top and bottom.

Including everything, the entire air armada available in the Fifth Air Force added up to four flying boats, twenty-two heavy bombers, eighty-six twin-engined bombers and a mishmash of seventy-three fighters.

A grand total of one hundred and eighty-five airplanes.

It really wasn't that much.

Whip and his crews were sitting in their bombers waiting to start engines when the first reports began trickling in. The lumbering PBYs had gotten away with their first-light torpedo strike by the grace of God, their audacious flying and running interference by ten P–40s. The fighter pilots, bless 'em, had deliberately drawn the Zeros away so the Catalinas could have at the plump targets waiting for them.

They put one fish into a destroyer, disabling its rudder, and the warship had already fallen well back of the convoy. A transport took a torpedo into its hull but it seemed not to bother the vessel, which was still maintaining full speed with the other ships, although trailing a long oil slick in the water.

The Catalinas confirmed the force at twelve destroyers and fourteen transports and a sky "thick with Zeros; they're like mosquitoes out there." The dusk strike, however, had kept the aerial score at a stand-off. No one had shot anyone else down.

"But they've got a nasty surprise," radioed back the lead Catalina. "Maybe two dozen PT boats. Fast, and loaded with flak guns. They'll try to weave in and out of the transports against the low-level attacks."

The B–17s went in with a first wave of thirteen bombers. Flying down at ten thousand feet did wonders for their accuracy. A string of heavy bombs walked across the deck of a troopship and tore it into about four major pieces, all of which fell away from the others and sank quickly. The second wave of nine heavies hit two or three of the transports, one of which was sending flames into the air from its stern.

But the B–17s had paid off in yet another way. A loose swarm of Zeros came down from their high cover to chop up the big bombers, and the low cover went scrambling for altitude. The P–38s made the high bounce, breaking up the enemy formations, and while the Japanese were occupied the first wave of A–20 Havocs, led by the Beaufighters, raced in against the troopships.

Before the low-level raiders were ready to commit, the

P-38s had shot down nine Zeros and the B-17s got another four. That meant thirteen less fighters in the air, and the Fortresses were already on their way down to load up again for a second strike.

The initial low-level run was a spectacular success. The Beaufighters led the way, hammering the flak positions on the destroyers and the transports. Four 20mm cannon and six machine guns add up to a massive punch, and the A-20s each had a cluster of four fifties riding with them. Two transports were left broken and burning.

By now the Zero pilots were frantic. Every time they came downstairs the P-38s were all over them, harassing their moves, forcing them to break off their own attacks against the raiders on the deck.

The B-26s timed their runs at four thousand feet with the Hudsons hugging the waves from the opposite direction. The Zeros clawed after them but had to contend with the P-38s on high, as well as all the remaining P-40s and the P-39s. Unable to mix it up to the best advantage, confused by the fighters and bombers coming in from all directions and altitudes, the Zeros proved ineffectual and kept taking heavy losses.

A transport turned into an inferno from the Marauder bomb run. Men hurled themselves into the sea to escape the broiling flames. As the transport erupted, the Hudsons went in all the way and took out one destroyer, damaging a second.

The big punch would come with the thirty-seven B-25s and their skip-bombing runs. There was no mistaking the target area even from a distance. Smoke towered thousands of feet into the air and milling fighters reflected the morning sun like tinsel.

"This is Blue Goose calling the Beaufighters. Over."

"Right, Yank. We're down here in the middle of them. How far out are you?"

"Three minutes. Can you people work over those torpedo boats?"

"Right-o."

"We'll take care of the big stuff on the way in. Thanks."

"Good hunting, Yank."

It was the best move. The torpedo boat crews had proved fanatical and dangerous, charging off in the direction of any incoming flight. They could mess up the low-level runs and Whip wanted no interference.

New Guinea was on the distant horizon. The transports were making full speed for land. *Any* land. The idea was to keep them from getting there.

"Okay, troops, we take them in elements. Looks like the people who got here first did some good work. I see only twelve transports. Forget those that are burning. We'll get to them later." Whip studied the expanding scene. "We'll go in first with the gunships. Fan out in elements, troops. You glass-noses hang in about a mile behind us so you have room to change targets. Anybody got any questions?"

None. Just the way it should be.

They would never have a better opportunity. The destroyers were trying desperately to flank the vulnerable troopships, but it was a losing battle. Of the twelve destroyers that greeted the light of day, one was far behind the others, disabled from the first B–17 strike, another had been sunk by the Hudsons and a third, also victim to the Aussie Lockheeds, was a mess with fires amidships. That left nine still in there fighting, but they had taken a terrible beating from the flak-suppression runs, with broken bodies littering the decks. Half their guns no longer operated, and as each wave of bombers came in low more and more guns fell silent.

Whip led the way in. On the deck, engines thundering, he went directly for the destroyer making up the outside screen. He saw the slab-winged Beaufighters well ahead of him, chewing up the brave little torpedo boats. Some A–20s were still in the area, using their four nose guns to good advantage by hacking away at flak positions on the ships. It was an incredible job; everybody was in there pitching, helping the new bomber waves coming in.

Whip took heavier fire than he expected, and he saw what he was looking for. The flanking destroyer with three massed gun batteries still operating on the side facing him. "Watch that tin can in front of Lead," he called out to the other bombers. He rolled the bomber from side to side in his famous weaving approach with tracers sparkling about him. They were taking hits but he ignored the thudding sounds in the airplane. At the last moment he cracked the bomber out of its gyrations, locked everything on the rails and squeezed the gun tit. The fourteen machine guns smashed the first gun tub into wreckage, and he eased in rudder to take out the second. Let the troops behind finish off the bastard.

He pounded low over the destroyer, back in his weave, never holding the airplane steady long enough for gunners to hold the B–25 in their sights. But there was a torpedo boat slicing away from the Japanese destroyer and they opened up with everything they had. A fusilade of lead ripped into the B–25. They felt and heard the impacts. Holes appeared in the wings.

"How's it going back there?" Whip called on the intercom.

No one answered for the moment. The gunners were busy hosing the destroyer and the torpedo boat as they went by. "We're busy!" Joe Leski sang out. "Would you mind calling back later?"

Whip concentrated on the transports. My God, they had men hanging everywhere. The holds must be packed with men, for the decks were awash with human bodies. Frightened faces looked up, and three gun tubs with single machine guns were already stitching their tracers toward the onrushing airplane.

"Make it a good one," Alex said quietly.

"It will be," Whip promised.

It was a textbook approach. Right out of the manual Whip had been writing in steel and blood. He rolled out of his wild maneuvers, steadied the airplane for a short, devastating burst into a gun position. Then he was holding steady and true on the bomb run. They had six 500-pounders in the bays. "We'll give 'em two bombs," Whip said curtly.

"Roger. Two to go," Alex confirmed.

"Fighters twelve o'clock high! They're diving on us!"

The dorsal turret was hammering. Whip ignored the Zeros after a glance showed him four fighters racing in to them.

"Oh, ho, they've got company," Alex said. "Long noses."

Four P–39s right on the Zeros, cannon and machine guns firing steadily. One Zero fell wildly off on a wing and splashed. The others kept boring in but their aim was off. The P–39 was a dog, but these didn't have to turn. They were diving and that made all the difference in the world. Zeros couldn't hack the bombers while getting shot up.

The swarm of fighters flashed low overhead. Whip's whole world was the troopship before him. He saw the rust streaks on the sides, the anchor hanging, the dirty smoke, hundreds of faces staring at him.

"Drop!"

Alex let them go, and Coombs called it out. "They're dead-on, Major!"

They were. Two 500-pound bombs exploded just above the waterline. Whip was climbing, turning, getting set to come back again. They were rolling out, falling off on one wing, doing their best to ignore the fire from the destroyers, the blurred streak of fighter wings, when the troopship they'd hit went up in an incredible blast. The boilers had been torn apart, the thin plates crumpled like tissue paper and the ship was coming to a dead stop in the water, broken and burning, already starting to sink. It was death rushing in.

Strange; the most important mission they'd ever flown and it was shooting gallery time. The sea was calm, with long swells, and the big bombs skipped easily across the water, once, twice, and then sheared into the transports. The first wave of eleven gunships took out most of the flak and shattered four transports. Two were already going down, the others had minutes left.

Twenty-six more B–25s bore in. The flak was only a shadow of what it had been. The pilots took their time, aimed carefully, timed it all exactly. It was a case of thirteen pairs of bombers ganging up on the eight transports waiting for the ax.

Five troopships took the death blow in that long, careful skip-bombing run.

Three were left. The B–25s blasted overhead, started their turns to come back a second time. Everybody still had four bombs left. The Zeros were frantic, but even the P–38s were on the deck, cutting fighters out of the air with their fine, devastating touch.

"This is Blue Goose to the B–25s. You glass-noses concentrate on the transports. Gunships, form up on me. Let's get those tin cans."

Two B–25s never made the run. The Zeros were all over them, ignoring the American fighters. Three Zeros out of ten went up in flames in seconds, but the others went in close and the bombers were simply taking too much punishment. As far as the ships were concerned it didn't really matter.

Two dozen B–25s hit the three remaining transports in two more passes by each bomber. Forty-eight bombs bounced and skipped across the water. Sixteen hit. Five in one transport, three in another, eight bombs into the remaining vessel. It didn't sink. It exploded in great burning chunks that fell back into the sea, steamed and disappeared.

Whip went after a destroyer, Hoot Gibson riding to his right and behind. MacIntosh and Dusty Rhodes took on another, and the other gunships picked their own targets. They put three bombs into one tin can, breaking its back, and then they went into their climb turns with their bomb bays empty.

"Hoot, Mac, Dusty; let's take this next one line astern."

"Roger that, boss."

"Let's see what all this hardware can do."

"Okay, troops. I'll go for the waterline just ahead of the stack. It's engine room time."

"That old boiler of theirs will never be the same."

"Here comes the Chatanooga Choo-Choo."

Whip led them in, aimed, held down the gun tit. Fourteen heavy machine guns blasted their firepower into the thin plates of the destroyer just above the waterline. Water boiled, metal punched in. He lifted up the nose, creamed a gun crew, arrowed overhead. The other bombers swept in, everybody drilling into the same spot.

When they came around for another run the warship was at half speed, listing badly. "She'll never last an hour," Mac announced.

The destroyers weaving in and out of thousands of panicked soldiers in the water got their dose from the thirty-one other B–25s.

They were still mopping up that night. The B–17s were out with heavy bomb loads, looking for burning ships. If it burned they could see it and if they saw it they went after it. Slowly, methodically, from well under ten thousand feet, without Zeros to bother them.

It was the greatest victory they'd ever known. All fourteen troopships were either sunk or in sinking condition; none were under way from their engines. Nine destroyers had gone down and the B–17s were out looking for the remaining three.

The price they paid was heavy in lives, but on the statistical ledger it was a lopsided win. Eighteen planes had gone down — two B–25s, one B–17, three B–26s, one A–20, one Beaufighter, seven P–40s and three P–39s. No Hudsons were lost. The P–38s didn't lose a plane.

All told, the fighters and bombers wiped more than seventy Zeros from the sky. No one knew exactly how many.

It was over, but there was still unfinished business. General Spaulding called in the pilots of the eleven B–25 gunships, the five Aussie Beaufighters that could still fly. The A–20s had taken a beating and only fifteen were in condition to get back into the air.

Thirty-one killers.

And they had hell in store for them.

30

IT WAS WRONG. All wrong. What the hell was going on here? They moved into the big tent at Seven-Mile that General Spaulding had been using for briefings. You couldn't miss the armed guards around the tent. Not just at the entrance but completely around it.

There was only the briefest order to get to the special briefing. Grim-faced men, confused themselves, going after certain pilots. Not all the pilots, Whip noticed. He recognized the replacements that had been assigned to the 335th before Kanaga Field was wiped out. Gunship crews. None of the glass-noses in here.

Before General Spaulding stepped onto the raised platform the tent flaps were closed, and two armed guards took up position *inside* the tent.

Spaulding's face was grim, his lips pressed tightly together. His conversation didn't make sense. Tired and bone-weary as Whip was, still rigid deep within himself at knowing his own outfit was no more, he couldn't help marveling at the *insanity* of what he was hearing.

Weather conditions . . . a weather report, for God's sake!

"Winds in the strike area remain light and variable . . . sea calm . . . excellent conditions still prevail . . . water temperature high . . ."

Hold one, his tired brain rattled at him. Some of the words had begun to penetrate. *Water temperature . . .* Without realizing the change in his posture Whip was now sitting bolt upright, the aching muscles and burning eyes forgotten, all his intensity thrown into listening. He clung to every word. The old man himself was running with the ball. No subordinates, no lackeys.

"We estimate there are anywhere from three to five thousand survivors in the sea . . . some lifeboats, but mostly rafts and debris . . . plus what barges and other vessels the Japanese have sent from all neighboring islands . . . to pick up those men . . . not that far from shore . . . temperature and winds make it clear . . . survival factor high . . ."

The words hammered in his head.

"Most will make it . . . can't let that happen. Several thousand Japanese troops landing on the north coast . . . shift the whole balance . . . can't let that happen . . . must not permit this to happen . . ."

Whip knew what was coming. It twisted a giant knot within his belly.

His whole frame of mind, his attitude, the position he had taken on everything, including death and life; less than a day ago, for God's sake, it had all been turned upside-down on him. It had taken him hours to understand how utterly weary he was within himself, how dangerously low the spark was burning. He had struggled for objectivity, had wondered in awe about killing taking over everything in his heart and his mind and his soul.

Psycho and Arnie Kessler and Mule and Irish and the Greek; oh, Christ, was the list really that long? Ted Ashley and Jim Whitson and McCamish and that . . . Octavio Jordan's face swam briefly before his mind's eye and he thought he would retch. He fought it down and he wrestled with his thoughts.

He had accepted the change.

Goddamnit, they couldn't do this to him! Not now . . . Jesus, *not now.*

He was hearing what he had always wanted to hear, the granting of the free hunting license, the permit to kill, to lust with murder, wanton and brutal killing, the enormous scythe of the gunship under his hands.

A killing machine and freedom to use it. Not against one plane or one ship or a runway, but against *men*, hundreds of them, thousands of them, the stinking Japs before his sights and his guns. Oh, he'd wanted this until it had been a fury beating its death wings inside him, and he'd justified that sort of burning desire to slaughter because of Melody, and that moment, when he realized that for weeks she had never been in his mind, and all those people who might still be flying with them if he hadn't pressed, pushed, hadn't anviled them between his kill lust and the enemy . . .

That's when he had quit. Smyth pulled the plug on him and Whip hadn't found anger. He'd come to grips with himself and he *had* gone out there — goddamn them all to hell! — and *said* goodby to that twin-engined brute in which he had lived all these months, and now, oh, the sons of bitches, the filthy rotten bastards, to do this *now* —

"There is not a man in this world I would ask to do this." The general's voice droned on; the cackle of death in every word. "Only one man may bear this responsibility and that man is myself. I must, therefore, make this a direct order, but I will hold it against no man who tells me, alone, after this briefing, that he will not or cannot do what you must do."

Why the hell didn't you ask me to do this only two days ago? I would have gone gladly, I would have rushed into the sky with my guns charged, lusting to kill. Why not two days ago? Why now? Why?

He heard no more. He heard the words but they had no meaning, no thrust, no importance, because his mind was shut out, and nothing was more terrible to him now than knowing that he would go out there and he would do what the general would not ask them to do, but would play conscience-critic and give them a direct order.

Which they did not have to obey.

Alex refused.

He made no speech, pleaded with no man, offered argument to not a soul. When he heard the mission he stood by his bunk and looked strangely at Whip and said, "No," and he walked from the tent, and Whip Russel never again saw this man he had come to love as a brother.

But *he* went.

And he hated himself because he knew there was no need. Not for *him*.

31

THERE WAS no way to miss. God had his cruel streak. They couldn't have missed if they wanted to. And after the first few moments there were few of them who still had the stomach for it.

They were everywhere in the water, heads bobbing, hanging to packing cases, to hatch covers, to life rings, clinging to rafts, holding to ropes from lifeboats, swimming, struggling; men who'd kicked away their shoes, tied knots in their trouser legs and made air pillows of them so they might not fill their lungs with salt water and drown.

To each side of his gunship Whip saw the men. The greatest concentration was before him. He eased back on the throttles, he slowed her down. He glanced to his left. Ten more gunships, the new silvery airplanes and the remainder of the Death's Head Brigade. How that name had come home to them!

He looked to the right. The A–20s and the Beaufighters were going in now, setting it up.

He wondered what they were thinking, those souls in the water, and as he wondered what they wondered, his thumb was moving almost as if it were a living creature unto itself, an appendage of death, caressing the gun tit. For an instant Whip thought of what his gunship must look like, those great curving teeth and —

He squeezed. In the first burst he knew he had killed more than a hundred men.

They didn't just die, the massed firepower of the fifties blew them apart. Grisly pieces of flesh and bone spattered and bounced and whirled through the air.

He walked rudder, the hammer scything through water, tearing into bodies, shredding and mutilating and ripping and tearing and chopping.

The ocean took on its ghastly red hue.

Pieces of flesh floated on the sea.

Was that screaming he heard? Could he hear those cries above the thunder of his engines?

The kid next to him, the copilot riding this mission as a volunteer, puked.

Whip eased into a climb and brought her around again, and saw the brilliant flashes of guns and cannon from the other gunships, the Beaufighters and the Havocs, and the great blades of death whirred again and he went down.

For the first time ever he closed his eyes when he squeezed and the hammering, bucking roar of the guns seemed a thousand miles away.

Death whipped forward in its giant hose and the ocean churned and exploded in froth. He couldn't take any more and this time he simply held down on the gun tit while the fifties became overheated and began to glow and then thank God he was out of ammo.

They left thousands of men behind them.

No one knew how many were dying, leaking their life into the water; they had been hacked, punched, cleavered, and the sharks came to feast.

The kid next to Whip — he didn't even know his name — couldn't throw up anymore. His body shuddered in dry-heave spasms. Finally he turned to Whip, his eyes pleading.

Whip found his voice. "Go to hell," he said.

32

"THERE'S NOTHING to say, is there?"

Whip shook his head. "No . . . no, there isn't, Lou."

A hand rested briefly on his shoulder, pulled away. "Let me know where you end up."

"Sure. I'll do that."

"Damnit, Whip, I'm not just talking words!"

He looked up from the dust. "I know that. Christ, Lou, I didn't mean to —"

"Oh, shit. I know what you mean. I'm sorry, kid." Lou Goodman looked across the runway. They were waiting at the B–17 for Major Whip Russel. The living, flying legend who walked slightly stooped because his belly was filled with barbed wire.

They walked together toward the waiting bomber, and they stopped a short distance away. Something tried to fight its way out from both of them. They shook hands. The words didn't come. Whip turned away, started off. He seemed to stumble, stopped, turned around.

"Lou?"

"What is it, Whip?"

"We had to do it, didn't we?"

Goodman nodded. "We had to."

"Do you think it will help to . . . make it end sooner, Lou?"

"God knows it should, Whip."

"God don't know shit. He wasn't out there. I was."

"Then maybe only you can answer the question."

His eyes went wide. "Only *me* answer —" Whip's voice broke off in a harsh laugh.

"Lou, uh, no one knows what will . . . I mean, if something happens to me, would you? I mean — "

"I know. Melody."

"Yeah. Melody."

"You know I would. No matter what. But somehow, Whip, I think you're going to make it."

Whip sighed. "Maybe you're right, Lou. I mean, how can you kill a man who's died inside, right?"

"Does it hurt, kid?"

"It hurts, Lou."

"Then you're alive."